ALSO BY SOPHIE LARK

Minx

Brutal Birthright
Brutal Prince
Stolen Heir
Savage Lover
Bloody Heart
Broken Vow
Heavy Crown

Sinners Duet
There Are No Saints
There Is No Devil

Grimstone
Grimstone

GRIMSTONE

SOPHIE LARK

Bloom books

Published by Bloom Books, an imprint of Sourcebooks
P.O. Box 4410, Naperville, Illinois 60567-4410
(630) 961-3900
sourcebooks.com

Originally self-published in 2023 by Sophie Lark.

Cataloging-in-Publication data is on file with the Library of Congress.

Printed and bound in the United States of America.
LSC 10 9 8 7 6 5 4 3 2 1

This is for anyone who's ever made a terrible mistake...
And for Ry, who forgives all of mine ❤
XOXO

Sophie Love

Yesterday, upon the stair
I met a man who wasn't there
He wasn't there again today
Oh, how I wish he'd go away...
　　　　　—WILLIAM HUGHES MEARNS

Soundtrack

1. "Oblivion"—Grimes
2. "Fire"—Two Feet
3. "Hush"—The Marías
4. "Fangs"—Younger Hunger
5. "Eyes on Fire"—Blue Foundation
6. "Yellow Flicker Beat"—Lorde
7. "Running with the Wolves"—AURORA
8. "Love Story"—Sarah Cothran
9. "Creep"—Kina Grannis
10. "Heads Will Roll"—Yeah Yeah Yeahs
11. "Baby I'm Dead Inside"—KOPPS
12. "Criminal"—Fiona Apple
13. "Black Magic"—Magic Wands
14. "Werewolf Heart"—Dead Man's Bones
15. "Lust"—The Raveonettes
16. "Wires"—The Neighbourhood
17. "Nightcrawlers"—Widowspeak
18. "Bitter and Sick"—One Two
19. "The Hanging Tree"—Angus & Julia Stone
20. "Special Death"—Mirah
21. "Ghost"—Confetti
22. "Aurora"—Snow in April

Music is a big part of my writing process. If you start a song when you see a 🎵 while reading, the song matches the scene like a movie score.

Spotify   Apple Music

CONTENT WARNING

This book contains elements of BDSM, post-partem depression, harm to an infant by a parent, filicide, parenticide, suicide, stalking, violence/blood, and attempted sexual assault (on-page).

WELCOME TO

DINER 1

2

3

14

16

15

Town Square

GRIMSTONE

9

8

7

6

5

4

MAIN STREET

10 11 12 13

17

Echo Park

CHAPTER I
REMI HAYES

♫ *"Oblivion"—Grimes*

WHEN WE PULL UP IN FRONT OF THE RUINED MANSION, IT'S WORSE than I expected. Jude pretends like it's not so bad 'cause he's the one who pushed for this.

"Oh yeah…" he says, getting out of the car and stretching his legs. "That's really…something. Look at all those trees. And, uh… it's definitely big."

Big isn't a benefit when we have to renovate every square inch of this place. And by *we*, I mean *me*—Jude can barely hold a hammer.

"You suck at being optimistic," I inform my brother. "It doesn't suit you."

"All right." He grins. "It's a huge pile of shit. And probably haunted."

That's one thing I don't have to worry about—I don't believe in ghosts.

Although, if a house *were* haunted, this would be the perfect candidate.

The ancient Victorian has a baleful look, the peeling paint giving it a diseased appearance, the many gabled windows dark and shuttered. The porch yawns like a mouth, the broken steps like crooked teeth.

"Do you think maybe Uncle Ernie was a murderer?" Jude whispers in my ear, making me jump.

I turn around and raise my fist like I'm gonna pop him. "Don't *do* that!"

Jude smirks. He knows I'm a big softie. I've never hit him in my life—even when he really deserved it.

"Uncle Ernie used a wheelchair," I remind him. "Which is probably why he didn't get around to cutting the grass."

The front lawn is a jungle of waist-high weeds, not to mention trash and broken machinery. I'm going to need a brush hog to clear this out—a normal lawn mower wouldn't make it two feet.

I'm already tallying up the tasks required to make this place livable, let alone flippable. The weight of those tasks is immense compared to my own pathetic little shadow creeping up the rickety front steps.

"Do you have the key?" Jude says.

"Yeah."

But when I touch the knob, the front door swings open with an eerie groan.

"*Oooo...*" Jude does shivery spirit fingers at me.

"Shut up." I push past him.

The interior of the house is dark and cool, dampness in the air. The only light comes from the hole in the roof that's let in drifts of dead leaves and a whole lot of water damage. The rotting boards sink beneath our feet.

Mold bleeds down the walls like black tears. In the distant rafters, there's the fluttering of a bird. Or maybe a bat.

The dank cold and the oppressive weight of trying to fix this could crush me. But I don't crush that easy.

"You want to go pick out your room?"

Jude sniffs the air and makes a gagging sound. "I'm sleeping in the car."

"No, you're not."

"You made me sleep in the car in Green River."

My neck gets hot like it always does when I have to think about money. "The hotel was full."

"You could have checked the other one."

"The other one looked expensive. It was only one night—I got us a place in Boise."

"Only 'cause you were starting to stink." Jude wrinkles his nose.

My brother is ridiculously prudish. That one night in the car is the closest he's ever gotten to camping. Well...until tonight. Depending on how many holes are in the bedroom ceilings, we might be sleeping under the stars.

"Grab the bags, will you?" I say. "I'm gonna check out the electrical panel."

Jude heads back outside, while I search the main floor. I was hoping I wouldn't have to open the narrow door in the hallway and descend the steps to the cellar, but, of course, that's exactly what's required.

I hold up the flashlight on my phone so I don't break my neck on the steep staircase. This part of the house was never finished; the stone walls weep water that pools on the cement floor.

My phone sweeps a feeble light around the space that makes the shadows loom up, huge and menacing. Dusty glass jars line the far wall, full of unknown sludgy substances. Something rustles in a far-off corner, setting my teeth on edge.

I don't like small spaces—places with no windows and no escape. Cold sweat drips down my back.

Dry leaves crunch underfoot—or I hope it's only leaves. Drifts of glossy blue-black leaves lie everywhere inside the mansion, glittering like beetle carcasses. They're from the grove of ninebarks that circle the property, the reason Uncle Ernie named his house *Blackleaf*.

I find the electrical panel, but it's so full of cobwebs that I'm even more certain I shouldn't risk flipping any switches. Not until a professional takes a look.

There's a lot of things I can handle myself—almost anything if I've got YouTube and my tool bag. But I don't want to risk a fire.

Just the thought brings the sharp scent of smoke into my nostrils. I shake my head hard to clear it, my heart stiff and jerky in my chest.

No fucking fires. I know all too well that even wet things can burn.

I'll get an electrician here. It'll have to be on a budget because renovating this place is already going to take every penny I have saved, plus more—especially since I'm already down seventy-eight dollars for the speeding ticket I got from some power-tripping sheriff on the way into Grimstone.

What an asshole. He didn't even pretend not to look down the front of my shirt while he was writing the ticket. I was glad Jude was in the passenger seat—I'd hate to think what might've happened if I were pulled over all alone on an empty road by Sheriff Shane.

But it'll all be worth it if we can successfully flip this place.

While one part of my brain has been cataloging every broken window and rotting floorboard, the rest of me had been noting the untouched stained glass in the observatory and the silver ceiling tiles in the kitchen that are definitely salvageable…

This house could be gorgeous. It could be something truly special—with the right amount of elbow grease. And the one thing I've got is elbows.

When I ascend to the main level once more, Jude hasn't retrieved the bags. I find him poking around in what used to be the servants' quarters in the olden days and became Uncle Ernie's bedroom suite once he was in a wheelchair. He had the bathroom outfitted with the kind of tub that opens on the side and metal guardrails next to the toilet.

His medical equipment still sits next to the hospital bed where he spent the last months of his life. A bird built its nest on the EKG machine. I don't know if the empty bedpans were scattered by squirrels or by the teenagers who have clearly broken in here at least once to leave their empty beer cans and used condoms.

"Gross," Jude says.

I'm not sure which disgusting thing he's referencing, but yeah, I agree.

"So, I take it you don't want this room?"

"Not a fucking chance."

I thought he'd pick the main suite like he did in our last place, but my brother exists to defy my expectations. He chooses the smallest bedroom next to the library instead.

"Think any of these books are still readable?" He pulls a leatherbound tome off the shelves, and it immediately falls apart in his hands.

"Sure…if you don't mind a face full of dust."

"Some of these could be worth something… They're from way before Uncle Ernie's time."

"Knock yourself out. Anything you can sell from this place goes right in your college fund."

Jude makes a sour face. He hates when I remind him that, yes, he is 1,000 percent *absolutely* going to college, and we aren't fighting about it anymore. Because I really might punch him if he tries again.

"You could start in January. I have enough to get you through your first semester. And by next fall, this place will have sold for sure."

"I don't want to start midyear. And anyway, you're going to need my help."

"Oh, you're actually gonna help?"

"Ha, ha." Jude rolls his eyes. "If I don't help, then how come I know how to tape and paint a room, despite the fact I never consented to add that knowledge to my brain?"

"You've never taped."

"I've seen you do it. And I *have* painted."

He's got me there. Jude has, occasionally, painted. And he's pretty good at it, too, for however long he lends his attention.

My brother is brilliant at everything he tries; that's the tragedy.

He was a middle school chess champion, a cello prodigy, and top in every test at his fancy private school. But not top in his class because he's never handed in a homework assignment. Nor practiced anything for more than a few hectic, obsessive months.

I'd kill to have an ounce of his genius. But I'm B+ across the board—and that's with me trying my hardest and studying my ass off. Without the work ethic, who knows how stupid I'd be.

"I need to head into town," I tell Jude. "Get groceries and all that. You want to come with?"

I thought his answer would be an automatic yes because I never learn.

"I'll stay here and explore," Jude says.

"Okay. Just be careful… Some of these floors aren't too stable."

"You're worried about the floor falling out from under me now? God, I need to give you something real to stress about."

"Please don't."

I know he's only kidding, but I hate to leave him here all alone, his face thin and pale in the gloomy light, his eyes huge and dark and childlike. My brother turned twenty last week, but he looks so much younger. He always has.

I ruffle his hair. "I'll be back soon."

He smooths it with a long-suffering expression. "Don't hurry."

It only takes me an hour to drive into Grimstone and load up my ancient Bronco with groceries and a few other supplies. I make a cursory examination of the local hardware store, knowing that'll be my top shopping destination in the upcoming weeks.

I'm pleased to see two new restaurants on Main Street, plus some bougie-looking boutiques. The resort is booming, which is exactly what I'm counting on to turn this flip from profitable to life-changing. Uncle Ernie's house isn't so far in the sticks anymore—for the right buyer, it could simply be considered private.

I'm feeling pretty good on the drive back up the long, winding road to Blackleaf until I come to a chained and padlocked gate that was most certainly *not* here the last two times I passed through.

"What the fuck?"

I get out of the Bronco and walk right up to it like it might be an optical illusion. Fifty-seven minutes ago, I blew through here on my way into town, not even noticing the fence posts on either side of the road. Now it's barricaded by an eight-foot-tall, rusty, but extremely solid iron gate. I shake the chain like that's gonna help.

This would be a problem, except that I have my tool bag in the back of the Bronco—containing one very large pair of bolt cutters.

Bolt cutters are fucking awesome. However, they do not magically make cutting through inch-thick steel a piece of cake. I'm sweating and grunting, and I've torn my T-shirt before I manage to break the chain.

"I could shoot you for that."

I drop the bolt cutters and the chain, making a sound that could only be described as *screaming like a little girl*.

"Arghhhhh, what the fucking fuck?"

Those are my first words to the man standing in the shadow of an oak tree. Or *hiding*, one might say.

He's tall, with a shock of thick dark hair streaked with silver. It's hard to tell how old he is. His face is cold and stern and so colorless that I think he must be sick—especially since he's wearing a dressing gown at two o'clock in the afternoon. But the bare chest beneath his robe looks anything but ill.

Old money flashes into my head. Only that kind of rich could stand there looking haughty in pajamas. Granted, his velvet robe and embroidered slippers are ten times nicer than anything I own. I'm the sweaty ruffian in a torn shirt, chains puddled around my ankles.

"Trespassing is one of the only crimes they give a shit about around here," the man informs me calmly. "I think our sheriff might actually squeeze out of his favorite booth at Emma's to investigate."

My heart is still hammering my ribs, but I've recovered my voice, at least. "You can't trespass on your own land."

He raises an eyebrow. That's the only part of him that's moved so far. He's leaning against the trunk of the oak, his arms folded loosely over his pale chest.

The sleeves of his robe drape back at the elbows, showing the sleekly masculine shape of his forearms and hands. I don't want to notice anything appealing about him, but it's impossible not to. He's stark and striking, cruel and beautiful. It makes me feel a lot of conflicting emotions, especially when he talks.

"Brilliant observation," he says dryly. "But we happen to be standing on *my* land."

His confidence is so powerful that I can't give him the answer I'd planned, which is *Fuck off, you lunatic.*

Instead, I go with the marginally more polite "And who the hell are you?"

"Dane Covett," he says. "That's my house. And all this"—he gestures on both sides of us—"is my property."

Through the trees, I spy the gables of a grandiose mansion in much better condition than the one I just inherited. Every bit of it—gutters, shingles, shutters—is painted midnight blue. The visible parts of the garden look pristine.

I might be a little bit jealous as I snarl, "Congratulations. You still don't own the road."

Dane smiles. His teeth are straight and white, but they bring no warmth to his face. Quite the opposite. "Wrong with conviction. Do you think repeating it makes it true? I own the road and all the land on either side of it. That's what it means when I put a gate across it and say, 'Stay the fuck out.' But I guess the chains and the padlock were a bit too subtle."

Wow. It's been a long time since I've hated someone this much on sight.

I wish I had something devastating to say instead of the slightly whiny "Then how the fuck am I supposed to get up to *my* house?"

He shifts his position against the tree, frowning slightly. "What house?"

"Right up there…"

I point in the direction of Blackleaf, which you can almost see from where we stand. Really, I'm just pointing at the dark halo of trees around the house.

Dane straightens, stuffing his hands in the pockets of his robe, looking, if anything, as if he now dislikes me even more. "You're Rosemary."

His level of distaste for my given name almost matches my own. "It's Remi."

"And what are you doing here, Remi?"

The way this guy poses his questions is really starting to piss me off.

"I'm trying to get home. But some asshole blocked the road."

"And now we're back to that." He runs a hand through his hair, which makes his robe pull open to show a little more of his hard, pale chest. I hate him, and I can't stop looking at him—like he's a venomous snake or a poisonous mushroom.

"I blocked *my* road," he repeats, like a goddamn broken record. "That you don't have access to use."

"Then how the fuck did Ernie get up here?"

"I gave him an easement," Dane says smugly.

I could fucking explode.

Instead, I stuff that emotion down inside and try to plaster on my sweetest smile. This is something like trying to wrestle an orangutan into a closet—my smile is shaky and feels a lot more like gritted teeth.

"Then could you please also give *me* an easement?"

His response is cold, calm, and immediate: "No."

It has never been more crucial or more soul-destroying to keep hold of my temper. I want to scream so fucking badly. But I'm starting to suspect I might have a serious problem...

This motherfucker could ruin everything.

Just because he wants to.

Just because he doesn't like watching me drive by.

I wish he'd come out on the road to talk. He's lurking in the shadows beneath the oak, which means I have to leave the road and join him under the trees to come close enough for civil conversation.

It's ten degrees cooler under here and a whole lot darker. I suddenly remember how far away we are from any other people. Days must go by, even weeks, without a single other car cruising down this road.

Up close, Dane is both better looking and more off-putting.

His eyes are amber colored, and his lips are the only soft thing in his face. Maybe a little too full and soft—it makes me shudder to think of them touching me. But I am thinking about it.

I could probably handle a new neighbor who is either gorgeous or threatening, but both at the same time is breaking my brain. Curse you, dichotomy! I try for a reset.

"Listen, I think we got off on the wrong foot. I inherited Blackleaf from Uncle Ernie. He died three years ago—"

"I know," Dane interrupts, colder than ever. "I was his doctor."

I cannot picture this man as a doctor. An undertaker, maybe. "I didn't know that."

"I'm not surprised." His lip curls. "You never came to visit."

That lights my fuse. This judgmental fuck doesn't know a thing about the past ten years of my life.

Red noise buzzes in my ears like hornets—all the painful moments, everything I've had to do, my stresses, my fears—they build and they build and they never release...

My hands ball into fists. Dane's eyes flick downward, amused, like he can't wait to watch me lose control.

Don't!

I hear it like a whisper—my better self.

If I pop off, it'll provide the perfect excuse for him to deny access to the house.

But if I stay calm, he's got to be reasonable. He has to—as long as I stay calm.

Stay cool, baby girl. Stay cool…

"Ernie left Blackleaf to me," I repeat. "And I'm going to renovate it. So I'm going to need to come and go on this road. A lot, actually."

"That's not happening."

That's all it takes for me to lose my tenuous grip on diplomacy.

"Why the fuck not? Seriously? Why do you even care?"

"I don't want crews of people coming up here so you can turn that house into some modernized monstrosity and flip it for a buck."

"There's not gonna be crews—it's just me! And maybe an electrician," I admit.

That gives him pause. He looks me up and down again, his eyes lingering on the hole in my shirt.

"You're going to do the whole renovation yourself?"

Disbelief I'm used to. I'm five-four with purple hair and piercings, and while I don't look as young as Jude, I don't exactly scream *responsible adult*, even though that's exactly what I've been for longer than most.

"Yeah, I'm going to do it myself. Because I'm fucking spectacular with power tools."

That draws a ghost of a smile from him. It doesn't show any teeth, but it's nicer than the one that came before—by a tiny margin.

"Congratulations," he says. "I still don't give a shit."

"Please!" I'm truly desperate now. We need this fucking road. "What did my uncle give you for the easement?"

"Ten thousand a year."

He says it flatly and casually, like that kind of money means nothing to him. It probably doesn't.

Or he's lying. How can I find out?

He's not lying. This is exactly my luck.

My body's made of lead. "I don't have ten thousand."

Dane gives as few fucks as ever. "Then how are you going to renovate the house?"

"I need every penny I've got, and it still won't be enough. Please, it's just me and my brother. I'm begging you! We need this."

I'm pathetic and I don't care. I'll get down on my knees if I have to—I have no pride where Jude is concerned.

Dane looks like he'd enjoy it. In fact, I fucking know he's getting a kick out of this. Why else did he string that chain across and watch me cut it loose before he said anything? Why is he standing there, his hands in his pockets, like he'd love to draw this out all day?

Because he would.

Look at him: he's enjoying it…

Don't appeal to his better nature; he probably doesn't have one.

Be smarter.

Offer him what he actually wants…

That's the worst part of me talking, but this time I think it's right.

Jude and I gambled everything we've got on this place—I have to make it work. Whatever it takes.

"I don't have ten thousand, but there has to be something I can do to pay you—on your property? I don't just do house repairs. I can cut your grass, haul trash. I can do anything…"

I'm deliberately listing degrading tasks because I feel like that's what will appeal the most to this sadistic motherfucker. He's loving holding this over my head.

And he takes his sweet time considering, his eyes crawling over my face, my body, the sweat on my lip, the tear in my shirt… I can't tell if he loathes me or wants to eat me.

"All right," he says so abruptly that I jump. That makes him smile, too.

"So...I can use the road?"

"Every damn day."

"And...what do I have to do?"

This smile is the worst of all because it's the most genuine.

"You'll do whatever I ask. Come tomorrow evening—and bring that tool bag with you."

CHAPTER 2
DANE COVETT

I HADN'T PLANNED TO GIVE THE GIRL THE EASEMENT, ESPECIALLY once I realized she was the neglectful niece.

I made the choice in the moment because of the look she gave me when she said *I can do anything...*

It was part desperation, part stubbornness, and 100 percent too tempting to resist. My mind filled with a flood of twisted fantasies.

Plus, I liked how her body looked, sweating and straining to cut through that chain. The sun shone through her thin shirt, revealing the shape of her dark nipples and the silver glint of rings.

That was the first filthy thought I had about her—the impulse to tie her to the bed so I could slowly tug and twist on those rings...

A dozen others followed. The temptations came hard and fast, images of what I'd like to do with her hands, her mouth...

It surprised me because I hadn't felt anything like that in a very long time. I haven't even been hungry, and all of a sudden, I'm craving a ten-course feast...craving it from her...

The rusty orange Bronco and that ridiculous purple hair...it's eye searing, and I should hate it, but I'm fixated like I've discovered some entirely new flavor combination, something you almost want to spit out until you find yourself reaching for another handful...

I want to watch her work on my property, doing whatever I ask. I want to watch her lift and haul and sweat for me.

The annoyance of someone passing on my road is a small price to pay for the leverage it creates against a girl that desperate.

I head back inside to doze through the heat of the afternoon. In the evening, I cook and then read because I have no appointments tonight.

I take my plate of food out on the upper deck. From here, I look out over a carpet of green bordered by a black smudge of ocean. I can't see Grimstone or that ugly fucking resort, thank god, but to the east, Blackleaf is glowing.

It's been three years since a light burned in any of the windows. Even though I know it's only the nephew and niece, I still get a feeling of warmth like Ernie's there, too. The body doesn't pay attention to the brain, sometimes.

I don't know which is in charge when I get the urge to walk over to Blackleaf—probably some part south of my brain, because that's where I feel a low throb when I picture the girl sweating in the sunshine.

I cross the woods and fields between the two houses, a familiar walk, even in the dark. But I approach Blackleaf like I never would have in the past: from the side instead of the front.

It's easy to locate the siblings by the bobbing lights of their lanterns moving from room to room.

Half the windows on the main level are smashed. The industrious Remi has already nailed up fresh boards. Her voice leaks through the gaps in the planks.

"—so I'm going over there tomorrow night."

"How are you going to fix our place if you're fixing *his* place?" comes a peevish voice—presumably the brother. "And why are you going at night?"

"I don't know. He probably works in the day. And I don't exactly have a choice, Jude, I told you"—her voice muffles momentarily as she exits the room, still talking, and returns a moment later—"best I can do."

Whatever the brother says in response is lost as Remi drags something heavy across the room. She sets it down with a grunt, then clatters about for a bit before commencing a repetitive rough scraping sound. I move to the next window to see if I can get a better view.

This window is unbroken, bubbly glass bisected by lead strips. Peering through, I get a watery view of the two siblings in the formal dining room. Their dinner was peanut butter sandwiches. The jar sits open on the table, a knife stabbed handle upward in the peanut butter, next to a bottle of cheap wine. Jude sneaks a quick glance at his sister before topping up his glass.

He's slim and good-looking, with pale hair and dark eyes. He's quick and impatient in his movements, picking up a book, setting it down, his eyes returning often to his sister as she works.

Remi kneels in the opposite corner, scraping wallpaper in long peeling strips. The dark green covered at least two previous wallpapers in burgundy floral and navy stripes. The piles of curled paper show the hours she's already spent.

She's dogged, relentlessly attacking the wall. Sweat drips down her face, and her shirt sticks to her back. She's tied up her purple hair, exposing the vulnerable nape of her neck.

"Play something for me, Jude," she begs.

Her brother regards a moldering grand piano with a cracked lid. "I doubt it plays."

"Try anyway."

He ignores his sister and sprawls across the couch instead, picking at the loosening buttons on the tufting. After a moment, he mutters, "I saw Gideon texted you."

"Don't fuck with my phone," Remi replies without raising her head.

"I wasn't. I saw the text coming in as I walked past."

Remi keeps scraping, a little more aggressively than before. Her face is flushed.

"I thought you blocked him," her brother persists.

"I did. I'm going to."

"He's trying to suck you back in."

"I *know*."

I can't tell if Remi is more annoyed at Jude or this Gideon person.

Her brother waits a few beats, then says, "You don't want to be the kind of woman who—"

"Jude, enough." Her voice is low and exhausted. "It doesn't matter if he texts me. It's over."

Her brother doesn't reply, but it looks as though his shoulders relax. After a moment he says, softer than before, "Never mind, Remi; he's an asshole. You were always too good for him. Didn't I say that?"

She laughs, though even that sounds sad. "You're biased."

She's not scraping the paper with as much vigor.

Jude watches for a moment more before abruptly standing and crossing to the piano, where he takes a seat on the creaking bench and begins to play. His sister pauses her work and turns, a smile already breaking on her face.

Her smile changes everything about her looks. Without it, she's barely pretty, but her grin throws the switch at the amusement park and her whole face lights up, neon bright.

The piano is old and out of tune, but Jude's fingers plunk across the keys with mad genius. He draws out a mocking melody that dances around like it popped live from his brain.

Remi listens, her eyes locked on her brother, delight all over her face. She doesn't move an inch while he's playing, her scraper held loosely in her lap. When he finishes, she claps, then puts two fingers in her mouth and whistles.

Jude tosses his hair out of his face. "Go on, go on…" He pretends to fan himself.

I'm watching Remi.

Her eyes shine, and her face glows with adoration.

I can see why her brother's lapping it up.

Love is a drug, especially love that blind.

I thought I wanted to make her scream, but now I want to make her smile, too. It doesn't matter what order.

I want Remi to look at me like that.

In fact, I just might make her.

CHAPTER 3
REMI

BY THE END OF THE FIRST NIGHT, WE'VE GOT RUNNING WATER, though it takes twenty minutes for the water to run clear instead of dark with rust. Jude sweeps out his room and sets up his camp bed while I'm nailing boards over the most egregious holes in the walls, windows, and ceilings.

I thought I was really gonna be hot shit living it up in the main suite, but it doesn't take long for me to regret my choice. The space is cavernous, my lantern hardly casting light around the bed, let alone the rest of the room. The wood paneling is as black as the heart of a mine, the large four-poster surrounded by musty hangings that I pull down at once. The mattress has some nasty stain right in the center, so I yank it off and swap it for my inflatable.

The wind moans over the chimney and whispers down into the fireplace. The ashes stir as if shifted by invisible fingers.

The idea of a haunting seemed laughable by daylight but less so at midnight. I'm having a hard time falling asleep with a thousand projects zinging through my head, plus intrusive thoughts about my new neighbor.

Why do hotness and assholery go hand in hand?

Probably because nobody would dare punch that aristocratic nose.

Dane intimidates me, like he must intimidate a lot of people. He's fucking scary. I bet nobody says shit to him.

Wish I could say the same.

He was so calm and controlled throughout our encounter, while I could hardly keep from exploding. Of course, that's exactly what he wanted—he set the whole thing up to confuse and upset me.

And what does he want tomorrow?

Probably to hold his leverage over me and rub it in my face.

I know guys like him. I've encountered plenty, working in construction—men who want to feel big by making me feel little. Well, I am little. But I don't let anyone make me feel small.

I'll fix or clean or haul whatever I have to. Then I'll give him two middle fingers straight up in the air while I cash the check for this house.

I am curious to see his place. I could only spot the gables through the treetops, but it looked dark and airy and elegant compared to the shambling, peeling mess Blackleaf has become.

I wonder if he really was my uncle's doctor. Ernie never mentioned him. But it's not like we were that close—we only exchanged letters a couple of times a year. Ernie was more than "eccentric." This house was falling down around him long before he got sick.

My uncle fancied himself an inventor, and he actually did invent a few things over the years—a garden tool with an exchangeable head and color-changing candies—among a hundred abandoned projects and outright failures.

His shed is still stuffed with old equipment and beakers, plus notebooks full of his mad scribbles.

I loved Ernie because he was the first person to teach me to use a lathe and a circular saw. When we'd visit him as kids, he'd give us the full run of the place and let me fuck with all the leftover bits of pipes and boards he wasn't using.

My parents sure as shit didn't know how to do anything practical. My father was a trust fund baby, and my mother, a Southern belle—she did cotillion but never held an actual job in her life.

They loved us, though. God, how they loved us. That was the best thing about my parents: life was a game; it was purely for fun. They took us to Africa on safari, Thailand to wash baby elephants, Brazil for Carnival, Paris for Christmas...

Every day with them was play and laughter, my mother's quips, my father's arms around my shoulders.

That's how I know there aren't any ghosts. My parents would send a message to us if they could—my dad for certain.

I watched for years. Through the hardest, most fucked-up times, I never heard so much as a whisper, never felt so much as a cool hand on the back of my neck. Wherever they went, there's no coming back.

Still, the creaks and groans of the settling house sound disturbingly alive. It could be bats, squirrels, raccoons... We aren't the only residents of this place. But some of the movements sound heavy.

I sit up on the inflatable mattress, lighting the electric lamp once more.

The main suite is on the third floor. The double doors were locked when we arrived, so it's been spared the depredations of teenagers. I jimmied the lock with a screwdriver, entering a space that felt like it had been sealed for decades.

All the windows up here are intact, but the drapes are so full of dust that I left them open. The trees stand close to the house, their branches waving right outside the glass. The motion makes me whip my head around, thinking someone's peeking in the windows.

Downstairs, boards shift like somebody is crossing the main level. The wind mutters in the chimney.

I tell myself it's nothing—old houses are noisy, especially ones that are barely standing up—and I lie back on my inflatable. Until a sharp creak sends me bolt upright once more.

I wait, listening.

Two long creaks and a groan sound from the hallway below— like someone pausing and stepping around the soft spot in the floor.

The silence that follows is worse than noise. My mind fills the gaps with all kinds of horrors.

"I'll just...take a quick peek," I whisper out loud. Talking to myself is a bad habit I got into when I didn't have anyone older and wiser to turn to for advice.

I slip my bare feet out from under the blankets and find my sneakers on the floor. Anything's better than lying here driving myself crazy. I'll make a circuit of the house to prove it's nothing, and then I'll be able to sleep.

I'm not quite brave enough to search the attic by night, and anyway, the noise was coming from below.

I descend the first set of steps to Jude's bedroom on the second floor. I listen, then turn the knob quietly, peeking inside to confirm the shape of his back beneath the blankets. Then I close the door and slowly release the latch, making less sound than the mice scurrying around in the walls.

I'm glad Jude didn't have trouble falling asleep—I'm just surprised he's not snoring.

Next door, the library shelves are full of gaps, the missing books splayed across the floor like fallen birds. My own reflection startles me in a silvery mirror. I cross the room to look at myself, bare legged in an oversize DMX shirt. The T-shirt belonged to Gideon. I stole it with no remorse—it's the least he owes me.

Another creak sends me spinning on my heel, shadows whirling as the lantern swings around. From down in the dining room comes the distinct sound of piano keys...

My scalp tightens, and my skin goes cold.

One note plays, then another, then another: *bing, bong, bing...*

I'm frozen in place, my heart a lump of ice in my chest. Then all at once, I'm sprinting down the staircase, my lantern swinging madly. I leap over the broken steps at the bottom, only to slip on a wet patch on the tiles and go sprawling. My lantern smashes against the wall.

I haul myself up and limp into the dining room.

It's empty. The keys of the open piano glint like bone in the moonlight. The room is closed up tight, boards across all the broken windows.

I search the space anyway, my heart wide awake now and hammering. I heard someone moving down here. And I *know* I heard that piano play.

I fumble my way into the kitchen, groping for the matches and candles I left on the countertop. Candlelight is less powerful than the lantern, illuminating only a couple of feet in front of my face. I check the back door, then the front, and even the door to the glass conservatory. All three are locked and bolted.

The house feels empty now, dark and quiet. The windows are boarded, all the doors securely locked.

Following a hunch, I grab my car keys and climb into the Bronco, driving back along the one and only road away from this house. When I near the point with the iron fence posts, I turn off my headlights and creep a little closer. Then I park and get out.

I walk into the woods in the direction of the dark-blue gables, voids against a starry sky.

I ought to be more terrified than ever, alone out here in the dark, but I'm driven by a strange certainty. My feet crunch over twigs and dead leaves.

It's past two o'clock in the morning.

Yet, just as I suspected, a single light burns in Dane's house.

I would have liked to confront him right then and there, but I was feeling a little vulnerable without any pants.

Instead, I drove back home, got a few fitful hours of sleep, pulled on jeans and a clean shirt, then sped back to pound on his door.

Dane answers, looking rumpled and extremely annoyed.

"You're twelve hours early." He runs a hand through his thick streaky hair, which only makes it spring up more. He's wearing the same robe, no shirt, loose trousers, bare feet. I smell the warm, spicy scent of his sleeping and can't help imagining what it would be like to climb under his sheets.

Somehow he's even better looking fresh out of bed. It might be because he looks a little more human with his hair wild and his face slightly flushed. His skin looks softer, but his stomach is harder before he's had anything to eat.

He's beautiful in a terrifying way, like a glacier or a sword, those golden eyes cruel as a bird of prey. It's all extremely distracting, and if that makes me shallow, then yes, I must be. Because it's hard to make a sentence, and not only from the three hours' sleep…

I blurt, "Were you in my house last night?"

Dane gives me a long look I can't read. "Did you see me in your house?"

"That's a weird way to answer that question…"

"Not as weird as you pounding on my door at seven o'clock in the morning. Which is a terrible way to ingratiate yourself with me, in case you were wondering."

"I'm not sure I'm trying to ingratiate myself." I squint at him. "Kind of depends on if you broke in."

"Why would I do that? I've got my own house right here."

He isn't smiling, but something in his tone makes me think that was his version of a joke. It's certainly a reminder that the house behind him is massive, beautiful, and in excellent shape, while mine is a hunk of junk. Even a ghost would have better taste than to haunt me while this is an option.

"I heard someone downstairs," I say rather lamely. "Playing the piano."

"What song?"

That trips me up again. He's so…infuriating.

"They weren't playing 'My Heart Will Go On,'" I snap. "It was a couple of notes."

"Maybe a mouse ran across the keys." Dane looks bored and like he'd prefer to head back into the house for coffee or more sleep. From the shadows under his eyes, I'd guess it's the latter.

"It wasn't a mouse," I say, though I'm not quite so certain anymore. In the garish light of morning, the idea of someone breaking into my house to play the piano sounds about as stupid as ghosts.

"It also wasn't me." Dane yawns and doesn't bother to cover it up.

"Why were you awake, then?"

His eyes sharpen and the yawn disappears. "How do you know I was awake?"

"I drove over here. I saw your light."

His mouth quirks slightly. "Now who's stalking whom?"

He leans against the doorframe, which makes his robe fall open and exposes more of his long, lean body. He has the kind of muscle definition I've only seen in magazines, not on an actual human person two feet away. It's a lot more intense in 3D—4D, actually: every time he moves, I get a draft of his warm bed scent, and my face flushes hotter.

"I wasn't *stalking*." I'm staring at his bare feet, which are actually really nice for a man's feet—clean and smooth like the rest of him. I force myself to look at his face instead, which is especially intimidating when he's leaning so close. "I thought maybe Ernie gave you a key."

"Do you give your doctor a key to your house?"

His calmness makes me feel idiotic. How does this guy manage to maintain the upper hand when I've never seen him out of pajamas?

"I thought you might have been friends."

"We were friends," he says, surprising me. "God knows he needed one."

His expression has gone hard and disdainful again.

I've had about enough of that.

"Yeah, I wish I could have visited him, too." I force my voice to remain low and steady, though I want to shout. "Unfortunately, I was living two thousand miles away, working three jobs, trying to keep my brother from getting expelled."

"Are you his sister or his mother?"

"Both! I've had to take care of him since a week after I turned eighteen, and it's been fucking hard, so you can get off your high horse about it—I already feel shitty enough that my uncle died alone!"

I'm humiliated to realize that there are tears in my eyes, and my face has probably gone the color of a smashed tomato. Fuck this guy and his fucking judgments.

I've already turned away when Dane's voice calls me back.

"Seven o'clock tonight. And no need to bang on the door; I'll be waiting."

Jude is in the kitchen when I return, eating the best breakfast he could manage without a working stove, fridge, or toaster. He's cut a banana into uniform slices and topped each one with a dollop of peanut butter. He spears the slices with a fork, placing them carefully into his mouth. Since he was a toddler, Jude has hated getting his hands sticky. He even eats pizza with a knife and fork.

"Where'd you go so early?" he mumbles, his mouth full.

I give him a brief recap of my encounter with our neighbor. Jude laughs in my face, which doesn't improve my mood.

"You accused him of breaking into our house? Jesus, Remi, this is why you don't have friends."

"I have friends!"

"Yeah, but I'm your best friend." He grins. "Which is a little pathetic."

"Why is that pathetic?" I ruffle his hair. "You're my favorite person."

He smooths his hair back, frowning. "Better make yourself Dane's favorite person, or we're screwed."

"I bet his favorite person is Ted Bundy."

"Then start stabbing, 'cause we need to stay in his good graces."

"That's not funny."

"Whatever it takes—isn't that your motto, sis?"

"I guess."

I grab a banana and an untoasted piece of bread, wishing Jude wouldn't use my mantras against me.

I eat my food on the drive back into town to buy our first haul of construction supplies.

"Back already?" the lady behind the counter says. She's in her sixties, wearing a green apron with the name tag RHONDA and cat-eye glasses with jewels at the corners of the frames.

"You'll probably be seeing a lot of me. I'm renovating the Blackleaf house."

"Oh, really?" Rhonda pauses in scanning my items, giving me a much more intensive up-and-down. "Where are you staying?"

"At Blackleaf."

"Inside?" She shudders. "You wouldn't catch me within five miles of that place."

"How come?"

"Well, it's creepy, of course! Just the look of it gives me the heebie-jeebies."

"It's not so bad." I'm hoping prospective buyers don't feel the same as Rhonda once I'm finished with it.

"And the man who lived there before..." She makes a face. "He was crazy as a soup sandwich."

"Ernie was my uncle." I try not to make it sound like a reproach, but I'm kind of bugged at this lady all the same. Ernie was crazy, but he was also warm and funny and generous. I doubt Rhonda knew him at all.

"Oh, I'm sorry," she says in a sweet, high voice that doesn't approach sorry. "That's what everybody called him around here: Crazy Ernie."

I'm torn between the urge to defend my uncle and the desire

to get out of here as quickly as possible. I'd like to tell this lady off, but Ernie isn't here to care, and I'm probably going to have to see Rhonda three times a week until the renovation is done. This is the only hardware store in town.

I satisfy myself by saying, "He was an incredible uncle. And he left me his house."

Rhonda snorts. "Don't know if that was a favor—living way up in the woods next to Doctor Death."

She's a catty old gossip, but I still catch a chill.

"Why do you call him that?"

"Well…" Rhonda looks around the store to make sure we're the only people close.

An old man is puttering around the fishing supplies, and Rhonda's husband is restocking the nails, but neither is paying any attention to us. At least, I'm assuming it's her husband over by the nails. They look exactly alike, Mr. and Mrs. Potato Head in matching green aprons, except his glasses are square.

Rhonda has abandoned the remaining supplies waiting on her conveyer belt. She peers at me over the top of her glasses and purses her lips, as if deciding how much to tell me.

"Everybody else calls him 'the night doctor,' on account of how he handles cases that happen at night. The clinic on Elm closes at six, and it's more'n an hour's drive to the hospital for anybody who lives outside Grimstone. But I wouldn't let him into my house if he were the last person on earth with a stethoscope."

She waits for me to ask, "Why not?"

Then, gleefully, she whispers, "Because he killed his wife! And his baby son, too."

My stomach drops. That is not what I expected.

"Now, Rhonda…" Her husband straightens, pressing his hands against the small of his back, like he was waiting for this. "You can't say that to people."

Rhonda raises her eyebrows and puckers her lips. "Well…he did."

"You don't know that."

"I do know it! My cousin Annie works at the morgue, and she told me."

"She did not tell you that he killed his wife," Rhonda's husband repeats patiently. This is clearly a conversation they've had many times.

"Well, she told me the coroner's report was changed, and why do you think Billy changed it? If he didn't do it for Dane Covett, then he let him do it himself, 'cause who else would know how to fix it up besides a doctor?"

"You didn't see any report." Her husband shakes his head, grabbing another bucket of nails. He gives me an apologetic look. Rhonda sees the look and puffs up like a hen.

"Annie saw it, and she told me! That baby dies, and a month later, the wife dies, too? He killed the baby, and she knew it, so he killed her, too!"

"You can't say things like that." Her husband is shaking his head so hard, he looks like a bobblehead doll turned the wrong way. He stuffs both hands into the nails and busies himself with restocking, like that's the end of it.

It isn't close to the end of it for Rhonda. She's flushed and bright-eyed, determined to have her say.

"I'm telling you: he never wanted that baby!" She points her finger at her husband's back, then turns to me. "Everyone knows what he did. And that's why he lives up there, all alone, only coming out at night. He's ashamed, as he should be."

My stomach is churning. I don't like Rhonda one bit, but she seems extremely certain.

But then, she was certain about Ernie, too, and she doesn't know shit about him.

Except...Ernie *was* a little crazy.

I'm sick and clammy-handed, and I just want to get out of here.

"Do you take cards?" I ask, to remind Rhonda that I want to check out.

"Of course." She resumes her scanning. "All of 'em except American Express. Who do they think they are, demanding three percent?"

She scans my items with extra vigor, chucking them into the bag like she's ripping them directly out of the hands of the greedy corporate executives at Amex.

Dane doesn't seem ashamed of anything.

But he does seem a little bit like someone who might murder his wife.

And he's asked me to come to his house. Alone. Tonight.

CHAPTER 4
DANE

THE BRONCO COMES COUGHING UP THE ROAD AT 6:58 P.M. MY NEW neighbor is punctual. Or eager to get this over with.

I watch through the window as she parks in the yard and takes her tool bag out of the trunk. The tool bag is laughably huge compared to her small frame, but she hauls it out and marches up my steps with surprising strength. She's strong like a little French pony.

She has her hair pulled up today, purple pieces hanging down, revealing the silver rings along the rims of her ears to match the ones in her nose and lower lip and nipples. Which makes me wonder if she's pierced anywhere else…

She's wearing jean shorts, work boots, and a T-shirt with the sleeves cut off. The T-shirt is gray, but when she moves, I can tell there's no bra beneath. She probably thinks she doesn't need one because her tits are so tiny, and I guess she doesn't if her only concern is big breasts bouncing around. But she definitely needs one if she doesn't want my cock to stand at attention anytime she's near.

"Oh," she says when I open the door. "You do own clothes."

"That makes one of us." I raise an eyebrow at her shorts and T-shirt, which have both been hacked to shit with a pair of scissors.

"Sorry I didn't wear my Sunday best to scrub your floors."

"You're not working in the house." I come out onto the porch and shut the front door firmly behind me. "I can do that myself."

"Then what am I doing?"

Remi looks tense and nervy, much more so than this morning when she was pounding on my door. When I step toward her, she flinches back.

I wonder if they've been talking in town...

Of course, they have.

I can feel my face hardening.

"For starters, you can fix that fence." I point to the perimeter fence around my orchard. It's about a mile long and so decrepit that half the slats are missing or hanging loose.

Remi regards the immense amount of work before her with a stoic expression. "Then I better get to it."

Without another word, she turns on her heel and hauls her tool bag back down to the fence.

I stand in the shade of the porch, watching her, not even hiding my smile, because she's determinedly not looking at me.

I love how intent she is on appearing strong and composed, while it's obvious she's completely fucked up inside.

Takes one to know one, baby.

She pulls a sledgehammer from her bag and starts knocking the broken slats off the fence. She scowls as she swings the hammer, smashing the slats with all her might. I bet she's pretending each one is my face.

I head back inside, but only so I can watch her more comfortably through the polarized windows. I don't expect her to keep up the furious pace, but she keeps swinging the hammer like that for two full hours. Her stamina is impressive, especially since I know she already spent all day working on her own house.

I'd know that even if I hadn't walked over to see for myself. She's clearly the type who burns her own body for fuel, who takes out her stress in labor. Plus, she doesn't have much choice. The car alone tells me how broke she is—the bumper's tied on with rope.

The sun is sinking before she stops for so much as a water break.

Sweat drips down her face. She takes out the sort of metal canteen used by construction workers, drinks a huge draught, then pours the rest over her head.

Her shirt was already drenched, but the pose—her head thrown back, eyes closed, chest thrust forward—shows me the exact moment the cold water hits her face and her nipples harden like pencil points. The water runs all the way down to her strong thighs and into her boots.

She lifts the front of her shirt to dab her face on the only dry patch near the bottom. The movement reveals a tiny slice of the underside of her bare breasts.

The flash lasts less than a second and was completely unintentional, but Remi couldn't have devised a more devious way to send me into a tailspin. I've always found underboob ten times sexier than cleavage.

My cock is so stiff, it no longer feels like human flesh—more like a homing missile determined to drag the rest of me exactly where it wants to go.

I slip my hands in my trousers and squeeze hard around the base.

My cock throbs with each bend and flex of her body as she fixes my fence. Her soaking shirt clings to her tits. Her bare skin glows in the sun. She has the deep tan of long hours spent outdoors and the broken nails and bruised knees that show it was in work, not in leisure.

We don't get that kind of sun in Grimstone. Clearly, she's not from here.

You could tell anyway, just from the way she talks, just from the way she looks around…

She's living in a dream, that one.

I remember what it felt like to dream.

Dreams fuel you. Look how hard she works…because she believes in what she's doing. She thinks she's building something.

That fence is almost always in the sun; it's why I haven't fixed it.

Remi switches to a claw-head hammer so she can lever out the straggling nails.

Watching her work is so goddamn arousing. Watching her bend and move and sweat for me...

I'm lost in fantasies of what else I could get her to do.

It's not my fault she drove down my road...

She practically came knocking on my door...

I stroke my hand lightly up and down my raging shaft.

This girl is nothing like what I'd usually be attracted to. I'm not into tattoos and piercings and ridiculously colored hair.

But there's something vivid about her, like a firework, like fresh-squeezed orange juice. I'd like to put my mouth on her and see if she crackles against my tongue.

As she yanks and wrenches at the nails, the hammer slips. The claw comes down on her leg, cutting a gash out of her thigh. She clamps her hand against it, but blood seeps through her fingers, shockingly fast.

I'm sprinting across the yard before she's had a chance to move, scooping her up in my arms and carrying her into the house. I had no intention of bringing her inside, but it's instinct.

"Fuck," she says, lifting her hand. "That's a lot of blood."

"Keep pressure on it!" I bark, pressing my hand down over hers.

She's solid in my arms, warm from the sun. Even her blood is bright and vivid.

I have my own tool bag, a lot sleeker than hers. I grab my doctor's kit and lay her down on the couch in my living room.

"I'll get blood on the cushions." She struggles to rise.

"Shut up and lie back." I push her down. "I don't give a fuck about the cushions—and I assume you don't give a fuck about these shorts."

I cut them off with shears, baring the underwear beneath. She's wearing a white cotton thong, and she'd have to be a lot closer to death for me not to notice how it clings to her pussy lips and the little nub in between...

That's all the time I have to perv before professionalism takes over. I move her filthy hand, relieved to see there's no arterial spray, just heavy bleeding from a ragged cut.

I irrigate the gash on her inner thigh, cleaning out the dirt and splinters.

Remi stays silent and still, though her face has gone gray. I think that's from squeamishness, not blood loss—she's staring at the wound, transfixed.

"I've never...seen inside myself before," she croaks.

The raw flesh could be a lot worse—she didn't sever any major veins.

"I'm going to give you a shot so this won't hurt so much."

She nods, her lower lip trembling.

I inject novocaine around the wound and then a shot of Demerol in her arm to calm her down. By the time I've got the sutures ready, her breathing has slowed.

She sits up on the cushions, her leg extended. Her eyes flit down to her exposed underwear, and her face reddens.

"Thank you," she mutters. "For fixing me up."

"Can't have you dying in my yard."

When I glance up, our faces are closer than I expected.

I'm struggling with something that's never happened to me before...

I'm really fucking turned on.

I've been turned on before, of course, but never while attending to a patient. I don't know if it's because I was stroking my cock two seconds before she hurt herself, but I'm still extremely aroused.

Blood doesn't bother me. What *does* affect me is the scent of Remi's sweat and her warm flesh under my hands. Her body is firm and overheated from all that labor; her scent is everywhere in the air, sweat and copper and her own unique essence.

I've never had to focus so hard just to put in some simple stitches.

My cock isn't calming down—I shift my weight to hide the fact it's swelling every time my hands touch her body.

Her legs are spread, the injured thigh propped up on the cushions, the uninjured leg bent over the edge of the couch. I kneel on the ground, my hands high up on her leg, the tight delta of her pussy inches from my face. Only millimeters of cotton prevent me from turning my head and swiping my tongue in her warmest, wettest place. If I breathe slowly through my nose, I can smell the faintest hint of her sweet, sweet cunt.

I've never smelled a woman's pussy before I've even kissed her lips. It takes everything I have not to hook my finger under the cotton gusset and pull it to the side so I can see if her pussy is as velvety as the rest of her skin...if it's pale pink or dark like her nipples...

Even the sutures are starting to turn me on. I plunge the needle into her flesh and pull it tight, closing the gash. I'm penetrating her with biting steel and fine thread, leaving something of mine inside her for the next seven to ten days until the stitches come out.

Remi watches, her eyes fixed on my hands. She won't look away. I wish she would, so I could confirm if that little nub between her pussy lips is metal or flesh...

When I'm finished, her eyes move to my face. Hers are blue green with black rings around the irises, like the wings of a blue morpho butterfly. It's her only feature I'd call truly lovely, and yet I've never felt attraction quite like this. Her blood is under my fingernails. Her scent fills my lungs.

"I know it's asking a lot," she says. "But I'm also gonna need a pair of pants."

CHAPTER 5
REMI

DANE GIVES ME A PAIR OF THE SOFT COTTON TROUSERS HE WAS
wearing on our first two encounters. They're way too big for me,
even after I roll up the legs and tighten the drawstring. He's at least
six-three, which makes us a full foot apart in height. Probably at
least a decade in age, too, though it's hard to tell. His hair is thick
and springy, the sort that might have gone prematurely gray.

I wonder if these are the same pants he had on the other day.
And if he wears underwear beneath.

That's a bit of a stupid thought to have about someone I just
learned might be a murderer, but since I'm already inside the potential murderer's house, it probably doesn't matter if I have pervy
thoughts about fabric that might have recently touched his cock.

My hormones don't seem to give a fuck about the circumstances
of this encounter. It shouldn't be hot to be bleeding all over someone's
couch, especially not when it hurts like a son of a bitch, but I think
I'd have to lose the whole leg not to notice how fucking sexy Dane's
hands look on my body.

Hands are my kink—they show everything about a man's compe-
tence. The way they move, the way they touch…a well-shaped hand
resting on a steering wheel or shifting gears… I could come just
thinking about it.

Dane doesn't just have a surgeon's hands; he has the hands of an artist. I was mesmerized as he elegantly sewed my ragged cut into a neat, smooth line.

Maybe it was the pain that made his touch feel so good. Heat seemed to spread from his palms, infecting my blood, setting fire to my brain...

I never wanted the stitches to end.

That's fucking crazy considering what I just learned about Dane.

Do I believe it?

Rhonda's a gossipy old bitch, but that doesn't mean she's wrong. If anyone was going to get away with falsifying a medical report, it'd be a doctor. And I *was* here just twelve short hours ago accusing Dane of breaking into my house.

But now he's making me a drink and a sandwich. And I'm very susceptible to bribery.

"Eat," he orders, like there was any chance I'd let a good sandwich go to waste. "You lost a lot of blood. And you were going hard out there."

"Were you watching me?"

He obviously was—he ran out the moment I hurt myself.

And he doesn't try to deny it.

"It looked like you were trying to fix the whole fence in one night."

"I was. I like getting shit done."

"You'd need an army to finish that fence before dark."

"I can still try."

"That's...a little delusional."

"I call it 'motivated.'"

His mouth makes a funny downward motion that I think is one of his smiles. A dimple appears on the downturned side, a surprising interloper on his cold, stiff face. It's kind of adorable.

I bet his wife thought that, too...

Oh, shut the fuck up, Rhonda. I don't even know if he actually had a wife.

Yes, he did. Her husband said it, too...

Small-town gossip.

A lot of things get swept under the rug in small towns...

I take a huge bite of the sandwich. If Dane wanted to poison me, he could have done it when he injected whatever the fuck that was into my arm. Also, even if he *did* kill his wife, I doubt he bumps off every random girl who crosses his path. This is fine. I'll be fine.

As long as I can stop staring at his body under that shirt...

I liked it better when he was bare chested, but goddamn, can this man fill out clothes. He's wearing charcoal slacks a few shades darker than his hair and a crisp white dress shirt. Or at least, it used to be crisp—now blood blooms shockingly bright on the body and sleeves, with a bonus streak down the leg of his trousers.

I set my sandwich down, feeling guilty all over again.

"Now I owe you for some clothes, too."

Dane glances down at himself. "Why—because of this? You think I don't know how to get bloodstains out of clothing?"

"A person could take that the wrong way."

He gives me a sharp look.

Is it better to say it or not to say it?

Hey, did you ever have a wife?

And if so, did you happen to kill her?

Nope, can't do it. I'm too fuckin' chicken.

Instead, after an awkward pause, I ask, "Are you working tonight?"

"In a couple of hours."

"Do you always work the night shift?"

"I pretty much have to."

I let that hang until he adds, sullenly, "I have a condition that makes me sensitive to the sun."

"Oh." I'm trying not to examine him under the lens of this new information. "Like a vampire?"

Too late, I realize how often he must have heard that stupid joke.

"Sorry," I mutter.

"Not as bad as that." Dane lets it pass. "But I get a hell of a sunburn if I go out at midday."

"Kind of a waste, living in a beach town."

"I don't live in Grimstone." His face darkens, like the idea is offensive. "I live right here."

He's deep in the woods in this house painted the shade of a night sky, dark film on all the windows. The trees grow even closer around his house than mine, creating a den of perpetual shadow. Only the orchard receives full sun.

This is all making sense now, in a sad kind of way—I'm leaning more to the interpretation that Dane is a misunderstood outsider, and superstitious old biddies like to talk shit.

"Have you always lived here?"

"Yes," he says simply. "I was born in this house. My father delivered me—he was a doctor, too."

"Does your house have a name?" I love houses with names. I'm planning to build a signpost for Blackleaf.

"Someone called it 'the Midnight Manor,' and it stuck," Dane says with a strange, unhappy smile.

I couldn't think of a more perfect moniker. His house is sleek and dark, the walls and ceilings painted glossy indigo, the woodwork a deep mahogany. His furniture is more modern than mine, but he's kept the old glass doorknobs and the brass chandeliers.

What I'm really looking for is any hint of a woman's touch. How long ago did his wife die? Is he dating anyone now?

More stupid thoughts because it doesn't matter if Dane is dating anyone. He won't be dating *me* because he's probably not interested, potentially a murderer, most definitely coercive, and if that weren't enough, we have nothing in common. The books on the shelves and the art on the walls tell me Dane is a hell of a lot more highbrow than me. I like to pour vodka into a Slurpee and get plastered watching *Rick and Morty* with Jude.

Now that I've decided we will never date and he probably won't kill me, I feel a lot more relaxed. Enough to set my empty plate down and start poking around.

"Have you read all these?" I trail my finger down the spines of his books.

Touching his stuff makes Dane uncomfortable. He watches me everywhere I move.

I like his eyes on me, even while I can barely stand it.

"Every one," he says stiffly.

When I was his patient, he was in complete control. He's not quite so certain how to deal with me as an unwanted guest in his living room.

This is the first time I've had anything like an upper hand, and I can't help dragging this out a little just like Dane did outside the iron gate. It might have something to do with the shot in the arm he gave me, which makes this all the more his fault—I'm floating on a wave of wicked glee with zero sense of consequences. I can't even feel my injured leg beneath me.

He's got a lot of odd books on his shelf—stuff that looks mystical and occult right alongside the nonfiction.

"Are these your old textbooks?" I pull a tattered leather-bound copy of *Gray's Anatomy* off the shelf.

"No." Dane narrowly resists snatching it out of my hands. "That's a first edition from 1858, and it's worth about sixteen grand, so unless you want to be scrubbing my toilets until the end of time—"

"Thank god." I laugh. "I was afraid that's what they were handing out back when you were in college."

"I'm not that old." His mouth quirks up, though his expression has saddened. "Though, fuck, sometimes I feel like it."

"Me, too," I say with too much honesty.

We stare at each other for a long moment.

Dane seems like he's looking at me for the first time, really looking at me: as a person, not an obstacle. And I do the same back to him—I stop ogling his body through his clothes and fucking with his stuff and really look into his face, feeling that moment of connection where an emotion is the same, even if all the circumstances are different.

"What's the deal with your brother?" he asks abruptly. "Why are you his keeper?"

The moment is broken. I look away, flustered. "Because our parents died."

Dane doesn't ask the next obvious question—*How did they die?*—and for that, I'm grateful because I loathe the way acquaintances will casually ask me to relive the worst night of my life.

Most people can't resist their curiosity.

If Dane really had a wife who died, I'd guess he isn't asking 'cause that's the exact question he hates pointed at himself.

Instead, he says, "How old was your brother?"

"Ten. But he looked about six." I smile, remembering how small and slight Jude was, how huge his dark eyes were in his tiny pointed face. "He was such a sweetheart as a kid. He used to lie at the foot of my bed for hours while I was studying. He'd draw or read or write in his journal, but never do his own schoolwork."

Dane snorts. "Sounds like my brother. Just the last part—not any of the nice stuff."

"You have a brother?" It's good to know Dane has family members still breathing.

"He owns the Monarch in Grimstone. He took that in the inheritance, and I took the house."

"Who got the better deal?"

"We both got what we wanted. Or so we thought at the time."

The Monarch is the beautiful old hotel on Main Street, the only one actually inside the town itself. Its competitor is the hideously opulent Onyx resort built on the opposite end of the beach, loathed by the original residents but possible salvation for me in the way it should skyrocket my property value. Dane's, too, though it sounds like he doesn't need it.

"So, you're *rich* rich," I say. "I thought so. It's the velvet robe—most people wear fleece these days; I don't know if you know that."

When I make a joke Dane doesn't want to acknowledge, he has to pause and unclench his jaw. It's becoming my favorite thing to watch.

"The Covetts were one of the founding families of Grimstone," Dane says, like he's admitting something, not bragging.

"Were you the ones who named it? Because you might want to rethink your marketing...doesn't exactly conjure up images of sunny skies and sandy beaches."

Dane raises an eyebrow. "Have you seen our beaches?"

"No, actually." Uncle Ernie hated the ocean. He took us into town but never down to the water.

"Let's just say it was the one time my ancestors were honest."

"Can't be that bad if they built a whole resort around it."

Dane gives me an odd look. "People come here to visit, but they don't stay."

"Why not?"

"Because they can feel there's something wrong with this place. Especially down there." He nods in the direction of the town and its caves and beaches, though we're long past seeing even the trees in his own yard. It's fully dark outside now and only a little better illuminated inside Dane's house. The sole lamp in the room wouldn't give nearly enough light to stitch up my leg anymore.

I hadn't realized how much light we'd lost. Dane's eyes have gone from honey to stone, his skin like marble. The darkest bits of his hair are black as jet, the lightest streaks pure silver. He's more metal than man.

I should go...

Instead, I ask, "What's wrong with Grimstone?"

Dane looks at me, his head tilted. "Why is any place the way that it is? Why is everything in the Amazon poisonous? The people who grow here aren't good people."

"Including you?"

"Especially me."

All at once, I remember that I'm in the house of a complete stranger. With a terrible reputation.

I lick my lips. "What does that mean?"

"What?"

"That you aren't a good person?"

The silence between us is smooth like lake water—you could notice the tiniest ripple across it.

Dane's face is expressionless while a thousand thoughts flicker behind his eyes.

If I could read them in a book...would I open it?

Yes. Every fucking time.

"What do you think it means?" Dane says. "To be a bad person."

"It means you hurt people."

He smiles slightly, his light breath tickling my arm. "Remi... everyone hurts people."

"I mean intentionally. Taking pleasure from it."

"Does it matter if the person who hurt you did it on purpose?"

Gideon flashes into my head. "*Yes,*" I say fiercely.

"I don't think so." Dane stands close to me in the dark. "I don't think it matters at all when you're bleeding out on the floor."

His words are threatening, his presence is terrifying, but there's a dark amusement dancing in his eyes that draws me irresistibly closer, instead of out the door.

I lift my chin. "I was bleeding out on your couch. You stitched me up. Doesn't seem like a bad-guy move to me."

Dane's hand whips up quick as a snake and seizes my ponytail, yanking my head back. His body presses against mine, and he's not metal at all anymore, not coldness or steel—he's pure molten fire, flickering behind his eyes, breathing out of his lungs. His lips burn against the rim of my ear.

"That was purely selfish. You owe me a fuck of a lot more work than that—and I'm going to take every dollar out of your body before I let you fall apart."

His mouth crashes down on mine, hot, wet, and aggressive. His other hand slips under my shirt and seizes my nipple, squeezing hard.

"I do enjoy pain in a beautiful woman. I enjoy what it does… physiologically." He twists his fingers, making me cry out against his mouth. His lips trail down my jaw, and he presses his nose behind my ear, inhaling my scent. "The adrenaline in your sweat…" He swipes his hot tongue up the side of my neck. "The way your pupils dilate…"

He kisses me, and my spine bends back over his arm, all the strength gone in my legs. I'm lost in the dizzy heat of his body pressed against mine.

A bright bolt of pain from my tit brings me back.

The pain is sharp and throbbing; it jolts me upright again, my fists clenched helplessly in his shirt. He pinches my nipple relentlessly, pinning me in place, forcing one blazing point of focus while the rest of my mind tries to dissolve in the softness of his lips, the warmth of his arms around me.

"So, no, I didn't stitch you up to help you…" he whispers in my ear. "I did it because I want my fence fixed…and because I liked cutting off your shorts."

With one last sharp twist that makes me screech, he lets go of my breast and releases me.

My tit is on *fire*. The nipple throbs like he ripped out the ring, a pounding heat that spreads across the entire breast. My lips are swollen and throbbing just as hard.

Dane stands back, cool and composed once more, adjusting the cuff link on his blood-drenched dress shirt. "Now, if you don't mind…I need to change clothes before I leave."

He walks over to his own front door and opens it.

My legs are shaking. My nipple is blazing. I don't know what the fuck is wrong with this guy.

But he just dismissed me like a dog, and I'm not going to walk out of here like a little bitch.

So, as I'm leaving, I turn and pause on his doorstep, sweaty, bloodstained, and completely filthy from working in his yard.

"You know, according to you," I say, "if you were enjoying that... it means you think I'm beautiful."

CHAPTER 6
REMI

"How did it go?" Jude calls when I haul my tool bag into Blackleaf at last.

He comes into the kitchen to meet me, his clothes dusty and his eyes bright. "What did he make you do?"

"Fix some old fence." I turn and open the fridge so Jude can't see me blush. I'm terrible at lying.

"There's nothing in there," he reminds me.

"Oh yeah. What'd you eat?"

"Peanut butter sandwich."

"You can't eat that every single day."

"You keep saying that, and yet here I am." He gestures to himself like his continued aliveness means it can't possibly be doing him harm.

"I don't know." I shrug. "I just thought someday you might aspire to have the muscle mass of, say, a twelve-year-old girl."

"Strength is overrated," Jude says. "I prefer to use my brain."

"Is that what you've been doing all day? How come you're filthy?"

God knows it's not 'cause he finished clearing out the library like I asked—I didn't see any tattered books tossed on our trash heap.

"I've been in Ernie's workshop."

"Yikes."

Jude's eyes are wide and manic. "You wouldn't believe the shit he's got in there."

"I was kind of thinking we should douse the whole place in lighter fluid and throw in a match. We don't need the outbuildings to sell the house."

"Don't do that!" Jude cries. "The barn's still good. I'll clear it out."

"You need to help me in the house. Did you even touch the library?"

"Come on," he wheedles. "You could turn it into, like, a really bougie four-car garage."

That *would* be a good selling feature. God damn it.

"All right," I relent. "But you have to do the whole project yourself. I'm not helping until it's empty."

"You do what you're good at, and I'll do what I'm good at." He points between us, grinning.

Actually, this could be perfect. Jude is excellent at finding valuables in the houses we flip. He sells them on eBay and Craigslist and on strange little forums where he can off-load hard-to-find items at inflated prices. Convincing him to put the cash in his college fund is a separate issue.

When Jude gets a bee in his bonnet, he's surprisingly productive. I'm much better off giving him his project of choice than trying to make him do what I want. If he can get the whole workshop cleared out, that's a hell of a lot better than burning down the barn, which I'm pretty sure is illegal—not that it would stop us, but I'd like to keep our felonies to a minimum.

"Fantastic," I say. "And I've got the electrician coming tomorrow."

"Thank god. I'm so fucking tired of warm drinks."

Tom Turner is the one and only electrician in Grimstone, so I hope he knows what he's doing. And doesn't charge too much. I doubt he accepts fence fixing in payment—or semiconsensual kisses.

My face burns. Jude notices, and all of a sudden, his eyes are flicking everywhere, finding evidence.

"Whose pants are those?"

Fuck.

"Dane's. And get your dirty mind out of the gutter. My shorts were covered in blood."

"Whose blood?" Jude says, going still. Jude can't stand gore of any kind. He's practically vegetarian, and not only out of laziness.

"Mine," I admit. "I cut my leg."

"Let me see."

"No, you don't need to see. It's way up here on my—"

"Let me see," Jude insists.

I watch his face as I slip down Dane's pants, concerned that he might get pukey just from the sight of the stitches.

Sure enough, what little color was in his cheeks drains away. He licks his lips. "Did he do that to you?"

"The stitches? Yeah."

Jude stares at the long gash down my inner thigh.

"I'm fine," I say, pulling up his pants. "It doesn't even hurt anymore."

Jude blinks. "That fucker. He was probably worried you'd sue his ass."

"What for? I'm the one who hit myself with the hammer."

"On his property. Working for him."

"Is that our new plan?" I snort. "We're gonna get rich filing workers' compensation suits?"

"Well, you picked the right guy to stick with a lawsuit. He's rich as hell, isn't he?"

"Yeah. Apparently his brother owns the Monarch."

"Wish our parents were as rich as they thought they were." Jude sulks.

"Not as much as I do."

After our parents died, Jude and I learned that they never actually owned our lovely, bright colonial in the Garden District of New Orleans. It had always been the property of a sweet old lady named Brenda, who gave us exactly thirty days to grieve—then informed us how much rent we owed, including arrears.

My father's trust fund was down to its dregs. My mother never had money; she was just fucking gorgeous. She was raised to marry rich, and she had—though not as rich as she thought.

By the time we paid off all the debt and set aside what we needed for Jude to stay at his private school, there was barely enough left for half the rent on a cheap walk-up. I got a job with a painting crew the very next day. I was eighteen years old. I'd never even been kissed.

"Never mind," I say to Jude. "I charged my laptop off the battery pack—you want to watch a movie tonight?"

Jude grins. "I've got something way better than that."

He takes me out to the back garden, overgrown with blackberry bushes and pumpkin vines. He's set up a couple of rickety lawn chairs and tacked a sheet against the back of the house. A projector sits on three spindly legs, the fourth side propped up on books.

"Ernie had a generator!" Jude says gleefully. "Only took me a few hours to get it working again."

He cranks it up. The generator roars to life, spitting black smoke and the stench of gasoline.

"Bit loud for a movie, isn't it?" I yell over the noise.

"That's why I built this." Jude slaps a pillow-stuffed box over top.

His makeshift soundproofing works well enough that we can hear most of Han's lines in *Return of the Jedi*. Jude yells out all the best ones anyway.

The characters make ghostly shapes on our wall, their faces distorted by wrinkles in the sheet. Moths flutter across the projector's lens, throwing shadowy wings a thousand times larger across our movie.

My brother is surprisingly tender about the wound on my leg, insisting on propping my foot up on pillows and wrapping a blanket around my shoulders. He even builds a little fire so we can toast marshmallows.

"Jude," I say after I've eaten about a hundred s'mores. "This is really nice."

"I know." He nestles back smugly on the pillows. "I did a good thing."

"Well, don't get too cocky—you have chocolate on your face."

"No, I don't," he says, looking haughty.

I laugh because he absolutely does—a big streak across his nose.

Jude falls asleep in the middle of our second movie. I clean up the mess and haul my brother up the stairs because sleepy Jude does not give a fuck about my leg. He can't even make sentences.

"Brush your teeth," I say.

"*Mrghashwa*" is his response.

As I'm following my own advice and brushing my own damn teeth, my phone buzzes next to the sink.

Can't we just talk?

I spit, all the warmth of the evening sucking down the drain with the toothpaste.

Another message flashes up:

Remi, I swear I don't know how—

I don't open the message to read it. Instead, I do what I should have done weeks ago and block Gideon's contact.

It's like I turned off a buzzing fan in the room. My suite becomes calm and quiet and cool.

I pad across the room barefoot and slip under the covers, my inflatable mattress crinkling beneath me on the comically opulent four-poster.

Tonight, the creaks and groans of the house are gentle as sighs. I don't hear anything that sounds like somebody moving around. And definitely no piano keys.

My body is heavy with exhaustion, my muscles aching. God, I'd kill for a long, hot shower instead of the minute and a half I managed under the icy spray.

Still, I feel surprisingly peaceful. Even with my left tit throbbing.

I examined it in the mirror: the piercing was perfectly fine, though the nipple was swollen and red.

Unconsciously, I reach up and pinch the other one, like I'm evening them out.

The bolt of pain causes an unexpected response lower down. My thighs squeeze together.

I touch myself, still pinching my nipple. My fingers slide across my pussy lips, shockingly slick. My wetness is thin and slippery and already spreading down my thighs.

I twist my nipple between my fingers and thumb. It's only a fraction as hard as Dane did it but much rougher than how I've touched myself before. The bite of pain is soothed by the soft pressure of my fingers against my clit.

I picture Dane's amber-colored eyes close to my face and the heat of his lips against my ear...

I did it because I want my fence fixed...and because I liked cutting off your shorts...

I pinch my nipple furiously, rubbing my fingers against my clit. The harder I squeeze, the harder I rub, until the sensation blasting through my body is a twisting bullet of pleasure and pain.

The face in my mind is Dane's—no thoughts of Gideon at all.

And that night, I sleep deeply, no phantom footsteps or keys played by restless ghosts.

It doesn't mean anything.

But I do find it interesting since I know Dane was away working all night.

CHAPTER 7
DANE

IN THE DEEPEST HOURS OF THE NIGHT, WHEN I RETURN HOME from delivering a baby and setting a broken arm, Lila is waiting for me, as I knew she would be.

I feel her close as I'm washing in the sink. I straighten, her flawless face reflected in the mirror just behind me, her dark eyes looking into mine.

You brought her into our house.

"You prefer I let her die in the yard?"

She wasn't going to die.

When I turn, there's nothing there.

I know there's nothing there.

But I saw her all the same.

I enter the bedroom, stripping off my clothes so I can slip naked between the sheets.

Only an hour or two of night remains. Lila's still close. I pull back the covers, the scent of her perfume—pear and bergamot—rising from the sheets. If I lie here in the dark long enough, she'll come to me.

But as my head hits the pillow, the image that flashes on the black canvas of my mind is of two eyes startling open, wide and blue as butterfly wings.

My cock swells. I grab it in my hand.

I think of Remi's nipple between my fingers, thick and stiff and run through with metal...

The sheets aren't cool anymore; they're heating.

And the scent of pear is nowhere to be found.

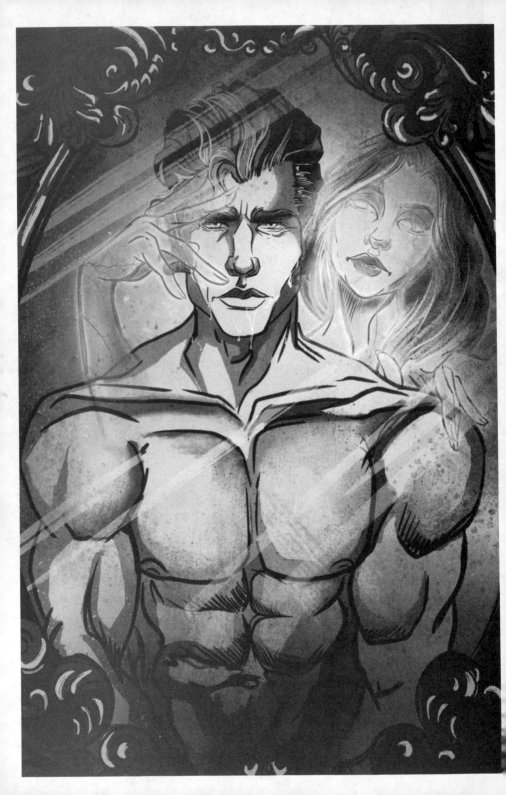

CHAPTER 8
REMI

THE NEXT MORNING, JUDE'S UP EARLIER THAN USUAL.

"Will you drive me into town?" he says the moment I step into the kitchen.

"Sure. What for?"

"'Cause I'm sick of sitting around here all day."

"You could try not sitting around."

"You know what I mean," he says. "I'm stir-crazy, cooped up here in the sticks."

"Well, it has been two whole days."

Jude doesn't even dignify that with an eye roll. He's spearing apple wedges on a fork and dipping them into the jar of peanut butter, the fancy fondue version of his usual breakfast.

I can't stand the idea of peanut butter for another meal. I'm fucking starving from all that work yesterday; I need protein.

"Why don't we get some real food while we're in town?"

I'm sure we can afford a couple of plates of bacon and scrambled eggs from the diner. Or, in Jude's case, pancakes and possibly a poached egg if I can convince him.

"Sure." He shrugs.

"Don't trip over your own feet in excitement."

"Only one of us does that." He ambles over to the back door and slips said feet into a pair of canvas boaters. Jude's wardrobe would give you the impression he's going yachting in the afternoon, or if he's gloomy, he dresses like a cleric.

He's been gloomy often since graduating from Newman. For all the trouble he got into, Jude loved that school. He had a pack of friends he'd roam around with, and I think it was easier for him to pretend we were still part of the upper crust, despite what our apartment looked like—and smelled like.

I'm hoping once he's at college, he'll find his feet again. Maybe start dating. He's never had a girlfriend, at least not one he told me about. I've wondered if he might be gay, but I haven't noticed any particularly intense connections with his male friends either.

I worry about him constantly because I'm always afraid it goes back to losing our parents or, worse, to the way I raised him afterward. I was barely more than a kid myself. I had no clue how to properly help him through his grief except for scrounging up the funds for a therapist Jude refused to see more than twice.

Fuck, maybe *I* should see a therapist. I haven't been dealing well lately, especially after all the shit with Gideon. My nightmares are back, and the pressure in my head is building. Sometimes I thought I was going insane—but I guess that's what gaslighting does to you. Maybe I could have forgiven Gideon if he'd just been honest with me, but he wouldn't even give me that closure.

Now he's texting and calling nonstop after I asked him to leave me alone.

Blocking him solves that problem. I should have done it weeks ago like Jude said. I guess I wasn't as ready to let go as I wanted to believe.

Thinking about my ex yanks my mood down several notches. Jude notices before we've even climbed in the Bronco and handles it with his usual grace.

"What're you moping about all of a sudden?"

"I blocked Gideon last night."

"Oh." He glances over as I start the engine. "Well, that's a good thing. He had too much power over you."

"It's called 'being in love.' You wouldn't get it—your most devoted relationship is with peanut butter."

"After all the trouble I went to with movie night." Jude sniffs.

"That was thoughtful." I rest my hand on the nape of his neck, tickling the short hair back there, something that has relaxed him from the time we were kids. Our mom was hilarious and adventurous but not physically affectionate. It was me Jude came to for snuggles.

"Gideon was controlling." Jude can't resist taking a few more shots at my ex now that we're on the topic. "Always telling you what to do and how to spend your money."

"Well…I think he thought he had the right once we got engaged."

Gideon seemed supportive when we were dating, but as soon as the ring was on my finger, he had some things to say about my plans and budgeting. Most especially my need to pay for Jude's education, not that I'd ever tell Jude that.

He and Gideon already had a prickly relationship. They were polite, but I could tell they didn't exactly adore each other, like two cats forced to live in the same house. And we didn't even cohabit—Gideon and I planned to get our own place once Jude was in college.

Thank god we never did. It would have been a hell of a lot more difficult to untangle our lives.

All I had to do was drop off a box of the stuff Gideon left strewn around my place. Minus his DMX T-shirt.

The box looked so pathetic there on his porch. A three-year relationship, and it all fit in three cubic feet.

"It's over," I promise Jude.

"We'll see." He gives me a look.

I know why he doesn't trust me. Gideon and I have broken up before and gotten back together. He's very convincing, and if I'm honest with myself, I'm too easily convinced. Sometimes I believe what I want to believe—that I have someone who loves me and will be there for me when I feel so goddamn alone.

Well, I'm not going to do that anymore. I'm going to believe the evidence in front of my face. And I have more than enough when it comes to Gideon.

A fresh start, a real change—that's why we're here. I left the old Remi in New Orleans; her soul lies abandoned in the smiling couple's selfies on Gideon's porch.

Now I'm here in this tiny diorama of a town, quaint as gingerbread, dark as a fairy tale.

Jude looks around with interest as we drive into Grimstone. He hasn't been here since he was small.

It's a gorgeous autumn day, the bright drifts of leaves making Main Street look particularly picturesque. The buildings are old-fashioned and mostly neat, though some of the newer shops and restaurants sit next to stranger, shabbier establishments. A tattoo parlor and a dodgy-looking tarot shop bracket the opulent Monarch hotel. Its gold-scrolled facade brings Dane to mind—as a throb located right around my left tit.

I have the oddest urge to peek inside and see what his brother looks like. But I doubt anyone with the last name *Covett* would work the front desk—the brother's probably holed up in some back office making the maids' lives miserable.

I park in front of Emma's Diner instead, which sports a chic turquoise awning and *Best Pancakes in 100 Miles!* written across the window in gold script. The tables are packed, lending solid support to that boast.

Jude and I squeeze into the last available two-top right next to the window. The waitresses are hustling. The girl who comes to our table has a mischievous face, bright-orange hair in two buns, and an adorable gap in her teeth.

"Hiya!" she says. "What can I get you to drink?"

"Black coffee," says Jude.

I ask, "Do you make lattes?"

"Absolutely. In fact, I'm the only one who can make that hunk of junk work." She points her pen at a contraption with so many brass knobs and tubes that, at first, I think it's a church organ and not an espresso machine.

"Latte it is," I say, smiling.

"You got it." She doesn't bother to write that down on her pad.

I watch her fire up the espresso machine, with as much steam and chugging as a locomotive. Next to the machine sits a notice-board papered with local jobs, advertisements, and a MISSING poster for a friendly-looking dog.

"You can leave me here in town," Jude says. "I want to explore a bit."

"You'll call me later when you want a ride home?"

"Yeah, or hitch partway back."

"No way! That's super sketchy."

"I'm not the type who gets kidnapped," Jude says. "On account of the penis."

"That doesn't keep you safe."

"My goal in life is not to be safe."

"Well, my goal *is* to keep you alive, unfortunately. So call me for a ride. I mean it."

Jude shrugs irritably. He's getting tired of my coddling. I know I should stop, but if anything, I feel more protective than the average parent—if only because I know how easily you can lose the ones you love. Jude is all I have. And I'm all he's got, even if I'm annoying the hell out of him.

Our waitress returns with the most beautiful latte I've ever beheld. She's made a little scene in swirls of brown and cream—a pumpkin, bat, and ghost. I finally understand the urge to post a picture of my food because this is too pretty to drink without ceremony.

"You're an artist!"

"Only with food." She laughs. "You two in town for the weekend?"

"Longer than that. We're renovating the Blackleaf house."

She gasps. "No shit—my cousin's coming over this afternoon! Tom—he's an electrician."

"Oh!" I laugh with her. "I've never been more excited to see somebody. We're dying for hot showers."

"I'm Emma." She sticks out her hand.

"This is your place?" I'm impressed. She can't be past her thirties, and plus, she's hot. I know that shouldn't factor into my being impressed, but it does. I've always suspected if I were truly stunning, I'd lack motivation. "I was kind of expecting an older lady with a beehive."

Emma grins. "I've only been up and running for two years—give me another twenty, and that's exactly what I'll be."

"This is my brother, Jude."

"Welcome to Grimstone!"

"I love it already," Jude says, unsmiling. "This is my first hot coffee in three days."

"He's really been through it," I tell Emma. "You could never understand his pain."

Her laugh makes the whole day better. "God, I'm so glad to have somebody new in town for longer than a week. You've got to come out with me and meet everyone else—there's a bonfire tomorrow night."

"Sounds great," I say before Jude can make a face or an excuse. He's always nervous about meeting big groups of people.

"Fantastic!" Emma scribbles her digits on her order pad and rips off the top sheet. "Text me something so I have your number—I'll send you the details."

"Can we also order?" Jude says plaintively.

"Depends on what you want." Emma's smile is saucy. "You're way too late for my famous blueberry pancakes."

"Good thing I would never put a blueberry in a pancake."

"He's such a charmer..." Emma winks at me, secure in her pancakes.

When we're alone again, I tell Jude, "Knock it off. If we're gonna be here a while, we should make friends. The locals seem nice."

Dane acted like everybody in this place would rip your head off and drink your blood come nightfall.

Jude is unconvinced. "You think everyone's nice."

"They mostly are."

"No," he says with seriousness. "They're not. This is why you always get burned, Remi, because you only see the best in people. Like Gideon."

"Okay, okay." I'm sorry I even brought it up.

"There were a hundred signs before you'd finally admit—"

"Okay!" I cry. "I won't think people are nice. Especially Emma. Look at her over there"—Emma is currently laughing with a darling old man, and I'm pretty sure she's offering him a bag of free muffins to take home—"she's clearly awful."

Even Jude has to snort at that. "All right, so Emma's a saint. What about everyone else?"

I reach over to mess up his hair. "It's sweet that you're being protective."

"Don't get used to it." He sips his coffee, his pinky in the air. "One good deed per day out of me."

"Wouldn't want you to exhaust yourself." I snicker.

Against my better judgment, I leave Jude to poke around Grimstone on his own and head back to the house to meet Emma's cousin.

Turns out there was no need to hurry because Tom is two hours late. He finally rolls up in a truck even older and uglier than mine, looking distinctly rumpled and smelling of last night's beer.

I can't really give him shit about it, since he's my one and only option.

"Remi," I say, sticking out my hand.

"Well, hello there." He pushes back the brim of his cap to give me an up-and-down. "That's some hair."

"Hark who's talking."

The curly mullet escaping from under his hat is the same carroty shade as Emma's.

"Fair enough." His grin is bright and charming, also like Emma's, minus the gap in the front teeth. The cousins are infinitely more similar than Jude and me—but we're like a joke of genetics. "So how can I help?"

"I might have the worst job in the world for you...." Fuck, my sales pitch sucks. I should have practiced.

Tom only shrugs. "Used to work at a slaughterhouse. Can't nothin' in your walls can be worse than that."

"I like your attitude...and your fluorescent hair discount." I add that last bit hopefully. It's hacky, but I'll try anything.

Tom eats it up. "Absolutely..." His gaze lands lazily on my face and stays there as he smiles. "Us miscreants gotta stick together."

It's kind of fun following Tom's hulking frame as he crawls through the attic, shimmies across the roof, examines the electrical panel in the cellar, and even drops inside the walls to peek behind the old appliances. We're really getting into the bones of the house.

We're filthy and grinning by the time we emerge. Tom scribbles up a quote for me.

"It's not too terrible. If you help a bit, I can probably do it for...I dunno...about this."

He passes over his scrap of paper with the estimate at the bottom. It's a hell of a lot better than I feared. Generous, even. He's hooking me up.

Which could create its own set of problems. Fuck, I hope I didn't lay it on too thick about the discount—I haven't quite sunk to sucking cock for construction favors, and I'd prefer to keep my terrible blow job decisions centered around drunken late nights and guys named Alonso.

"Thanks," I say, trying to strike exactly the right balance. But because I'm an idiot, I add, "I know you could have stuck it to me way worse than that."

Tom gives a low, huffing laugh. "That's not how I like to stick it to pretty girls."

Someone shoot me so I can stop making things worse. "Well, thanks again."

I don't know if that makes it better or worse.

Tom just grins. "Let me get my tools."

Bless him—Tom is my new best friend until we have lights and a stove that works.

"Can I see your kit?" I ask, already peeking in.

Tom hauls the dusty bag out of his truck. "You really are gonna make me fall in love."

CHAPTER 9
DANE

IF I'M AWAKE, I CAN HEAR EVERY CAR THAT PASSES DOWN MY ROAD. I could be in a coma and still hear Tom Turner's truck. I glance out though the polarized glass and watch him roar past, his muscular tanned arm resting on the open windowsill.

The bolt of jealousy that hits me when I see him heading up to Remi's place is swift and alarming. I barely know this girl, and I shouldn't give two shits who visits her, but I haven't been able to get her out of my head.

She's the reason I'm awake so early, after fevered dreams of sun-warmed flesh and nipple piercings cool as a sliver of unmelting ice.

She draws an aggression out of me I thought was long gone.

Until that kiss, I barely lived inside my body. I was trapped in my brain, tortured by thoughts, while the rest of me moved around, cold as an automaton.

Now I'm living, breathing, walking again, full of impulses and strange new purpose.

I ate a monstrous breakfast when I woke: half a pack of bacon, an omelet, and buttered toast.

I ate right by the window, looking out at the back garden. It's completely different in the day, dull and unassuming. But to me, it's always beautiful because I planted every bit of it myself. That garden saved me. I'd burn my whole house down before I'd lose it.

The thought flashes in my head to show it to Remi. As she's someone who works with her hands, who builds things, I have a feeling she'd appreciate it.

Having her in my house yesterday was...strangely enjoyable. Nobody but my brother has crossed the doorstep in years. The women I fuck are almost exclusively vacationers. I pick them up at the local bar and take them back to their own hotel rooms, when I feel like doing that at all...

I haven't had the urge in months. Maybe even a year. Time is a thief and a liar—until Remi showed up, I hadn't realized Ernie's been dead for three years. How pathetic is that? My closest friend was the ailing lunatic who happened to live next door.

Fuck, I miss him. Ernie's mind worked at about ten times the speed of anybody else's. He talked a mile a minute, a thousand ideas and jokes and connections, leaping from topic to topic too quickly for others to keep up. He'd hold an entire conversation himself, both sides, doing different voices for each speaker, impressions of the people in our town, politicians, celebrities, characters of his own invention. He inhabited a world six inches in front of his eyeballs, and when he'd come back to me, he'd be panting and sweating, and I'd be laughing so hard, my sides hurt.

Remi's funny. Not like her uncle, but also a little bit like him in the way she talks straight from her brain, telling you things she really shouldn't.

The thought of Tom Turner up at her house, probably half-drunk, sneaking looks at her phenomenal ass, puts me in a dark mood.

Is she helping him work? Swapping hammers?

I never thought I could feel envious of that pickled turnip. God, look how far I've sunk.

He won't even have to beg for her number because he'll already have it.

He'll ask her on a date—that's a given.

Will Remi say yes?

I'd like to think she has better taste, but I've seen her clothes.

She's not coming back to work on my fence until the day after tomorrow.

I'd drag her out here every damn day, but I want to fuck with her, not bankrupt her. It'll already take a miracle for her to successfully flip that house.

I bet Tom has lots of good advice for her...

The idea of that mediocre fuck worming his way into her good graces with his construction talents is maddening. Rewiring a socket is probably the only thing in this universe he can do that I can't.

That, and take her to the beach at noon in July.

Well, guess what—I don't want to take her to the beach, and I sure as fuck don't want to rewire her sockets.

What I want to do is string her up in my basement and whip those tiny tits until they're rosy as apples, and then I want to turn her around and do the same to her ample ass. I want to build her pleasure and pain in layers until she's sweating and shaking and begging, until the slightest flick of her nipple brings her to tears and the touch of my tongue against her clit makes her scream my name until her throat is raw.

The thought of Tom fucking Turner putting his hands on what I've already claimed makes me want to do terrible things.

To him, and maybe to Remi as well for granting him permission to drive down *my* goddamn road to see her.

They're probably alone together right now. The brother's even lazier than Remi will admit.

Are they playing music? Is Tom making her laugh? How will they celebrate when he gets her lights running?

Only one way to find out.

I slip into my shoes and head out the back door, careful to stay under the trees to avoid the late-afternoon sun.

I hear their voices before I reach Remi's property line, and I duck into a grove of birches, knowing it was risky to come in the day instead of at night.

It looks like they've just come down from the attic—Remi's blinking in the sunshine, filthy with dust, cobwebs in her hair.

"—and that's all it takes," Tom says.

"Easy peasy!" Remi laughs.

"Yeah." Tom grins. "Just a quick hundred hours of work."

Hundred hours? I knew it. This fuck is drawing it out as long as possible so he can skulk around her house for weeks.

"It won't really take that long, will it?" Remi's eyebrows crimp in concern.

"Not if you can help me. Hot out today," Tom remarks, pushing up the brim of his cap to wipe sweat off his forehead with the back of his arm. "You want a drink?"

He hops up into the cab of his truck, dragging forward a large and filthy cooler. He flicks the latch and pulls out two bottles of beer.

"Thanks." Remi takes the drink and gives her bottle cap a sharp downward rap against the truck's gate so it pops off and goes flying into the uncut grass.

"Cheers." Tom clicks his beer against hers.

They each take a long pull, drops of melted ice sliding down the brown glass bottles.

The late-September sunshine is golden, bits of chaff floating through the air. Remi's tan glows bronze, her black eyebrows making funny shapes as she chats with Tom.

Tom's lazy smile gets wider. He leans back against his truck, resting his arms along the gate. He's shucked off his plaid shirt to show off the undershirt beneath and his freckled brown arms.

It's a moment I could never share with Remi, and not only because it would turn my face as red as Tom's hair to stand in the sun. Remi looks calm and relaxed, like people never do around me. Even half my patients are afraid of me. Probably more than half, but they don't have a lot of options after 6:00 p.m.

Most of the time, that's exactly how I like it.

But right now, when Remi's lit up like a sunset, all golden skin and violet hair, dazzles of silver in her nose and across her full lower lip, when she throws her head back and gives her cackling laugh, it's almost enough to make me want to trade places with Tom.

Especially when she lets her hand rest just a moment on his arm.

Almost, but not quite—'cause Tom's a fucking idiot, and I'm going to get exactly what I want out of Remi.

I decide it for certain, right there in that moment.

I'm going to taste that mouth again. I'm going to feel her firm little body in my arms. And I'm going to make her respond to me exactly how I want.

And Remi—my messy, stubborn, rebellious little treat—is going to look up into my face with so much more than calmness. She'll look at me with the kind of desire that makes her legs go limp and her thoughts melt out of her brain.

CHAPTER 10
REMI

FROM WHAT I CAN TELL, TOM'S DOING A PRETTY GOOD JOB ON THE electrical work, though he does drink six or seven more beers over the same number of hours' work. He rigs a couple of lamps to Jude's generator so he can continue working well past dark, and he's still going hard at eleven o'clock, when Jude finally putters into our yard astride a battered gray moped.

I'd just been about to drive out looking for him. He never answered my many texts and phone calls asking when he wanted a ride home. I wasn't in full panic mode quite yet—Jude frequently forgets to charge his cell phone even when we have proper outlets, not just battery packs—but I was definitely in that state where my mind was creating a thousand horrible imaginings of my baby brother beat up in a ditch or drowned on the beach. He's not a strong swimmer.

"Jude!" I run out to hug him. "Where have you been? And what the hell is this?"

"My new wheels." He tosses back his pale hair, damp with the exertion of holding the chunky moped upright. "Now you won't have to drive me around."

"When did you learn to ride a moped?"

"Today."

I could have guessed that from the way he wobbled into the yard. I bite my tongue on the probability of him getting pancaked by a semitruck and on the stupidity of him not wearing a helmet, but I can't hold back asking, "How much did that cost?" with queasy concern for his college fund.

He shoves down the kickstand. "Relax—eight hundred bucks. The thing barely started, but I tinkered it up enough to get back to the house."

Jude is a genius with small machines. As long as he can sit while he's working and concentrate for longer than ten goddamn minutes, he can fix almost anything.

"Okay," I say, like he'd return it if I withheld permission.

"Whose truck is in the yard?" he asks suspiciously.

"The electrician."

"He's still here?"

"Yeah, lucky for us—we could have lights within the week."

Tom comes out of the house hauling his tool bag, an extension cord wound 'round his arm like a lariat.

"That's it for tonight," he says. And then, "Hey, there," to Jude. Jude gives him a nod.

"Thanks for coming out." I give Tom my hand to shake, feeling warm and grateful at the prospect of hot showers.

His hand, rough and dusty, closes around mine. "My pleasure."

His fingers slide across my knuckles as he lets go. Jude raises an eyebrow.

To distract him, I say to Tom, "I met your cousin."

"Emma?" He brightens. "You try her food? She's the best in town. Better than the chef at the Monarch—ask anybody."

"I don't have to ask. I had her biscuits Benny this morning."

Tom groans. "Don't even mention her biscuits; I'm starving."

I'd like to offer him a snack for all his hard work, but I'm not sure if we've even got peanut butter. Jude sucks at rationing.

"How about you?" Tom gives me a certain kind of look. "You want to grab a pizza or something...? You could come, too." He invites Jude as an afterthought.

"Wow, thanks." Jude doesn't even pretend to smile.

"Maybe next time." I step between them to block Jude's dirty glare. "I'm beat. Thanks, though."

"What are you up to tomorrow?" Tom persists. "There's gonna be a bonfire down on the beach; a bunch of townies are coming. Locals, I mean."

"Emma mentioned that." I glance at Jude to gauge his resistance. "Sounds fun."

Jude looks sullen but not impossible to convince.

"Cool," Tom says. "Well, see you in the morning!"

"Yeah, thanks again! We really appreciate it. Both of us." I give Jude a nudge.

"Thanks," he says expressionlessly.

As Tom's truck rattles off, Jude mutters, "He sure doesn't waste time, does he?"

"Guys can't help themselves. If you've got tits and you're breathing, they're gonna shoot their shot—spoken as a solid six who gets asked on way too many dates by horny dudes in hard hats."

Jude gives me an odd look. "You think you're a six?"

I can't tell if he thinks that number should be higher or lower, and I'm damn sure not going to ask because if Jude thinks I'm a four, he'll tell me. That lucky little bastard got our mom's looks and our uncle's brains. But I got Dad's singing voice and Aunt Betty's ass, so I'm doing okay.

"I just mean—you know, I'm not everybody's cup of tea. And that's fine. I'm not trying to be."

Miserably, I imagine for the billionth time what Gideon's new girl looks like. I never did find out. Probably tall and blond like his exes. I guarantee she's got bigger tits than me 'cause it would be hard not to.

Jude mutters, "Did the redheaded amoeba get anything done, or was he scamming on you the whole time?"

"He did a lot."

"Did you have to babysit him?"

"Nope. I was down in the kitchen breaking up the old tile."

Jude's shoulders hunch, his hands stuffed in his pockets. "I don't like you out here alone with some dirty dude. I shouldn't have left when I knew he was coming. I thought he'd be old, with his ass crack hanging out of his jeans."

I laugh. "We should be grateful we don't have to look at that for the next couple of weeks."

"It's not going to take weeks, is it?" Jude lifts his head, horrified.

"I hope not. That's a worst-case scenario. I bet we get hot water way before that."

Jude nods, though he hasn't quite relaxed. "Just…be careful, Remi. We don't know these people. If that guy says anything to you, if he bothers you again—"

"He won't." I'm laughing a little, but also, I'm touched.

That's the second time today Jude was looking out for me.

I fall onto the four-poster, every muscle aching just the way I like. Exhaustion helps me sleep. If my body is tired enough, my mind can't fight for long.

When I work my hardest, I barely even dream.

I had constant nightmares after the accident. All night long I'd thrash around, sheets full of sweat, then wake with my head throbbing like I hadn't slept at all.

It was good luck I got a job with a painting crew right after. Ten-hour days hauling buckets and ladders—those were the first nights I slept more than a couple of hours in a row.

Oblivion is rest; absence is peace.

I don't want to dream.

But I guess busting up all those kitchen tiles wasn't enough to wipe me out—almost as soon as my head hits the pillow, the room seems to tilt and spin. The shadows of branches reach across the floor like fingers…

The bed tosses beneath me, rocking back and forth. I roll like a ship on the waves.

The wind washes against the windows, branches scratching. Raindrops lash the glass. Damp and cold leak down the chimney. On my mattress of air, I rock and shiver.

Gusts of wind, icy black waves…

Darkness so deep, the moon floats above an ocean of oil in a sky made of ink…

Hammering on Dad's door, a small hand clutched in mine…

I moan and writhe on the bed.

Banging, banging—why doesn't he answer?

Smoke rolls down the hallway. We start coughing, Jude worse than me. I make a fist and pound hard on the door.

The wood splinters. The door swings open. Dad hangs on the handle, lurching. The whole ship is tossing; nobody's steering.

Smoke rolls into his room. He blinks in the haze, his eyes glassy and dazed.

"Wh-what's happening?"

"Fire, Dad!" I'm screaming. Smoke burns in my throat. "The ship's sinking!"

He stands there frozen and dumb, like he can't understand, like he can't even hear me.

In the dream, his paralysis infects me… It spreads like frost up my legs, through my body, down my arms…

Cold grips my chest, my heart, my lungs. I can't breathe, can't scream, and I'm pinned in place, unable to do anything but stare upward through the spiraling darkness…

My eyes are open.

I'm seeing the room around me but also the shape of my dream laid over the top.

A pale face floats in the window, staring down at me.

I see the figure but with my father's blank face.

We're locked in place, this faceless man watching and me pinned to the bed, paralyzed.

Until at last I scream, and he drops out of sight, the dream dissolving, the hold broken.

I bolt up in the bed, sweating, my T-shirt drenched. There's no face in the window, nobody around. But he was there a moment ago—someone as dark and solid as the trees outside, except the dream blurred his face.

My heart is rabbiting a thousand beats a minute, my breath coming raggedly. I force myself to inhale and exhale, deep and slow...

First get control, then take action...

I picture my father saying those words. I'd rather think of him calm and encouraging instead of remembering his awful frozen white face.

I picture the way his eyes crinkled at the corners and the little brown freckles at the edges of his beard.

Only one problem, Dad... I haven't had control in a very long time.

I cope, and I make it work. Those aren't the same things.

Still, I make myself count breaths until my heart slows a little.

I hate the paralysis dream. This isn't the first time I've had it, or even the thirtieth. On my list of most hated nightmares, it ranks around the middle, behind the ending where fire sweeps down the hallway and burns us all alive and the one where the ship rolls over and everything hangs upside down.

The ending I hate most of all is the one closest to what actually happened—Jude and I escape the ship alone in the life raft.

But in the dream, instead of being tossed around for eight miserable hours in the dark before the Coast Guard arrives, Jude and I float on still black water. Until, without warning, our raft tilts, and Jude is pulled down into a whirlpool. I try to hold on to him—I cling to his hands—but I'm not strong enough. He's yanked away and dragged down under the water. And I'm left all alone because I couldn't save him.

It doesn't take Freud to explain why that one fucks me up the worst.

Jude is all I have left. Taking care of him matters more to me than anything—and he doesn't always make it easy.

I understand my nightmares.

What I'd like to know is how to stuff them back where they belong so I can get a decent night's sleep.

I should pull the covers up right now—I'm going to be exhausted tomorrow fixing Dane's fence after all my own work. But I hesitate, more cowardly than I'd like to admit at the possibility of slipping back into the same dream.

The mood in the room is cold and sickening. My worst fears cluster around me. They whisper down the chimney with the wind.

And distantly, on the bottom floor of the house, I hear the piano...

Bing...bing...bong...

CHAPTER II
DANE

REMI STOMPS OUT OF HER TRUCK LOOKING SLEEPY AND SULKY. I'D been expecting that and maybe something worse, so I'm waiting on the shaded porch, sipping gin.

"I'm gonna need some of that," she says by way of a greeting.

I already brought out a glass for her, not that she'd notice. Poor Remi had a restless night.

I pour her a double, rubbing lime around the rim.

"Thanks." Remi tosses back the drink and wipes her mouth on her arm. She has a comically practical way of doing things, like she forgets other people can see her.

Today she's wearing jeans that have more holes than fabric. Patches of her bare brown legs gleam through shredded denim.

Remi wears expressions her own way. Dark circles and a sullen look are kinda sexy on her—her black eyebrows hang low and her lower lip pouts.

"You look tired."

"I am tired."

"Rough night?"

She gives me a leery look over the rim of her glass. She already drank the gin, but she lets a little ice slip into her mouth and moves it around on her tongue. It's sexy, and she knows it's sexy.

I fold my arms across my chest, leaning against the doorframe, staring right back at her. If she thinks she's going to beat my poker face, she's dreaming worse than last night.

I watched her thrash and groan on that bed for over an hour...

What was torturing her in her sleep?

What was she seeing when she stared up at me and screamed?

She swallows the ice, practically glaring at me. "No worse than usual. Can I pee?"

"Pardon?"

"Can I use your house to pee?"

I really can't figure out whether she recognized me or not.

Her eyes were blank, but she was staring right at me...

I knew it was a risk, climbing up to look in her window. But when I saw her sprawled out there on the bed, tangled in the sheets, wearing just that thin white undershirt...

She writhed like she was caught in a web, sheets wrapped 'round her legs, her back arched. It was raining just a little, the droplets pattering on the glass casting freckled shadows across her skin. Each quick flash of lightning bleached her white and turned her underwear to tissue...

I crouched in the tree, inching out on the branch, knowing how insane this was but unable to resist her body thrashing on the bed, her tits pointed up...

I looked down into her face.

Her eyes flew open, and she screamed...

"Come on in." I stand in the doorway so she has to brush past my chest.

Just that slight touch sends a jolt through us both.

Remi glances up, her hair tickling my jaw. Our eyes lock, and she lifts her chin like she's threatening me...or daring me to kiss her again.

I stare at her mouth for a long moment.

"Bathroom's over there." I point.

When she closes the door, she doesn't bother to run the water or the fan, so I hear the distinct sound of her hot piss hitting the bowl. My cock hardens.

The creak of her sneakers on the floorboards turns me on. Her jeans rasp against her legs as she pulls them up, an unspeakably intimate sound.

I slip back into the living room while she washes her hands. She reemerges, pressing her thumb and index finger into the inside corners of her eyes.

"Thanks." She heads for the exit, not looking at me.

I step in front of her so her face meets my chest, knocking her off-balance. I grab the outsides of her arms to steady her.

"You okay to swing a hammer after that drink? I don't want to have to stitch the other leg."

That's a lie—I'll happily put my hands on any part of her.

Remi shakes her head. "I'm fine."

Another lie.

"You need coffee." *Shut up, idiot.* I've been looking forward to watching Remi sweat and bend in my yard for two whole days, and now I'm undermining my own plan.

She opens her mouth to decline, but a wave of exhaustion must roll over her. She sighs and sinks down on my couch instead. "Okay, you convinced me."

I leave her there while I brew a fresh pot. Less than a minute passes before the sofa creaks as she heaves herself up so she can peek around at my shelves. I give her plenty of time to snoop, silently berating myself in the kitchen.

What the fuck am I doing?

She makes me so impulsive.

Remi is an agent of chaos. All women are—but her more than most.

Everything about her is wrong and not what I like. But that's exactly what keeps me craving her, like sour and spice.

My cock is halfway hard in my pants. It's been that way from the moment I heard her Bronco rumbling down the road.

I press down with my palm, squeezing against its low, hot ache.

When I carry out the mugs, Remi's pulling books off my shelves again. She struggles to look and not touch.

She lifts *The Lotus Sutra.* "You meditate?"

"Every day."

"Really."

"You sound surprised."

She shrugs restlessly. She looks exhausted and a little reckless. "Seems a little woo-woo for a doctor."

"Doctors know that the mind is powerful. For better or for worse."

"What does that mean?"

I press the mug of coffee into her palm. "You might not like everything your mind does. An uncontrolled mind is...uncontrolled."

"Nightmares," Remi murmurs.

"I'm more concerned with what happens when I'm awake."

She glances up sharply. "I'm fine when I'm awake."

"I can see that."

She scowls at me, then snatches *Lucid Dreaming* off the shelf.

"I'm borrowing this."

"No."

"Why not?"

"Because you'll get crumbs in the pages, and it won't help you anyway."

"I won't— I don't *have* to get crumbs in it." Remi sets down her coffee and clutches the book to her chest, tattoos running down both her bare arms. She lifts her chin, haughty as her brother. "And what makes you think I can't master my dreams?"

"Because dreams reflect real life." I snatch the book back out of her hand and toss it aside.

She's empty-armed and suddenly flustered. "What are you saying?"

"You know exactly what I'm saying."

Her mouth falls open in outrage. "You don't know shit about my life."

"Probably not. But I know what I see."

The bags under her eyes could hold two weeks of luggage. Her nails are bit to nubs.

"You think I can't control myself?" Remi's lower lip trembles, and she blinks several times.

I step closer.

She sucks the edge of her lip into her mouth, fingers tugging nervously at the frayed threads of her jeans. She tries so hard to project strength, but she shakes like a baby bunny the moment I get close.

I lean down and look right in her face, our noses an inch apart. "I *know* you can't control yourself."

I grab her at the nape and shove my hand down the front of her jeans, thrusting my middle finger inside her and hooking there, my hand clamped on her pussy.

Remi gasps, grabbing my arm with both hands.

My hand is like a saddle, practically lifting her, all her weight on her clit pressed against my palm, my middle finger stuffed deep inside her. When I move my finger a millimeter, Remi's fingers dig into my biceps, and she groans.

"You're a fucking mess," I murmur in her ear. "Chaos, mistakes, missed deadlines…isn't that the truth?"

Her eyes are wide, staring into mine, rimmed with black lashes. Her eyebrows are thick and dark, drawn together in shock and fury.

"You're out of control, and you have no idea how much because you close your eyes every time it scares you…"

My lips buzz around her ear, and my fingers press against her soft, soaking pussy, searching for the most swollen, most sensitive parts.

I find the firm nub of her clit, and the tip of my index finger touches the metal ring running through its base. I have never been harder.

At least, that's what I think until I tap the tip of my finger against that little ring, and Remi lets out a deep shuddering groan like I've touched the core of her soul. My cock swells like a balloon inflated to its bursting point.

I kiss her mouth, sucking her puffy lips between mine.

Her breath comes out in ragged gasps every time I wiggle that little ring in the slightest degree. Even if I just press it against her clit, her eyes close and she keens like an animal.

This is highly addictive.

In fact, I don't know if I can ever let it go...

I press my middle finger deep inside her and lift her practically on her tiptoes, making her cry out and cling to my arm, her cheek against my biceps.

I seize a handful of her hair and pull her head back to make her look into my eyes. "Who's in control right now?"

"I—*you* are!" she cries, as I draw back my hand back slightly and thrust in two fingers instead. "You are! You are! Oh my god, you are!"

I pump my middle and index fingers in and out, watching her eyes flutter. The heel of my palm grinds against her clit like a pestle. The rhythm is deliberate and relentless. Her pussy softens, her wetness sliding down my hand. She closes her eyes, her head tilting back.

"No!" I snap. I turn her around, placing her palms flat on the stone mantel, forcing her to face the mirror hanging over the empty fireplace. "Open your eyes—look at yourself."

I hold her with her back pressed against my chest, my arm in a bar across her body, my other hand shoved down the front of her jeans, rubbing furious circles on her clit. Her slippery wetness is outrageous; it's like a rainforest.

"Look at yourself," I hiss in her ear. "Look at your face. Watch how much you love this..."

Her head lolls against my shoulder, her eyes glazed, her cheeks flushed. Her hips roll against my hand, her soft, swollen clit sliding across my fingers.

I snake my hand inside her shirt and seize her nipple. Slowly, I begin to tug while her clit grinds hard against my hand.

"Look... *LOOK!*"

Her blue-green eyes find their twins in the foggy silver mirror. She gazes at herself, shocked and dazed. Her face is flushed, her hair plastered to her cheeks. She reaches up to touch her own swollen lips and shivers.

I'm rubbing, rubbing, rubbing, my palm the center of the melting heat and wetness that holds her pinned in place, her legs swaying, her hands white-knuckled on the mantle.

I rub her pussy and pull on her nipples, my hand moving back and forth between her breasts, plucking, tugging. Her knees give way after each shuddering wave, but I hold her upright, pinned to my chest. I force her to watch her own face so she doesn't miss a moment of her pleasure.

"Did you think you liked this? Look at yourself... You do..."

I pump my fingers in and out, the wet slapping sounds a mockery of her whimpers and moans, the proof of how it really feels...

But her face is the truest proof of all, and I force her look at it—her eyes glazed in lust, her mouth open, panting, her thick black brows drawn together, not in pain or fear but begging for more...

"Tell me to stop..." I growl in her ear. "Tell me you don't like this."

She can't.

She won't.

"I'll stop right now...just say 'red.'"

Her eyes find mine in our shared reflection. She opens her lips as if she'll speak, but then she presses them together instead, her pussy squeezing around my fingers as another wave rolls through.

"Have you ever seen such a greedy little whore? How many times are you going to come?"

She stares at herself, wide-eyed, as the pleasure sends her through the spin cycle over and over. I rub her soaking wetness and push my fingers up inside her.

"Oh, god—Jesus!" she cries, her knees bending, her body twisting away.

I yank her back against my chest, my fingers hooked in tight. I pump into her pussy, my palm slapping against her clit. Her little clit has gone erect, and I feel it nudging against my palm, red, swollen, pierced with that thin silver ring...

"You're not done—you can come harder than that...yes, you can... Look at yourself..."

Her eyes meet mine in the mirror instead—hers wide and glinting with tears in her flushed red face. She's begging, pleading, her lips moving silently.

I have no mercy. Not for her, not when I can see what she truly wants.

"Come for me," I order.

She covers my hand with hers and presses it hard against her clit, her thighs clamping while she turns and looks directly into my eyes. Her whole body convulses, wrapped snakelike around my arm, her legs crossed, holding my palm tightly against her cunt.

She seizes a handful of my hair and kisses me as she comes, her tongue thrusting, wet and hot. She's shaking and clinging to me, moaning into my mouth. She comes and comes, clenching, squeezing, pulsing, as each shuddering wave rolls through.

Even after she's finished, she still twitches with aftershocks. It takes a long time before the trembling completely stops.

I stroke my free hand up and down her back, leaving her face turned against my neck. She won't look at herself at all now; she's too embarrassed.

When at last we untangle, I pull my hand out of her pants, wet and marked with red prints from the seams of her jeans. I cup it over my nose, inhaling her scent. Then I grab her and kiss her again so I can taste it with her mouth.

"Who was in control?" I demand, not letting go of the back of her neck so she has to keep looking at me from only an inch away.

Her eyes drop in shame.

"You were," she murmurs.

"Did you ask me to stop?"

She shakes her head within the short bounds it can move.

"Did you want me to stop?"

Her eyelashes flutter as she glances up at me, and her heart pounds against my chest. "No," she whispers.

"Then who was in control?"

She shakes her head slowly, looking into my eyes. "I—I'm not sure."

"When I told you to come, did you come because I made you... or because you wanted to?"

"I had no choice," she gasps.

My leg slips between hers. Even now she can't stop—she presses against my thigh, letting out an urgent low moan.

I grip her hair and give her head a little shake. "You had a hundred choices."

My mouth comes down on hers, hot and fevered. I lick deep into her mouth, under her lips, all around her tongue. I taste every part of her, every nuance of her flavor.

"Don't lie to yourself," I say, my hand wrapped tightly in her hair, my lips against her ear. "You're getting exactly what you want."

CHAPTER 12
REMI

"WHAT KIND OF DOCTOR ARE YOU ANYWAY?"

The books on his shelves aren't what I'd expect from a cold-blooded physician: *The Unconscious Mind*, *Tranceformations: Neurolinguistic Programming*, and *Hypnotherapy*, to name a few.

Dane's eyes flick across the spines. "That's more of a personal interest."

My heart is still racing. He smoothed his silvery hair back, and now he's standing there with his hands tucked in his pockets like he wasn't just making me moan ninety seconds ago.

No, it was much more than moaning... He turned my brain inside out.

I've never come like that, looking at myself.

It was disturbing. Like watching someone I didn't recognize wearing my own face.

I don't like aggressive sex.

Or at least...I didn't think I did.

But that was before I felt that kind of pleasure.

My whole body is still warm and throbbing. Everything inside my skin feels like a hot tub: liquid and bubbling.

Dane hasn't broken a sweat.

You'd have to know how pale he is usually to see the hint of color in his cheeks. The shape of his lips could break my heart. His eyes are the darkest honey. His smile is white and wicked.

When we're outside, I'm bronze and healthy, while Dane is pale and sweating. But inside the Midnight Manor, I fade as he comes alive.

He's gorgeous like men aren't supposed to be gorgeous—like he's his own kind of creature.

No wonder they hate him in town. He can't fit in, even in a place as weird as Grimstone.

I don't believe he's a murderer.

Maybe that'll make me just another idiot on the news, but I don't get that vibe. He's strange—fucked up, even. But I don't believe he's some soulless killer. He's too alive in the eyes.

I want him to touch me again. I want it desperately.

But that feels like the worst possible idea.

So I keep babbling.

"What's it for?" I lick my lips. "Hypnotism?"

Dane's expressions are like the weather—sometimes they take a long time to form, and how they end isn't how they begin.

When he looks at me now, I see a flare of something angry and painful, washed away by cold, clear calm. "It's for making a change."

The word hangs in the air, vibrating like a bell.

It's what I've been saying to Jude for months: *We need a change…* And it's what he said back to me to convince me to pack up our shit and move out here: *We need a change, a fresh start…*

I broke up with Gideon, sold everything that wasn't tied down, and here I am, all the way across the country, but I'm still having nightmares worse than ever. I still feel that red noise, that pressure against my ears, constant stress.

Wherever you go…you're still your own damn self.

"What does it change?" I say to Dane.

He looks at me with his head cocked like a raptor, barely blinking. "Depends. What do you want to change?"

"I don't know…" I run both hands through my hair, grabbing at the roots in frustration. "I don't know."

"Yes, you do."

Dane hasn't moved, hasn't blinked. His three words are a surgeon's blade, cutting through the bullshit.

He stands there in the shadowy light, deeply calm. He played me like a puppet a minute ago. The only time I've seen him even slightly flustered was when I cut my leg.

I'm envious.

I wish I could be calm and deliberate.

I wish people were intimidated by me, instead of stomping all over me every chance they get.

I wish my house were clean and my bills were paid and I didn't feel this perpetual sense of fear, having no idea what will happen to me later today, let alone tomorrow or next week...

My heart is hammering like I'm about to make a leap.

But my voice comes out in a whisper.

"You're right... I'm not in control of my life. And it's making me miserable."

It feels so heavy to say it out loud.

My body seems to sink into the floor, and the sinking never stops.

"I work so hard. But the hours slip away, and when it's bedtime, the list of things I was supposed to do is bigger than ever. It's like a mountain of marbles, and I take off five, but ten more pile on top. And the whole thing's getting wobbly, like it's about to collapse..."

Even saying the words out loud makes my anxiety rise and my hands shake. I have the horrible feeling I might cry in front of Dane, and that can't happen because I've already embarrassed myself enough.

But I can't seem to stop.

"I'm starting to think it must be me. I must be the problem because no matter what I do, it doesn't get better..."

It's all pouring out. I haven't had anybody to talk to in so long. I couldn't trust Gideon, and there's only so much I can say to Jude when I'm trying to protect him from the trainwreck of our lives.

Dane feels safe *because* he's a stranger. Whatever I say to him will disappear in a matter of months when I sell Blackleaf and move again.

Yet we have this intimacy between us because of the cut on my leg, his hands on my body, the stolen kisses, and those strange, electric moments when it feels like he's talking to the deepest part of me and I'm speaking to the realest part of him.

It's like I can tell him anything and it won't matter—even the most painful things.

I should have been able to talk to Gideon like this. But I never felt like I could.

Even when things were the best between us, even before I knew what he was doing, I never felt like I could share my whole soul. I had to censor what I told Gideon so we wouldn't have an argument.

I think of our best and warmest moments. When I had the flu and Gideon canceled a work project to take care of me. When we visited the castles in Spain. All the times I was late at a job and he picked up Jude from school...

And then I remember the sick, sinking feeling of finding the first bobby pin in his car. Then the second, and the third...

Jude's voice whispers in my ear: *You only see what you want to see...*

"I wish I weren't so fucking blind."

The words come out of my mouth and hang in the air.

I didn't mean to say that, but the more I think about it, the truer it feels.

I was blind.

I didn't see what was going on all around me.

And it should have been obvious.

Dane lets out a sigh.

My shoulders sink, and I lose confidence. "You think I'm pathetic."

"Don't speak for me," Dane says coolly. "That's not what I was thinking at all."

"What, then?" I sneak a glance at him.

His face floats like a pale moon above the dark collar of his shirt. His hands are clasped loosely in front of him, carved from marble. His pallor is beautiful inside this indigo house, like they were made for each other. I've never belonged like that, not even in my own family.

My father was warm and confident, my mother bewitching, Jude a child prodigy... I was the odd duck. That was fine when we were all together, but then my parents were gone, and all my quirks became flaws and mistakes...

"I was thinking you remind me of myself."

That's the last thing I expected Dane to say. My chest gets hot with a red glow of pleasure that he thinks we're alike, mixed with a little panic at wondering exactly what he means.

"Is that a good thing?" I'm smiling a little.

Dane isn't. "Probably not."

"You really know how to give a girl a compliment."

"Is that what you want? Compliments?"

His mouth is sensual and cruel. He's so calm that he makes the air go still around him.

I shake my head. "I told you what I want."

"More control?"

"Yes."

"Less blindness."

"Yeah."

I don't even know if it's possible. Could I change the most broken parts of myself?

"And you want me to what...hypnotize you?" His lips curve, and his dimple flickers into being.

"I don't know..." The flush rises from my chest up my neck.

"Liar," Dane says softly. "You know."

"Yeah, then," I say recklessly. "That's what I want."

I have this image in my head of Dane swinging a silver watch like a pendulum, saying a few words in that low, silky voice of his, and suddenly I'll be the one with the cool, steady calm, all the holes in my brain sewed up neat and clean like the stitches in my leg.

But maybe that's stupid. Postorgasmic magical thinking, that's got to be it—my pussy's still throbbing; I'm not thinking straight.

Dane isn't rejecting the idea. He really seems to be considering it, a gleam of interest in his eyes.

I ask, "Have you ever hypnotized anyone before?"

He nods. "Once."

"Does it…work?"

"That's up to you."

Dane's voice is deep and rich and already hypnotic.

I feel a tug of attraction, too much space between us. I liked it better when his hands were on my body and his breath was on my skin.

When he looks at me, when he grabs me, it's so intense, I can barely take it, but as soon as it's gone, I want it back again.

I inch closer, like climbing onto a roller coaster. My heart starts racing, and I have to force myself forward.

I step inside Dane's circle and touch his elbow, looking up into his face.

He looks down at me, smiling. "That's the first time you've touched me first."

I get a thrill because he's right and he noticed. He sees everything; there's no hiding.

His hands drop to my hips, and he pulls me close, right against him.

My hand moves up the outside of his arm. Touching him like this, like I have the right to do it, feels bold and wrong and so fucking hot. He's too intimidating, too good-looking, too much older, and probably demented…nothing I should want or could ever pull off, but fuck, I'm salivating at the feel of his biceps…

Our stomachs press together, his arm hooking around the small of my back. His fingertips stroke my ribs.

When he touches me, when he pulls me in, I feel his strength, the press of muscle, the pumping blood. He looks so pale and cold, but that's not what he's like at all, not up close.

He feels so good and so wrong…

This slow touching is even more potent than the frenzy a moment before because it's so much more intentional.

Dane's face is close to mine. He takes my chin between his fingers and tilts it up, examining my features.

I look into his eyes, mesmerized.

With some people, the longer you look, the less you see.

With Dane, the sense of connection only grows…

His amber-colored eyes swallow me whole. His face isn't stiff at all, not this close—it's a shifting canvas of curiosity and amusement, of desire and even sympathy.

He lifts a finger and touches my forehead. "There's more than one mind in here."

He lets his hand trail down the side of my face, his fingers brushing my cheek, his thumb sliding over my lower lip. "More than one Remi…"

His hand moves down my body, cupping my breast. He seizes my nipple and tugs, a brief reminder with an accompanying flood of heat. "Have you ever wanted something you didn't think you wanted?"

His hand slips lower still, into my underwear, his fingers sliding between my pussy lips. "Have you ever done something you didn't think you would do?"

He kisses me roughly, wetly, the kind of kissing I didn't think I liked, but his mouth tastes so good…

His fingers rub hard against my clit as his tongue plunges my mouth. He figured out what works a minute ago, and now he presses his fingers unerringly against the softest, spongiest, most aching place.

"Who's responsible?" he says, his lips damp and full and warm against mine. "Who's in charge when you're out of control?"

My body is throbbing, blood pounding through my brain. "I—I don't know. Nobody, I guess."

Dane laughs softly. "If only that were true."

He licks my mouth, and then he licks the taste of me off his own lips.

"You taste like honey. And this…" He rubs his tongue against the ring through my lower lip. "I like this…"

He sucks my lip into his mouth and nibbles it gently while his fingers sweep big, warm, melting strokes across my clit.

The sensation builds like the beat of a war drum.

I'm tired of careening blindly through the storm.

I want power. I want change. I want wind in my sails…

I look up at him and kiss him once, softly, with my eyes open. "Do you really think you could hypnotize me?"

He cups my face between his hands and looks into my eyes like he can see the whole universe inside my head, close enough to touch. "Let's find out."

We sit facing each other on the same sofa, our legs loosely crossed.

"Hold out your hands, palms to the ceiling, and close your eyes," Dane instructs.

I hold out my hands, my fingers slightly cupped, with my lashes resting lightly on my cheeks. Just closing my eyes around Dane feels like an act of trust.

His fingertips come to rest on the insides of my arms, just below the elbows. "Take a deep breath…" he says. "And let it out."

As I exhale, his fingers slide down my forearms and all the way across my palms, to the ends of my fingertips. The motion is smooth and tactile, timed to my breath.

"Breathe in…" he says, "and out…"

His fingers track each exhale down my arms.

My skin sparks beneath his touch. The breath and the sensation are one and the same, and everywhere the air goes, the feeling goes, too.

His voice isn't in front of me anymore. It echoes on both sides in my ears. It floats through my brain.

"Deep breaths…deep breaths… Everything is black… See the ocean, black and empty all around you, in front of your eyes…"

His hands are on my shoulders now, warm and heavy, weighing me down. "Sink in…embrace it…inside your head and all around…"

I feel myself sinking deeper into the couch cushions. I might be falling back, too; everything is soft and dark, above, beneath, behind…

"Let go…let go and drift…and listen to the sound of my voice…"

"You're awake."

I blink.

Dane sits cross-legged on the couch, looking into my face.

I can feel the air in the room like water in a pool. When Dane speaks, the sound floats in waves.

"How do you feel?"

I'm not sure how to answer that.

I'm not experiencing most of the usual emotions. I don't feel happy. I don't feel sad. I don't even feel stressed. That constant red noise has disappeared, like a droning sound you don't entirely recognize until it's gone.

"I feel light," I say at last. "Clear."

The lightness isn't in my body. It's inside me and all the way through, like I've become transparent. A feeling of stillness everywhere at once, like the world is holding its breath.

"What did you do to me?"

"I didn't do anything." Dane's dimple flashes. "You did."

I stumble out of Dane's house and into the Bronco without a glance at his fence. The clock on the dash reads 10:40; I arrived at 7:00 p.m.

The sky is an endless black ocean. I don't remember a moment of the sunset.

My phone shows two missed calls and fourteen unread messages.

Emma: The bonfire's on Crow Beach. If you park close to The Fog Cutter, you can go down the steps. I'll prob head over around ten!

Tom: Do you want me to pick you up for the bonfire?

Tom: I'm heading over now if you want a ride

Tom: Lots of people here, tons of beer, don't worry about bringing anything

Tom: Just checking in

Emma: Call me when you get here! I'm down by the water

Tom: Got a drinks for you right here fuckIng gorgeus night

Tom: Where you at?

Tom: Hope yur coming soon

Jude: Can you please respond to the redheaded amoeba, he's texting me now

Tom: Hurry up baeutiful Im waitng

Jude: If he sends me a dick pic by mistake, I will never forgive you

Emma: Sorry, I have confiscated Tom's phone. And his keys.

Emma: Hope you're on your way :)

I start the engine, wondering if I'm okay to drive. I'm not dizzy, exactly. I just feel…strange.

The feeling persists all the way back to the house. Blackleaf looms in the darkness, shaggy as a beast, the roof humped like a back with all its peeling paint and hanging shutters. Ernie's workshop stands behind the house, almost lost within the overgrown garden.

I turn off the engine and sit in the dark car. Without the rumbling noise, a heavy peace settles in my ears once more. I roll down the windows, feeling the cool air on my bare skin. I can smell the pumpkins swelling in the damp earth.

Jude comes out the back door of the house with a bunch of books tucked under his arm. He crosses the yard, slips through the garden, and disappears inside the work shed.

When he reemerges a moment later, his hands are empty.

"Hey!" I call across the yard. "You're supposed to be cleaning things out of the shed, not carrying them in."

He jumps like a cat. "Don't *do* that!"

"Serves you right; you sneak up on me all the time."

It only takes him a moment to recover his cool. "Finished with your indentured servitude?"

"Yup."

I don't tell him that I didn't actually work on Dane's fence today. I haven't told him about the kiss either. Usually, I can't keep a secret from Jude to save my life, but with Dane it's different. I can't explain what's happening between us because I don't understand it myself.

Jude can tell something's fishy. "What happened to you? You look weird."

I shrug. The movement feels bizarre, like I just invented it.

"I'm gonna change clothes." I hear the words coming out of my mouth like somebody else is saying them. "You coming to this bonfire party?"

"Fuck no." Jude scowls.

I shrug again. "Suit yourself."

I stump inside the house, noticing how much effort it takes to lift my feet. The motion of walking no longer feels automatic. My heart rate increases. I feel the muscle squeezing blood like a hand wringing out a sponge.

"What the fuck?" I whisper. *"What did you do?"*

I don't know if I'm talking to Dane or myself. I must have been insane to invite that man into my head.

I don't know what I was thinking. It's got to be some self-destructive urge that pulls me back to him again and again.

There are ninety-six tiles in the main entryway, and sixteen steps to the second level, but only thirty-nine railings—one is missing. The chandeliers are made of brass, and the birds on the wallpaper are finches...

My eyes dart everywhere, counting everything. My heart beats way too fast.

I scale the second set of stairs to my room and throw myself down on the bed, covering my ears and closing my eyes.

When I lift my head again, everything is normal. The room is dark and cool. The silence is just silence.

My phone buzzes next to the bed:

Emma: I don't want to keep bugging you, but you're missing a whole lot of fun

My thumbs move across the screen. I type, change my mind, then send this instead:

Leaving now

Emma's response is instant:

Hell yes! Get your ass down here!

I smile as I tuck my phone in my pocket. It's nice to feel wanted, even just as another warm body at a party.

I flip through the six pieces of clothes hung up in the wardrobe, pulling out the shirt I'd consider the nicest, meaning there's no paint smeared on it or visible holes. The same can't be said of my jeans.

I brush my hair, add a little eyeliner and lip gloss, and spritz on some of Jude's cologne. In the cracked mirror, by lamplight, I'm looking pretty damn good.

Jude's out in the yard, elbow deep in engine parts.

"Sure you don't want to come?"

"No thanks." He leans all his weight on his wrench, trying to loosen a rusty screw. "I'm going to get this thing running smoothly."

My brother becomes incredibly productive when he's avoiding something he hates more.

"Don't stay up too late."

"Same to you," he says, giving me a look.

Okay, okay, message received.

For the hundredth time, I remind myself to stop babying him. Though that would be a hell of lot easier if he'd occasionally act like an adult.

He's twenty, I remind myself. *Not a kid anymore.*

And for once, as I look at him hunched over in the stark lamplight, I can actually see it.

CHAPTER 13
REMI

THE DRIVE INTO GRIMSTONE IS BECOMING FAMILIAR AND soothing—narrow, mostly empty roads hedged on both sides by towering forest.

All the shops are closed on Main Street, other than The Fog Cutter bar and the Monarch Hotel. I park outside the bar as Emma suggested, and then I descend the long staircase of wooden steps built into the cliffs to the black-sand beach below.

I teased Dane about the name *Grimstone*, but he was right—I've never seen a darker, more forbidding beach. The inky cliffs form a sheer drop to flat sand that glitters like black diamonds. Waves rush into the dark voids of the sea caves, pulled back again with a hissing sound.

The bonfire blazes a quarter mile down the beach, surrounded by figures whose long shadows trail across the sand like capes. The noise and laughter intimidate me, and for a moment, I consider turning around and driving back home.

Then I spot Emma's bright-orange head, and she turns and sees me, too.

"Is that Remi? Come here, I want to introduce you to everyone!"

Everyone turns out to be a motley mixture of twenty- and thirtysomethings who live and work around Grimstone. Half seem to be related in complex and confusing ways. Aldous and Amy are black-haired twins, both employed at the new resort—Aldous as a concierge and Amy as a maid. This is apparently offensive to Corbin, a dark and surly cousin to Emma and Tom, who mans the gas station just outside town.

"Nobody should work for those parasites."

"I've got to work somewhere," Amy says crossly, "and the Monarch wasn't hiring."

"I'd hire you," says Selina, a mellow brunette with a raspy voice who owns the tattoo parlor next to the hotel. "But only for the summer. Can't swing it in the winter."

"I'm fired after Halloween," her sister, Helena, says glumly. Helena is a curvy blond who does readings at the tarot shop and seems to have some connection to Corbin, though I can't tell if they're related or used to sleep together. Helena won't stop glaring at him, while Corbin pretends she doesn't exist.

Music plays from a tinny speaker. Farther down the beach, people are dancing and playing volleyball.

Tom is so hammered, I don't think he even remembers texting me.

"Remi!" he shouts, raising his cup so enthusiastically that half his beer sloshes down his arm. "Where'd you come from?"

"Pretend he doesn't exist until tomorrow." Emma grabs Tom by the shoulders, turns him around, and shoves him back in the direction of the kegs. "This is not the impression he wanted to make."

"REMI!" Tom bellows back over his shoulder, though Emma's only managed to push him two feet away. "You want to play beer pong?"

"The table's broken," Emma reminds him.

"Who broke the table?"

"You did."

"WHAT?"

"He's not usually..." Emma sighs, huffing a kinky orange curl out of her face. It's Tom's curl—he's lolling his head on her shoulder, forcing her to support most of his weight. "Actually, he's like this most of the time."

Tom grabs Emma's chin between his thumb and index finger and wiggles it like he's making her talk. "*I'm Emma and I'm mad...*"

She shoves him off into a pile of sandy blankets. The rest of Tom's beer flies and lands in Corbin's lap. Corbin leaps up, his fists raised. Helena grabs Corbin from behind, and Emma throws herself over her drunken cousin. Corbin rips free, and chaos descends.

Twenty minutes later, after Tom's been safely sequestered and Corbin has disappeared into the darkness with Helena, Emma returns, scratched and dirty and in a horrible mood. I pass her a cider from Tom's battered blue cooler.

"That ass," she says, chugging it down and grabbing another. "It's the least he can do."

"I already drank three."

Emma laughs. "I hope you did."

I've been chatting with the twins and Selina, all of us sitting on slightly sodden driftwood logs around the fire.

Emma rubs her knuckles under her nose. "I don't know why I even help him. Should've let Corbin beat the shit out of him for the tenth time."

"Because you love him," I say, taking a pull of my cider. "Makes anything seem worth it."

"*Hm,*" Emma says, in a tone like, *Maybe, maybe not.*

"Who's that?" Amy murmurs to her twin.

A figure is coming down the beach—tall, lean, broad-shouldered—swigging from a bottle of wine. Something in the way he moves sparks recognition long before he gets close. My heart kicks into double speed.

Selina squints down the sand. "Is that the night doctor?"

Emma mutters, "What's he doing here?"

Dane strolls right up to the bonfire and takes a long pull of his wine. He's barefoot, his trousers rolled partway up his shins, his feet sandy and damp. His silver-streaked hair is wind tossed, his face beautifully severe, his eyes dark and slightly mad.

"Hello, Remi." He nods to everyone else.

"Hi, Dane." My voice comes out tight and anxious. Somehow, he's even more intimidating away from his own house.

Emma gives me a look like, *Well, aren't you full of surprises?*

The stare she gives Dane is a lot less friendly.

Everybody's sneaking glances at him, even the people who were supposed to be dancing.

He's used to it or doesn't care—he hasn't taken his eyes off my face.

"Want a drink?" He holds out his bottle of wine.

I cross the sand to take it from him. The rim of the bottle is damp from his mouth. I taste his lips along with the wine. He watches as I swallow. Everybody's watching.

"Thanks."

He takes the bottle back, his fingers touching mine.

Nobody else is talking.

I can't stand the tension.

"Do you know Emma?" I blurt.

"I do."

Dane and Emma exchange a glance that's more an acknowledgment than a greeting.

Fuuuuuuck, I hate this.

Aldous comes to the rescue. "I'm Aldous," he says. "And this is my sister, Amy."

Amy shakes hands with Dane with a mixture of fascination and repulsion, like she's touching an anaconda for the first time.

"That's Selina," Aldous says.

Selina raises a hand. She's perched on her driftwood log, firelight dancing in her face, her hair blowing lightly around her bare shoulders. She's not looking at Dane like an anaconda but more like he's a zip line over a deep gorge and she's thinking about risking a ride.

Corbin returns with an unhappy Helena trailing behind.

"Hey, Dane." He nods.

"Corbin." Dane nods back.

Helena introduces herself with a reproachful look at Corbin; Corbin ignores her because he's back to that.

The tension has eased now that Corbin's here, accepting Dane as an unusual but not unwelcome addition to the group. It wasn't enough when it was just me.

Conversation flows again. Corbin and Aldous each grab a fresh drink.

I take the wine from Dane for something to do. And because I like this connection between us. Dane's not sharing his wine with Amy or Selina. Just with me.

"What are you doing here?" I ask when I feel like nobody's listening.

"Checking up on you." He looks me right in the eye.

I like that he doesn't hide it. Doesn't try to pretend. "How'd you know I was here?"

"You told me you were coming."

My spine goes cold.

I don't remember telling him that.

I don't really remember anything from his house today.

That scares the shit out of me but also makes me feel a deep, dark thrill, low in my guts.

What the fuck did we do?

I take a hefty slug of the wine, which tastes tart and expensive, and wipe my mouth on the back of my hand. "What did you do to me anyway?"

Dane is amused. "I did exactly what you asked."

"Then how come I can't remember? And why do I feel all... weird now?"

He tilts his head in interest. "Weird how? What are you experiencing?"

"Everything's loud, or bright, or..." I press my fingers against the tension points in my temples. "Doesn't look quite the same as before."

"Interesting." Dane lifts my chin and looks into my eyes like he's checking my pupils. His warmth surprises me every time we touch.

When he lets go, I see Emma watching from the other side of the fire. Selina is watching us, too, though less obviously.

"Did you fuck with my head?"

"Maybe," Dane says. The firelight makes his eyes molten and flickers across his skin.

"Maybe?"

"I made a suggestion to your mind."

"What?"

"It was only a suggestion; you don't have to take it. But it sounds like you did."

My heart feels fluttery in my chest, a thousand panicked butterflies hatching in a too-small box. "What suggestion?"

Dane takes the wine and drinks a long, slow swallow. He's smiling slightly and seems pleased, like all is going to plan. "I told it to your other mind."

I snatch the wine back. "You're insane."

He shrugs. "You should have researched your doctor better. I have terrible Yelp reviews."

"You're not my doctor."

"Oh, definitely not—or what we did earlier is a lot more illegal."

"Which part?"

"The hand-in-the-pants part. And maybe the rest of it, too—I'm a doctor, not a lawyer."

I squint up at him. "You're funny when you're drunk."

"I'm funny when I'm tipsy—I'm maudlin when I'm drunk."

"So, you're only tipsy?"

"You'll know I'm drunk when I start talking about the death of the universe."

"The whole universe?" I must be tipsy because I'm giggling. "That *is* maudlin."

Dane shrugs. "Don't say I didn't warn you."

I'm probably being rude, talking only to Dane when Emma invited me here. It's hard to include her in the conversation, though, when she's staring daggers at Dane.

"Sorry about, uh—"

"Her?" Dane doesn't have to turn his head; he knows exactly where Emma's sitting. "That's normal around here." He pauses, then says, "There's rumors about me in town."

"Yeah. I might have heard some."

"You did?" He glances at me, taking the wine. "I wondered."

That's all he says. He doesn't ask if I believe the rumors, and I don't have the guts to say anything at all.

Part of me is desperate for information, but the rest of me has to admire how stone-cold he is, like the looks and whispers can't touch him.

Did you kill your wife?

If he didn't, that's super fucking offensive.

If he did, he's not going to admit it.

Nothing can be greater proof of how fucked up I've become than my willingness to roll the dice.

Dating with Jude in tow was like being a teen mom. I never had a rebel motorcycle-boyfriend phase—I had to stick with the safe choice.

Everything about Dane is a waving red flag, with flashing lights and sirens on top.

But it also feels bright and burning and wildly arousing, the opposite of my usual instincts.

Gideon seemed safe—and look how that ended.

A manic little laugh sneaks out of me. Am I rebounding from a fake nice guy all the way to a possible murderer?

I can't be that bad a judge of character—no matter what Jude says.

Selina gives up watching us and makes her way onto the open sand to dance with a muscular guy in a backward hat.

Dane glances at them, then determinedly away.

I wonder if he dances. It seems like there's no way he does, but also, he might be really good at it. When he puts his hands on my waist, it feels like we're already dancing.

I'm not a great dancer, but the pull to take Dane out on the firelit sand is irresistible.

"D'you—you want to dance?"

Dane lifts his head, startled, like he didn't expect me to ask. His mouth opens, and then he shakes his head hard and says, "No," rude and aggressive and looking away.

The rejection hits like a slap.

We were warm and comfortable a moment ago, standing close together by the fire. Everything felt easy and natural.

Now I don't know what to say or how to hold my face. I don't want to seem like it matters, but it stung way more than I expected, and now I'm confused and blinking too hard.

Dane shifts uncomfortably. He turns the wine bottle in his hands, opening his mouth again like he thought of something else to say.

Too late—Emma grabs my arm. "Come dance with me."

Maybe she was listening, or else she saw the look on my face.

I let her pull me out on the sand, my body moving mindlessly to the music.

Emma puts her hands up on my shoulders, dancing close. She's a good dancer, barefoot on the sand, her hair brighter than the fire.

Dane watches us.

"How do you know him?" Emma murmurs close to my ear.

"His house is right by mine."

She turns so we're back-to-back, still dancing. Her fingers slide down my wrist until we're holding hands. Her head rests against mine. "You need to be careful around him."

Somehow, it's even hotter over here than right by the fire—too many warm bodies pressed close.

Dane stands with his arms crossed over his chest, watching us.

Emma turns behind me, putting her hands on my hips, staring back at him. Like she's taunting him.

"He's fucked up," she says right in my ear. "Dangerous."

Lips barely moving, I whisper, "I heard the rumor about his wife."

Emma keeps her eyes locked on Dane. "It's no rumor. He killed her."

"How do you know?"

"Because." Emma turns me around and tucks a piece of hair behind my ear as we gently sway. "Lila was my friend, and I know he's fucking lying."

I'm facing away from Dane now, but still, I'm sure he knows everything we're saying. "What happened?"

"He says she drowned in the river by their house." Emma takes my hand and twirls me around, her fingers sliding down the back of my arm and all the way down my spine. "Do you believe that?"

"No." It comes out in a sigh. "Not really."

A heavy arm drops around my shoulders, startling me. Tom's warm boozy breath bathes my face. "If you're gonna dance with anybody, it should be me... I met you first."

"Technically, I met her first," Emma says.

I can't shake off his arm. I duck my head, sneaking a glance back at Dane.

He's gone, the empty wine bottle abandoned on the sand.

CHAPTER 14
DANE

I CAN'T SLEEP FOR SHIT WHEN I GET HOME FROM THE BONFIRE, and the next day is worse. I keep waiting for Tom's truck to racket past, torturing myself with the idea that he might already be at Remi's house, that he might have been there all night long if he came home with her after the party.

I shouldn't have left like that, but I couldn't stand those carrot-topped fuckers swarming her. Whispering in her ear.

Emma never liked me. She looks sweet, but she's possessive.

Now she's latched on to Remi. Just my fucking luck. Apparently, we have exactly the same taste in women—who would have thought, when Emma and I have nothing else in common?

By all appearances, neither do Remi and Lila—but there must be something that drew me in, and Emma, too. Because here I am, obsessed with the wrong woman all over again and right back to making terrible decisions.

It was supposed to be highly pleasurable and mildly manipulative sex, no emotion involved. So why am I pacing the main floor of my house, watching the window?

Tom finally does drive past, alone in his truck and looking like shit, which cheers me up slightly. I hope Remi's pissed that he didn't show up to work until two o'clock in the afternoon.

She's due at my place at seven.

I watch the hours tick past, anxious and almost angry, like she's already decided not to come.

What did they say to her?

It doesn't matter. If Emma hasn't filled Remi's ear with poison, someone else will. It's only a matter of time.

I hate them all, those fucking hypocrites.

It won't matter…as long as Remi keeps coming back.

At 7:04, I hear that familiar rattling engine I've come to anticipate like Pavlov's dogs, saliva flooding my mouth. I come out onto the porch because I don't care if she sees me waiting.

"Sorry I'm late." Remi slams her car door to make it stay closed. "Tom wouldn't shut up."

She crosses over to the porch and joins me without even grabbing her tool bag out of the trunk. She's dressed for work, but all her gravity is toward the cool of the house, not the half-fixed fence in the sun-blasted orchard.

Inside is where I want to go, too.

I look at her, unsmiling. "Did you tell me that just to make me jealous?"

She tilts her chin up, those black eyebrows wicked in mirth. "Depends… Did it work?"

"No." I seize a handful of her hair and kiss her impudent mouth. "But only because I was already jealous."

I open the door, and the house swallows us both.

———

"What does he say to you?" I demand, my mouth all over her lips, my hands all over her body. "Alone at your house?"

"He's mostly trying to get me to pass him tools." She's laughing and shivering in my arms, exhilarated and terrified. "But I've got my own shit to get done."

Her lips are all over my neck, my jaw… Our mouths meet in

a kiss that's hot and wet and aggressive. Her lips are full and firm against mine; all the parts of us line up, like that's what they were made to do.

I'm kissing her like I haven't let myself before—like I missed her. Like I've been thinking about the feel and the smell of her all day.

I have. I fucking have... Why should I hide it?

I've been chasing Remi since the moment I got close. I'm attracted to her—and not just a little.

She looks up at me, those wide blue-green eyes incredulous. "Are you actually jealous?"

"Of course, I am." I bite the side of her neck. "I want you. And I don't want him to have you."

Or that little Emma bitch either...

I turn Remi around, tucking her up against my chest, holding her wrists pinned behind her back with one hand. Leaving my other hand free to roam her helpless body...

Why does this turn me on so badly?

Why do I like her best when I have her captive?

Remi makes me want to do dark things...

Dark urges, dark impulses...

It's something in her scent, in the way it goes spicy and sharp when I grab hold of her, a wisp of smoke before the fire ignites...

"Has he touched you?" I say, while my hand slides across her bare waist, in the space between her top and her jeans.

Remi's breath comes tight and quick, her stomach fluttering beneath my fingers. "And what if he did?"

It's barely a whisper, threaded with excitement. Her nipples point stiffly through the front of her shirt.

I growl in her ear, "Then I'd be *extremely* jealous...and maybe a little bit angry..."

Remi's body goes still. "And what happens when you're angry?"

My hand slides up her ribs, my fingers dancing across the soft undercurve of her breast. "After everything I've done to help you... I might feel that deserved punishment."

"Oh..." She pauses, her heart like a bird beneath my fingertips. "What kind of punishment?"

Her back arches, her ass pressing against my hips. She feels my hardness, and her ass slides up a little more so my length lands right between her cheeks.

Her body thinks it wants this.

But it has no fucking clue, any more than her brain.

Remi turns just a little so her breast slips into my hand. Close to my neck, she murmurs, "He tried to kiss me last night..."

I turn her around sternly. "Did you let him?"

She gazes up at me, fear and fascination battling in her face. "For a minute. Before I pushed him off."

The flare of rage and envy is so potent, it feels like I could drop my pants and my cock would glow red-hot like a poker.

"Take off your top."

"Wh-what?"

I say it again, slowly and firmly: "Take off your top."

She looks at me, then crosses her arms, grips the base of her shirt, and pulls it over her head.

Her tiny tits are bare beneath, pierced through with silver rings. There's just enough flesh to create a curve on the bottom, and a mole like a spot of chocolate sits on the left breast. Her nipples are firm and brown and stick out from her breasts, giving those tiny tits everything they need to be utterly perfect.

"Hold your hands behind your back."

Remi clasps her hands at the small of her back as if I still have them pinned. I noticed that in our last session—she likes to obey. This is a girl with Mommy *and* Daddy issues, trying to please the parents who left her holding the bag.

Well, they're not here.

But I am...and I love to be pleased.

I give her left breast a sharp upward slap. It bounces beautifully, the little brown nipple going painfully erect, a pale-pink print in the shape of my palm blooming like a butterfly, punctuated by the mole like a spot of chocolate.

Remi gasps. I slap her again in exactly the same place.

"Ouch!"

"Don't say 'ouch.'" I catch her face in my hand and hold her firmly by the chin as I kiss her on the mouth. "Say 'I'm sorry.'"

I slap her tit again, this time on the other side. I'm catching her in just the right place to make it lift and drop and sting the edge of her nipple.

"I'm sorry!" she gasps.

I slap her again, on the right side to even them out.

"I'm sorry!"

"Not as sorry as you're going to be."

I give her tits light slaps with both hands: *slap, slap, slap* with my right hand, and then *slap, slap, slap* with my left, back and forth, on one side and then the other, until her nipples stand out, wrinkled and hard, rosy red on the tips, and her breasts glow pink and swollen. Her rings glint silver white against all those pretty sunset shades.

Remi struggles to keep her hands clasped behind her back, her cheeks as flushed as her tits. Her eyes go bright, and her lower lip trembles.

Slap, slap, SLAP! I give the last one some extra sting, and she cries out, "Jesus! I'm sorry! *I'm sorry!*"

I'm not even close to done.

I turn her around and bend her over the arm of the couch, yanking down her jeans. Her ass is fuller than the rest of her and paler because it doesn't see as much sun.

Her pussy is dark like her nipples, a tempting patch peeking between the globes of her ass.

I grip her wrists and push her body down over the arm of the couch, forcing her ass up in the air. Holding her wrists pinned at the small of her back, I reach down with my other hand to spread her pussy lips....

Her back shivers beneath my arm, tight and thrumming. She can barely breathe with the tension, with the awful and intense sensation of exposure as I examine her...

I spread open her outer lips, revealing the dusky-pink inner folds. Her little cunt trembles at my touch, soft as plush, slippery as oil. I rub my finger around her opening with light, even pressure, watching her wetness seep like dew, gathering it on my fingers so I can lift them to my lips...

"Mm..." I let her flavor dissolve on my tongue.

I touch her again, slowly, sliding my fingers around and around. She's even wetter than before. I bring it to her mouth.

"Taste that."

Obediently, she parts her lips and sucks.

I want that mouth around my cock.

When I touch her pussy again, my fingers plunge in. She's fucking soaking...

I bring my fingers back to my tongue, and I'm drunk on her.

The world was an old gray TV screen, and when it smashed apart, I found a buffet behind it, in gorgeous shades of crimson and claret...

That's her body, like cherries, like pomegranates, like wine, like meat left bloody red...that's the taste, the smell, and the feel of her, in my mouth and against my skin...

I could devour her, and I do, nuzzling my face into her wet little cunt from behind.

Her hips wiggle, and she squeals. When I pull away, her back arches and her thighs part, as if she already misses me, as if she's begging me to come back...

I kneel with my face close to her gorgeous pussy and ass. Up close I can see how sensitive she is, how delicate. I watch her shiver in that softest part.

And when I touch her there, I see her melt. I watch it, and I feel it under my fingertips, that feeling that begins under my hand and spreads out, taking hold of her body in shivering waves until she's completely under my control...

For a moment, at least.

Until she wanders off and gets herself in trouble.

I give her a sharp upward slap on the ass, making her ass cheek bounce like I did to her tits. Remi yelps.

I slap her again, then again, at a steady cadence so she knows what to expect. I do it on the right and then the left—firm upward slaps, until both her ass cheeks glow as rosy as her tits.

Now we're ready to get started.

I reassert the downward pressure over the arm of the couch, pressing into her back, letting my body rest on top of hers, letting her feel my weight, my warmth.

Lips against her ear, I murmur, "Remi...I can't have you letting other men kiss you, even for a minute, even if I stormed off in a rage."

She goes still beneath me and turns her head slightly because we're talking with honesty now. "Why did you storm off?"

Images flash in my head: the looks, the whispers, Emma's hands on Remi's shoulders, her lips against her ear, those witchy green eyes locked on me. "Don't play stupid. You know."

Remi lets out a breath like a sigh. Her voice is low and soft when she asks, "What do you want me to do? A lot of people are telling me you killed your wife."

"Do you think I did?"

The question is out before I can wonder if I want it answered.

"No," Remi says, quick enough that I could almost cry. "Obviously, or I wouldn't be here. But I'm not going on anything but a feeling, so I might just be dumb."

"I don't like it when you talk that way." I grip her wrists, twisting them up behind her back.

"What?" she gasps.

"I don't like when you pretend you're not intelligent."

"I—I'm…" She shakes her head slightly, but she's smart enough not to finish that sentence how I think it started.

Then she does it anyway:

"Jude's the one who—"

I roll off enough to give her a sharp slap on the ass.

SMACK!

"Ouch!" Remi yelps.

SMACK! SMACK!

"I mean, *I'm sorry!*"

"Don't tell me your stories about your brother," I growl in her ear. "There's only one way you're stupid."

I drop my hand lower and touch her pussy instead, rubbing softly, gently, soothingly… "I *know* how smart you are. I've seen it. I've watched how you figure things out. You're tenacious. I'm attracted to you…"

Now, when I grip her wrists and pull them tighter, it's like I'm pulling her against me. Like I need to charge off her body…

"But I can't have you flirting with Tom Turner. Not even for free electrical work."

"It's not free!" Remi gasps, shivering against my warm, wet fingers. "It's discounted."

I spank her six or seven times for that. *Slap! Slap! Slap!* All in quick succession. "No," I say firmly, my fingers pressed against her clit. "You come to *me* for favors."

I touch her softly and then with pressure, teasing out the places that feel the best. My pleasure in her body feels deeply sinful and somehow tied to the dark desire to test and examine her, the ideas maybe linked forever from the first time I saw her with no pants.

I touch her until I've created exactly the reaction I want, which is her crying out involuntarily, writhing, her pussy soft like a living flower, and then a texture I can't describe as anything but melting,

melting, melting until I sink three fingers deep, her wetness running down my hand.

She's gasping, red-faced, embarrassed.

Her emotions are spice in the air, firecrackers in the room…little piquant explosions when everything else is pleasure and silk.

She's so beautiful in all her little reactions because she feels things so intensely, because she burns so brightly and fiercely.

I turn her over and sit her on the arm of the couch, releasing her wrists. She touches where I gripped, her eyes on my face. I kneel between her legs, hands resting on her inner thighs.

Her pussy sits before me, its own perfect shape, half-open petals, flawless like a flower in all its symmetries and asymmetries. Her scent pulls me in; there's no choice about it.

I lick and kiss and taste… My palms read her thighs like a seismograph…waves and tremors before the full-on earthquake…

Her hands cup the back of my head, her fingers thrust in my hair, her nails scratch my scalp. Her thighs spread, and she pulls me tightly against her cunt, her back arching, her head thrown back… I suck gently, gently on her clit…

She comes unglued, clinging, squirming, begging for it, begging for it, until she can't take it anymore and pushes me away.

"Jesus!" she cries, still shivering. "Jesus…"

I kiss her so she can taste what I just tasted—the pure fucking evidence of how much she loved it.

"That was a favor," I tell her. "Did you like it?"

She closes her eyes and shudders as an aftershock rolls through her. "Yes."

I kiss her again, softer this time, breathing in her breath. "I like doing you favors."

We look into each other's eyes, another layer deep in honesty.

When you want someone for a purpose, you see them in that role.

When you want them just because you want them…you see so much more.

I like this space we're floating in now.

Remi isn't so sure. She finds her jeans puddled around one ankle and pulls them up again. She's still topless but doesn't seem to notice or care, in an endearingly boyish way. Instead, she sits on the arm of the couch, her feet not quite touching the floor, her arms crossed, frowning slightly. "I don't know if you did me a favor the other night... I'm still having nightmares."

"You thought they'd go away in a day?"

She sighs. "I wished they would."

I stand between her knees and run my hands through her hair until my palms cradle the base of her skull and her face tilts up. "Fixing your brain's about as fast as fixing your house."

Her smile bursts up, unruly. "Is that what you're doing? Fixing me?"

"God, no. I can't even fix myself."

"What's wrong with you?"

I hold her with her face like a dish so I can find all the brightest bits of blue and green in her eyes. "A thousand things: I'm selfish, I have a temper, I can be sneaky, I'm curious and arrogant, I'm picky, and almost everyone annoys me..."

"Is that all?" Remi laughs.

"And I've made some fucking terrible mistakes in my life."

Remi's eyes go sad, and she lets out a heavy sigh. "Me, too."

I feel an urge to come clean with her, now that I've seen Remi in her most open and vulnerable state. It only seems fair.

"No matter how tidy my house looks or how well I press my clothes, I'm a fucking mess, Remi...it's how I recognized it in you."

"Are you really?" she says softly, looking up into my face.

"Yes. I'm barely holding it together."

That's something I haven't admitted to anyone, even my own brother.

I'm telling Remi because I know she'll understand.

And she does.

There's no judgment in her face, only sympathy.

"In a way, that makes me feel better..."

"Why?"

"Because you're intimidating. And if I'm honest..." She takes a deep breath, her cheeks turning pink. "I'd like to think we're not so far apart. The other day, when you said you saw yourself in me..." Her blush deepens until her whole face is red. "That really made me feel good. It made me feel...so much less alone."

Her gaze drops, and then she chances one quick glance back up at my face.

I don't know what she sees.

I can't separate the churning mass of emotions in my chest—surprise, pleasure, but also a hefty measure of guilt...

"You're not alone." I brush a lock of that ludicrous purple hair back from her face. It doesn't look so bright and outrageous inside the house. Actually, it's quite beautiful, the deep violet against her dusky skin. "Not right now."

I bend my head to kiss her.

This is a different kind of kiss than those that came before. This one isn't stolen—I pause with my lips an inch from hers and wait for her to tilt up her mouth.

When her soft lips press against mine, a pulse surges through my body.

Fuck. This girl has quite the effect on me.

I take a step back, though I can't convince myself to actually move away. Our knees are still almost touching.

Softly, looking at some unfocused point, Remi says, "I don't want to sound ungrateful. I did like it in a way, the hypnotism—afterward, I felt this incredible sense of clarity. Like I was transparent and the air could go right through me, and I could see everything in a whole new way..."

Her hand floats up and touches the back of my thigh. She closes her eyes and leans forward to rest her head against my stomach. "Until it got to be too much, and it all fell apart."

I feel a craving in the back of my teeth, but not for food.

Carefully, I say, "Would you like to try again?"

Remi presses her forehead against my abdomen, hiding her face. She grips at the back of my pants. "I…I don't know. Afterward, all this time had passed, and I couldn't…couldn't quite remember everything we did…"

She casts a furtive look up at my face, a flash of blue green tipped with lashes fluttering black. Her eyes are like a Rorschach; they've become the symbol of everything in my mind. I see a hundred images shifting like ink…what we did…and what we did next…

I remember every second of our session.

And I want more.

CHAPTER 15
REMI

Dane goes around the room, lighting candles. He keeps the light low in his house as a general rule, and as I've learned, candle-light is gentlest on the eyes…save for starlight.

The wind has picked up outside. The last golden days of September might be over—today was gray.

Flames flicker all around us like we're sitting in a hearth. The shadows of the objects in the room grow wild and strange, dancing on the walls.

The pull to sink back into that deep and restful state is an under-tow, but I resist, paddling on the surface…

"I don't like not remembering."

That blank hole in my day creeps me out, like someone took a melon baller and scooped three hours out of my brain.

Not *someone*—the man standing across from me, making a low snorting sound like memory is overrated. Or worse, according to him…

"Half your memories are lies." Dane lights one last candle over the mantel.

He says such odd things so matter-of-factly.

"How can a memory be a lie? It's what you saw happen."

"What you *think* you saw."

Dane shakes out the match he was using before it can burn his fingertips.

"Think about it: When two people disagree, how come they're each remembering the version of events that benefits themselves? The mind sees and stores what it wants to."

I make a disdainful sound. "Then how can anyone know what's true?"

"If you're honest with yourself," Dane says quietly. "But nobody is. You tell yourself a lie, and you tell yourself the lie again…and soon you can't see anything else. Even when it's right in front of your face."

Unbidden, I think of the stack of bills on my father's desk—bills months and years out of date, gone to collections, while we rode elephants in Thailand and took a freighter to the Antarctic. No life insurance for him or my mother. The lie was that we were rich. The lie was that nothing could hurt us when we were all so happy…

I could have seen signs: Times my father was stressed. Times he fought with my mother. Twice, I saw her swipe a credit card and it wouldn't go through. Once my father bought a new car, and a week later, it was gone from the driveway. And once, Jude's school called in a snit over tuition instead of his behavior.

Warning lights blinking all around, but they meant nothing to me at the time.

Most, I barely registered. It was only later, when I combed through the bills, that I remembered how, for a second time, the cashier at the grocery store swiped my mother's card and said, *I'm sorry, ma'am. It says it's declined…* And my mother got so angry…

I think of how often I smelled perfume on Gideon's clothes and tried to tell myself it was flowers in the room or someone he'd sat close to on a train…

You fucking fool.

"I don't want to lie to myself."

Dane gives me a look with a surprising amount of sadness in it. "We'll see."

He sits on the floor this time, across from me. His rug is thick, so we're comfortable. The flickering candles and the wind outside the

windows make it feel more like a séance than a meditation session…
which is fitting. My head is full of ghosts.

Including Gideon.

That's what blocking someone is—it's erasing their face, their
voice, out of your life like they're dead.

I ghosted him. I made him my ghost.

"What are you thinking about?" Dane's voice makes me jump.

"I…" *Fuck, why am I so slow…?* "…don't want to tell you."

Brilliant.

"Do it anyway."

"I…was engaged. Up until three weeks ago."

Dane sits very still, the candlelight turning his eyes orange and
amber. "What was his name?"

"Gideon."

"Mm." I can't interpret that sound or the slight smile on his lips.

Why is his mouth so beautiful and so cruel?

Why am I here, seeking mental clarity from the most disturbing
person I know?

Blame it on Grimstone… God knows, Dane would.

Lunatic.

And here I am, cross-legged before him, a lunatic acolyte.

Teach me, master…

If I can't get sane, I might as well get better at crazy.

He's crazy, I'm crazy, we're all crazy…

My mind will say anything to fill the void.

"What happened?"

Hypocrite! How dare he ask when I've barely said a peep about his wife?

No, he knows this isn't the real ugly.

Gideon hurt, it's true, but I was surprised when I examined the
wound—it wasn't even near fatal.

I should care more. I should be devastated.

Instead, it feels…inevitable. Like we were only playing pretend
all along.

"He cheated." This is the first time I've said it out loud. I've never admitted it, even to Jude. But he knew. I'm sure a lot of people knew. "That's probably why Jude never liked him. And now he rubs it in my face, and he should because there were a thousand signs."

"What signs?" Dane asks, unsmiling, unmoving.

The wind stirs the air down the chimney, wafting the scent of cinders, of smoke…

"I'll tell you the one that drove me insane. Because it was so… ephemeral. But it haunted me, day after day…"

I remember a hundred afternoons, evenings, mornings, even… smelling a floral scent in his apartment, his car, even on his sheets… not many florals—the same fucking one: jasmine.

"It was a woman's perfume. That's obvious now. But he denied it so convincingly. It was honestly like he really couldn't smell it. I'd say, 'It's on your coat. It's here in the car…'" After a moment, I find myself admitting, "He must have been seeing the same woman the whole time. It was always the same perfume."

Somehow that hurts more than the idea of many women, many casual encounters.

This means emotion. This means love. A deeper deception.

Did he miss her when he was with me?

Did he sneak away to text her?

The details shouldn't matter, but they do because they mean a thousand different cuts behind my back, a poison I never saw, but it ran all through my blood. That must have been the reason for the emptiness between us. Silences that felt so bleak. It must, it must, because otherwise it should have worked…

"I didn't leave him because of that." I'm admitting it all now—why not? I really don't like pretending. "I had to find a condom, a used condom, on my side of the bed… Like, I had to hold it up to the light before I'd believe it. And that's fucking embarrassing. I should have known the first time I found lipstick on his clothes. That only happens one way. The other 'reasons' I invented are ridiculous."

Dane smiles slightly and almost laughs—his breath comes out with that kind of a sound.

I wince. He notices and reaches out to rest his hand on my forearm.

"I'm only laughing because I'm the same. Everyone's the same—when we're being irrational."

Irrational.

That word has a certain bell-like sound.

I sit up, my palms pressing against the floor.

"What is it?" Dane says.

"Did you—? Are you—?"

I'm not even sure what I was thinking a second ago. It was all so clear, and then it faded…

True thoughts come back.

What was I thinking?

Irrational…

Right. The word *irrational*…it's wrong. It's not what I want to be. But it's not as imposing as a word like *mad* or *crazy*. You could never *really* trust a crazy person, could you? Like, you might love them and have them as a friend, but would you…leave them alone with your newborn baby?

No, admit it. You wouldn't.

But someone who's irrational or who had been irrational once or twice…that's everyone. That's not so awful.

I could admit if I'd been irrational.

And I could try to change.

Maybe someone who'd gone mad could never truly be sane, but I could be rational. If all I'd been before was irrational.

"He was cheating on me, and it took me way too long to admit it."

I say the whole thing out loud, low and distinct. It's pulling out a sliver of glass—fucking hurts, but then…less.

It was so much worse when it was still inside, cutting.

Dane nods like he understands.

"Did you…? Was your wife—?"

"No." His smile is flat and without humor. "Our problems were between us."

However he meant that, it doesn't invite further questions.

This feels one-sided. I'm back to distrusting him; I don't like the imbalance.

"I don't want you hypnotizing me again. What was I thinking? That must have been part of a complete breakdown—we barely know each other."

"*Barely know each other…*" Dane makes a disdainful sound. "Don't act like you believe that."

"What?"

"*What? What?*" he mimics me again. "How long do you have to spend around me to 'know' me? What, exactly, do we need to do together?"

He seizes me and kisses me on the mouth.

"You already know me because you answered the question right, while everyone in town answers it wrong. I didn't murder my wife. And you knew it, you felt it."

He kisses me softly, warmly. "Does that feel like a killer, like someone who would rip you apart? Some things can be felt. They can. Fucking try to find the killer in me."

He kisses me deeply, passionately, hungrily, even…but he pulls back without hurting. He's dancing with me; he's in control.

What does that mean? Is control an on-off switch?

Or is a monster always leaking through the seams of his suit?

Dane feels good; I can't deny it… He's a kind of good I've never touched before—the kind where each new sensation turns hot and molten: his lips on my jaw, his hand on my breasts…

It all feels better, more intense, more pleasurable than it has any right to…

Is that a guarantee of good or a sure sign that it's wrong?

Don't believe anything that's too good to be true...

But then...are we allowed to believe in any good things?

It feels so fucking transcendent when he kisses me.

Who told me to resist that kind of feeling? My body seems to think it's exactly what I need...

Dane lets go, and the room spirals back with a jolt.

"I'm not going to make you do anything," he says. "But if you want, this time I'll set up a camera. You can watch the whole thing."

This is a new, intriguing option.

If I never try again, I'll never know what happened.

But if I film a session... I'll see it with my own eyes.

What did I just tell Dane?

I don't want to lie to myself.

"Show me," I say. "Show me what I do when I'm hypnotized."

———

"You're on a beach," Dane says. "At the ocean. See the water. See the waves."

There's a rhythm in his voice, almost music...

Low, clear, and smooth, like a bell...

Thoughts go out, and then...they come back...

Each different, and yet...always waves...

"Do you see the sky?" Dane asks.

"Yes."

"Do you see the waves?"

"Yes."

"The sand?"

"No..."

I'd only been picturing rolling blue water.

I don't like the deep ocean.

In fact, it terrifies me.

That's how I feel when I'm scared and stressed...like I'm

drowning. I swim and I swim as cold water drags me down. Until I want to give up and sink into darkness.

"Don't jump in the ocean," says Dane with a touch of amusement. "You're on the beach—standing on the sand. The waves lap at your feet…"

I picture it how he says: blue ocean, white sand under my heels, sun overhead, cold water washing my toes…

I begin to feel warm and calm instead of afraid.

Dane's voice is as melodic as an instrument. He should have recorded audiobooks for a living—it would have been a hell of a lot easier than med school.

"How many waves are there?" he asks.

I watch them come in on the canvas of my mind. Wave after wave, today, tomorrow, and forever… "Infinite."

"That's right." I can hear that he's pleased, though my eyes are closed. "Infinite waves. And how many mistakes do we make?"

I pause, feeling the wash of cold foam again and again on my toes… "Infinite."

"That's right." Dane sighs. "Infinite mistakes."

CHAPTER 16
REMI

"YOU'RE AWAKE."

My eyes open.

I'm sitting cross-legged on the floor.

Dane sits just opposite, like he hasn't moved at all. But he has moved, I'm sure of it... The windows are opaquely black, and the candles have burned down. Even Dane himself looks altered—his hair rumpled and his skin flushed.

"How do you feel?" he says.

"I...I... I'm not sure."

I'm feeling that same sense of lightness, of clarity, but I'm also starting to freak out just a little bit. Why can't I remember what just happened? What the fuck is wrong with me?

"You look scared," he says.

"I am scared. Why don't I remember what we just did?"

"Because you don't want to."

That sure as fuck doesn't make me feel any better.

The burned-down candles flicker and smoke, shadows rippling across the room. Dane watches me, hair wild as a windstorm, eyes glittering. He's waiting. He already knows. I feel a deep sense of dread. Dane's phone sits on the bookcase, its red eye still recording. But I no longer want to look.

"Are you afraid?" he asks softly. "To see yourself?"

"Yes," I admit. "Why? Why am I afraid?"

"Because you want to believe you're in control. And you're afraid to see what you look like when you aren't."

I stand, disturbed by the deep, flat black outside the windows. How much time has passed?

There's more than one Remi...

My heart clenches, heat racing down each nerve. It's panic, it's terror, and it spikes each time I look in the direction of the phone.

"I don't want to see!" I cry suddenly. "Get that away from me."

"Remi—"

"No! I'm leaving. This is— I don't know what this is. I don't know what you want from me."

I'm in a full-out panic, searching for my stuff, forgetting what I even brought inside.

"Don't touch me!" I cry as Dane reaches for my arm.

He's not trying to catch me. He stands there watching as I storm out of his house, all the doors left open behind me.

———

Blackleaf is dark and quiet, and Jude's moped is absent from the yard.

Half of me worries about why he's out so late, but the other half feels relief. I'm so damn tired, I don't have the energy to talk, not even to my brother.

My body's throbbing, from sore muscles, blisters on my hands and feet, but also tenderness in more delicate places... My nipples rub against my shirt, the cotton rough as sandpaper against sensitive skin.

I've barely left Dane's house, and already I'm craving his hands on me again.

Half-remembered touches flit through my head—his lips on my neck, my bare pussy grinding against his thigh...

Are they real or only delirium?

I can't shake the mindfuck of all those blank, forgotten hours.

But neither can I shake the memories of his hands on my skin...

I take a short, cold shower, the pipes shuddering and groaning. Without a shower curtain, it's easy for me to see myself reflected in the cracked mirror, writhing like a wraith beneath the cold spray.

The magnet flips a dozen times, back and forth, back and forth...

Dane disturbs me, and I vow to avoid him...

While already longing to drive back to his house...

I climb into my own bed instead, determined to catch eight hours' sleep for the first time this week.

I'm tired enough that I'm out almost as soon as my head hits the pillow, but it's no restful sleep. I fall into a dream like the flick of a light switch: one moment in my room, and the next in our old house...

Jude is six years old but so much smaller. He's picked on at school. They put him straight into the second grade because he tested so high, but all the other students are a foot taller.

"We should have held him back, if anything..." Dad says.

"You can't hold him back. He's already bored." Mom's proud of Jude, fiercely proud. But when he throws a tantrum, she turns him over to me.

He's pitching a fit because he doesn't want to be a newsie. Mom made him audition for the school play; she was in a shampoo commercial, once.

"I don't like this hat!" Jude shouts. "I won't wear it!"

I take him to my room to soothe him.

He's flushed from crying, furious at Mom, but only because he's scared.

"You're going to be amazing," I promise him. "You know all your lines."

"I only have two."

"The best two in the show."

He buries himself in my pillows, his hat flung on the floor.

I dig him out and smooth back his hair, teasing and tickling until he finally laughs.

"There—I knew you didn't forget how to smile."

He's still adamant: "I won't do it."

"Come on," I coax. "I want to see you onstage! And Dad will take us for ice cream afterward..."

Jude loves ice cream, even though he always orders vanilla. "Did he promise?"

"Pinky promised."

"Fine," Jude says, giving his quick, jerky nod that reminds me of a samurai warrior in an old martial arts movie.

He snuggles against me.

"I wish you were my mother..."

"I'm your other mother." I wrap my arms around him, kissing him on the head. "Your backup mom. I'm always going to love you and take care of you..."

I promised with all my heart, with no idea it would actually come to pass.

The wind lashes the bedroom windows, no match for the storm inside my head...

I'm in the cabin of the SeaDreamer, *tossed like a jack-in-a-box. We've sailed through storms before, but never one like this...*

The next wave nearly throws me out of my bunk. Jude's chilly little hand grabs my arm. His eyes are huge and terrified. He's nearly hysterical. "What do we do? What do we do?"

The rolling ship slams us against the walls back and forth like pinballs as we stumble down the hall.

My parents' door is shut and locked. I knock, and then I pound.

I'm banging, shouting... Jude keens like an animal, cringing against my leg. The smoke makes him hack and gag.

At last, the door bursts open, its frame ripped off, leaving splinters and jagged metal points...

Dad hangs on the doorknob, reeling...

His eyes are dazed, unfocused. When he talks, he slurs…
"Wh-wha's happenin'…?"
"There's a fire, Dad!"
I'm screaming, but he hardly seems to hear…
"Get Mom!"
He blinks, slowly, so slowly… "I tried, but she won't—"

I wake to a crashing of keys.

It's the piano again, but not a few notes—a wretched, howling sound, like someone is pounding the ivories with both hands.

I'm out of bed and halfway across the room before I'm fully awake, hopping on one foot while I try to yank on a pair of pants.

I snatch up my phone, sending the charging block and everything else I had stacked on the dresser scattering across the floor. The piano still booms and clangs downstairs.

The noise halts abruptly as I sprint down the staircase, though the echoes hang in the air, confusing me as I finally reach the landing. Is that muffled sound coming from the kitchen, or is someone moving down the hall?

I take the latter route because it's closer to the dining room where I just heard the piano. I slow down, creeping cautiously, my phone light half shielded with my hand.

The house is quiet once more but not silent. The wind still moans against the windows, groaning, then dying down, then revving up again, like a fitful patient who can't find rest. Blackleaf creaks with each blast, ticking and groaning as it resettles.

I'm holding my breath, listening for any noise out of rhythm, anything that sounds human. Or animal.

A sudden explosion of glass and porcelain makes me shriek. I bolt away from the noise, halfway back up the stairs before I force myself to stop, cringing on the risers, clinging to the railing with one hand, my phone light jittering madly in the other, creating a strobe effect around the entryway.

"Come on, you chickenshit…"

I force myself back across the marble tiles, where water pools once more. Where the fuck does it keep coming from? My pale reflection tracks me across the floor, wavering in the ripples from my bare feet.

From the kitchen comes an irregular dripping, like a gutter overflowing. Did it start to rain outside? I thought it was only windy.

My feet slosh through an inch of cold water. I enter a kitchen that's become a shallow lake, the sink plugged and overflowing. When I raise my phone, the light glitters off shattered plates and glassware.

"What the fuck?" Jude says behind me.

His lantern light swings across the kitchen, illuminating in chaotic detail the mini–Niagara Falls pouring out of our sink and the mounds of broken dishes piled beneath the half-empty cabinet with its doors hanging open.

"Did you do this?"

"No!" I cry, my heart still galloping in my chest. "Why would I break the dishes?"

"I dunno." Jude stifles a yawn. "Thought you were sleepwalking or something."

"I don't sleepwalk."

"How do you know?"

"Because I was awake the whole time! I heard the piano—"

"What piano?" Jude says. "All I heard was smashing."

"Before that." I struggle to speak calmly. "The piano was playing again before."

"It was?" Jude glances at me. "I didn't hear that."

"It wasn't as loud. I mean, it was louder than the first time, but not as loud as the dishes…"

"Okay," Jude says. "I believe you."

Somehow that makes me feel worse, like there was a chance he wouldn't believe me. Like he's doing me a favor 'cause my story sounds crazy.

It does sound crazy.

It *is* crazy. What the fuck is going on here?

I shut off the sink, then wade across the kitchen to check the door that leads out to the backyard—it's locked and dead bolted. All the windows on the main floor are locked or boarded up; I checked and double-checked after the last time.

"Wait here," I say to Jude, and I dash back to the front door, though there's no way somebody could have gone out that way—or at least, I don't think so. I guess they could have snuck past me through the old ballroom; it connects on both sides. But the front door's bolted, too.

Jude joins me in the entryway, looking a bit like Charon as he carries his lantern across the dark water. "Still locked?"

"Yeah."

He watches my face. "You think it's the creepy doctor?"

I hesitate. "No. Well… I'm not sure."

Breaking into my house to smash my dishes doesn't feel like Dane somehow. But based off what? I barely know him, and he's fully capable of doing something just to fuck with me.

"He's not creepy," I add lamely.

That was stupid. Now Jude's fully awake and giving me his sharpest stare.

"Do you like him or something?"

"No!" God, I hope Jude can't tell how red I am in this light. "I mean, I don't dislike him. The more I get to know him, he's, uh…"

I really wish I wouldn't start sentences I don't know how to finish.

Dane's intense and provoking, and he says things that have me wondering for an hour afterward exactly what he meant. And when he kisses me…

Well, then it's not really a question of *liking* him. It's more like he shot me up to space and I need the air from his lungs just to breathe. It's like I'm composed of a trillion atoms and he's the force holding me together.

That's how I feel when I'm around him.

The rest of the time, I'm wondering if I should forget this impossible project, pack up my shit, and never see Grimstone again.

I came here for peace and stability, a fresh start, a shot at a better life.

But it's all become more confusing than ever, the red noise only building in my head.

Why does chaos follow me everywhere I go?

It really is starting to feel like *I'm* the common denominator.

Did I leave one shitty man just to latch on to someone worse?

"How long until you're done with his fence?" Jude says.

"I don't know; maybe a few more days."

I'm not looking at Jude because I hate lying to him. But I hate even more the idea of admitting that I haven't touched Dane's fence the past two visits because I was too busy letting him put his hands down my pants. And fuck with my brain.

Jesus, I really am losing my mind.

"I don't know what else he'll want me to do."

"Tell him to fuck off." Jude scowls. "The fence is enough."

"He kind of has us over a barrel."

"That doesn't mean he gets to break into our house!"

"I don't know if he did."

"Then who did all that?" Jude points in the direction of the kitchen. "A raccoon?"

"Maybe," I say, though I don't think either of us believes that for a second. There were piles of dishes on the floor, like someone cleared off the shelves with both arms. "But then who plugged the sink?"

"You ever see those YouTube videos where the raccoon tries to wash the cotton candy, but it keeps disappearing?" Jude smirks. "Maybe he was trying to do that."

I snort. "That's gotta be it."

I slosh back across the entryway, curious about what, exactly, is blocking the sink. We don't even own a proper plug.

I stick my bare arm down into the basin of cold water, its surface darkly opaque even when Jude holds the lantern aloft.

Reaching into the drain gives me an eerie feeling. There's no garbage disposal, but my mind still treats me to an image of blades suddenly whirling to life around my probing fingers.

"Hold on," I say to Jude, who's holding the lantern, "just a little farther…"

My fingertip touches something hard and slightly slimy, with a wet, fibrous texture wrapped around it.

"There's definitely something jammed in here…a tree root, maybe?"

I've dealt with plenty of tree roots growing into pipes, especially in basement renovations. This could be a bit of woody root tangled up with finer hairlike threads…

I manage to wedge my fingers down enough to grasp the knobby head. I tug and yank until finally it comes out of the drain with a horrid sucking sound.

I hold the root aloft in the lantern light, where it drips something darker than water…

The root isn't a root at all, but hard pale bone, hung with shreds of flesh and bits of bloodstained hair.

Jude takes one look, covers his mouth, and bolts from the room.

CHAPTER 17
REMI

SHERIFF SHANE DOESN'T ARRIVE AT OUR HOUSE UNTIL ALMOST four hours later, showered, shaved, and smelling of fresh coffee and bacon, so I guess he doesn't give a shit about trespassing either.

"You again," he says, as soon as I open the door.

I was holding out a faint hope that it might be a different sheriff than the one who pulled me over for speeding, but nope, same asshole.

He pokes around the house without touching anything or climbing any stairs. Then he hitches up his belt, chuckling a little as he says, "You think somebody tried to break in *here*?"

It does sound a bit like accusing someone of breaking into the DMV to wait in line.

By the light of day, Blackleaf does not look better. In fact, it looks a hell of a lot worse because I didn't clean up the water or the broken dishes, having much overestimated our sheriff's evidence-gathering capabilities. If I thought he was going to bust out the fingerprint-dusting kit, I was sorely mistaken—he doesn't even bag and tag the bone.

In the first awful moment, I thought it might be an ulna or a tibia.

"Nope," the sheriff says, tossing it in the trash. "Golden retriever."

That doesn't make me feel a whole lot better.

"Don't you want to take it anyway?"

"What for? DNA test it and see if he's got a brother?" The sheriff roars at his own joke.

I'm not smiling. "Aren't you concerned that somebody killed a dog?"

"Killin' a dog ain't illegal—unless you do it in a cruel and torturous way," the sheriff says with cold carelessness.

"Kinda seems like they did."

"No way to know from one bone."

"Oh. I thought they invented this thing called 'forensic science.'"

Now the sheriff isn't smiling either. "That sounds a lot like you tellin' me how to do my job, little lady—when you got a whole lotta work here to do all by yourself. And I'm not sure you've got the proper permits...so maybe keep your focus on your own list of chores"—his eyes flick up to my hair and down to my lip ring—"and try not to draw so much attention."

He holds his belt, his elbows flared like a gunslinger. I face him across the flooded kitchen, my hands stuffed in the pockets of my jeans, feeling about the same.

"What about all this?" I demand, jerking my chin at the pile of smashed glass and crockery.

"Maybe the wind blew it over." The sheriff's mouth is a thin, hard line.

I'd like to walk outside and take a baseball bat to his cruiser.

"Wow. Thank god I called you."

"Well, that's the kind of service you can expect here in Grimstone, little lady." He's steely-eyed as he bites off each word. "So anytime you get yourself in trouble, you just give me a call, and I'll be right over to give you the benefit of our state-of-the-art forensic science."

"Four hours later."

"That's right. Just as fast as I can."

Now that the sheriff and I have established that we wouldn't piss on each other in a firestorm, he's ready to be on his way.

"You got permission to use this road?" he calls out as he climbs back in his cruiser. "It belongs to Dr. Covett."

"We have an arrangement."

The sheriff snorts, giving me a look. "I bet you do."

"Well, I hate *him*," Jude says when the sheriff is gone. Jude made himself scarce the moment the cruiser pulled into the yard. Wish I could have done the same. "Did you have to make him mad, though?"

"Me make *him* mad?" I sputter, furiously sweeping shards of broken pottery into a wet, jumbled pile. "Didn't you hear that horseshit? He's not gonna do *anything*! He barely even looked around."

"Yeah, but now you got him looking at our permits…"

"That was just a stupid threat," I say sullenly. But now I'm second-guessing myself.

"You don't have to be so antagonistic," my brother remarks, with no apparent sense of irony.

"Oh, yes, please, give me all your pointers on etiquette, rudest person I know…"

Jude shrugs. "I was smart enough not to talk to him."

"I didn't have that luxury."

"Don't be a martyr."

I extend my arms on both sides and hang my head like I'm being crucified.

Jude laughs.

I tell him, "The sheriff said the bone came from a dog."

"Yeah, I heard."

"But how did it get in the sink?" I pause in my sweeping, leaning on the broom, staring at the dark hole of the drain.

"It is weird.…" Jude says with a sideways glance. "When all the doors were locked."

"I wasn't sleepwalking!"

"Okay, okay." He holds up his hands. "Then I'm back to thinking it was your new boyfriend."

"Don't call him that."

"Or maybe your other new boyfriend..."

"Please tell me you're not talking about Tom."

"Why not?" Jude shrugs. "He's always perving on you. And he's a total lush—he coulda gotten drunk and tried to break in and knocked all the shit off the shelves."

In a way, the chaotic mess does feel more like Tom than Dane, from whom I'd expect something a lot more...calculated.

"But that doesn't make sense either," I muse. "Because the first time I heard the piano, Tom hadn't started working here."

"The piano?"

"Yeah. The first time I heard it playing was the first night we came. I hadn't met Tom yet or even called him."

"Right..." There's nothing obvious in Jude's tone, but something in his expression, in the slight purse of his lips, is starting to piss me off.

"I heard the piano playing!"

"Nobody said you didn't."

"Your face is saying it."

"Relax, Remi." Jude rolls his eyes. "I believe you about your spooky magic piano."

I set the broom aside a little too roughly, so it slips off the end of the counter and clatters to the floor. "Someone's breaking into our house, Jude! This is serious! They could really hurt us, and the sheriff's not doing shit!"

Jude picks up the broom and hangs it up properly by the back door. "It's probably kids, the same ones who broke in here before. Or an animal, or fuck, who knows? I don't think we need to jump to 'murderous psychopath.'"

"Cool, cool..." I nod my head, my arms crossed over my chest. "Let's hope you're right, since the alternative is *us being carved up in our beds!*"

Jude shakes his head at me, unsmiling. "Remi, I'm saying this with love…you are wound way too fucking tight. We're out here in nature…you should go for a walk or something."

"You're telling *me* to get some exercise? Jesus, I must be a mess."

"I'm worried about you," Jude says seriously. "It's not just the Gideon stuff—you're exhausted all the time, not sleeping, forgetting things, picking fights, and, no offense, you look like absolute dog shit—"

"Why would I take offense to any of that?"

"I'm starting to worry if I ever do go to college, you're going to implode."

"There is no 'if'—you're going. And I'll be just fine."

"If you say so." Jude's eyebrows are so high, they've disappeared under his hair.

"I'm fine! I'm fantastic, actually—the sheriff was asking my skin-care routine."

Jude's mouth quirks. "He should have asked for mine—I don't look a day over fourteen."

"Don't sell yourself short—you could pass for sixteen and a half."

Jude joins me at Emma's for breakfast, his moped tossed in the back of the Bronco so he can make his own way home while I reload our supplies.

It only takes him about five minutes to devour his poached egg on toast and finish his coffee.

"What's your hurry?" I say when he scoots out of the booth before I'm halfway done with my omelet.

"I've got shit to do."

"In the shed?" I say pointedly.

"Yup," Jude replies.

"How's that going?"

"About halfway done." He blinks, which is not a good sign. That's always been Jude's tell.

I press a little harder. "You find anything worth selling?"

"A few things."

"Okay. Well—"

"See you later!" He barely waves before scooting out the door.

"Did he just dine and dash you?" Emma comes over to the table with a fresh latte in hand. She sets it in front of me and then drops down on the other side of the booth, taking Jude's seat before it's had time to cool.

"I always pay the bill, so...no more than usual."

Emma laughs. Her hair is piled high on her head, orange corkscrews spilling down. Now that it's October, she's wearing a spiderweb-printed apron and her nails are painted black. Paper bats hang from the ceiling, and the bud vases on the tabletops each contain a single ink-dark rose.

The foam on my latte is a wobbly moon dusted with a slightly wonky cinnamon cat.

"Not your best work," I tease.

"Oh, you had to point it out." Emma scowls. "I think that hunk of junk's finally on its last legs..."

The espresso machine lets out a gout of steam like a burp. On the board behind the machine, someone's added a notice for a missing cat.

"Can't buy another one until next year; summer crowd's already clearing out." Emma gazes around at the half-empty tables. "Most of 'em will be gone by Halloween. But we'll get a big boost that week."

"For the fair?"

I've seen the banners on Main Street, promising a Witches' Ball, Zombie Run, Haunted Hayrides, Night of a Thousand Jack-o'-Lanterns, and something called a Bloodbath...

"Yeah, the Reaper's Revenge," Emma says without much enthusiasm. "They do it every year."

"Sounds fun!"

"It is…but Grimstone gets packed, and all the masks and everything…something fucked up happens every year."

"What kind of thing?"

"Well…" Emma casts a quick look around and lowers her voice, leaning across the table so our heads almost touch. "There's this mascot for the festival, Mr. Bones. People dress up as him. Last year this girl from out of town got pulled into the park by somebody in a Mr. Bones costume. And I guess he assaulted her, but it wasn't just one Mr. Bones. There were a bunch, all dressed the same… She didn't know how many there were, just that they kept—kept taking turns…"

"Jesus." My stomach churns.

"Yeah. I'm sure it was all people from out of town, but that's why I don't like the festival; it brings in a rough crowd."

Emma's blaming the tourists, but it's the sheriff's table in the back where she casts her eye. Sheriff Shane is taking up half his favorite booth, his two deputies squeezed into the other side. As I glance backward, one of the deputies notices. He nudges the other and whispers, and they both laugh.

"Assholes," I mutter.

"Yup," Emma says bitterly. "I got robbed by an ex-employee last year, had her on camera entering and exiting the store, and Sheriff Schmuck over there wouldn't do shit 'cause you couldn't actually see her sticking the money in her pocket. I don't think he even bothered to interrogate her. Big fuckin' surprise, since her dad owns the golf course…"

From bits and pieces I've picked up from Tom, I get the impression there's some kind of vendetta between the people who consider themselves locals and the interlopers who live in and around the resort. I would guess the sheriff mostly caters to the latter 'cause they're the ones with all the cash.

The bell over the door jingles. A couple enters, looking around for a table.

"Need to help them?" I ask Emma.

"Nah." She motions to the other waitress to assist the couple instead. "Perks of being the boss."

"You're such a badass. How many employees do you have?"

"Six," Emma says proudly. "But most are part-time, especially offseason."

"That's so fucking cool. I'd love to have a real business, not just one-off jobs."

"Flipping houses?"

"Sure, maybe," I say, though that's not really what I'd do if I could pick anything.

"It's tough with employees." Emma sighs. "The girl who quit...we were pretty good friends, or so I thought. It gets complicated."

Moodily, Emma watches the other waitress, who successfully brought menus to the couple but is now lurking around the pass-through window, flirting with the line cook.

I'm not thinking about her.

I'm thinking about another mutual friend of Emma's...

"You said you knew Dane's wife?" The question slips from my lips.

Emma stops watching the waitress and fixes me with her pale-green eyes. "We were best friends."

"Really." My mouth goes dry. "What was she like?"

"Fucking gorgeous," Emma says at once. "The most beautiful girl I've ever seen."

"Oh."

I kind of suspected that would be the case, but I'm still filled with queasy jealousy.

"Lila was the princess of Grimstone," Emma says wistfully. "Literally—they crowned her the Pumpkin Princess our senior year, and she'd entered the pageant on a whim, didn't even have a proper dress... Here, I'll show you."

She pulls out her phone and searches through her photos. It

takes a moment, but not as long as scrolling back through years of images—she must have them saved in a folder.

"See?" She passes me the phone, showing an image of two girls on a makeshift stage, one short and orange-haired in a puffy pink gown, the other tall and elegant in a simple sheath, with a fall of shining black hair and large, lustrous dark eyes.

Teenager Emma is delightfully awkward with her braces-filled grin, while Lila could pass for twenty-two and already possesses the presence of a classic film star, an Audrey Hepburn or an Ava Gardner. She gazes out from the photo like her image will live forever, though the girl herself is long gone.

"Very pretty," I say, knowing how pathetically that describes the girl on the screen.

"Everybody loved her," Emma says, staring at her phone. "Nobody got why she dated Dane."

"They dated in high school?"

"Off and on. He didn't go to our school; he didn't go anywhere. Because of his…thing."

"His medical condition?"

"So he says."

"You don't believe it?"

"You ever heard of that condition before? *I* haven't—but I sure noticed how much he liked keeping her trapped in his house. The rest of us would go to the beach or boating—she'd want to come, but if she did, they'd have some huge fight after."

I think of a teenage Dane unable to attend school, visited by his wildly popular girlfriend on her way to the beach, her shoulders sun-kissed, the straps of her bikini visible beneath her shirt… I imagine the other kids waiting outside, their voices audible as they chatter excitedly, the guys ribbing and laughing because they're about to watch Lila undress and swim in that suit while Dane is stuck inside until the sun goes down…

"I think *he* was the one trapped in the house," I say to Emma.

She makes a soft amused sound. "Lila used to defend him, too."

"You really think he killed her?"

"I know he did."

"How?"

"She told me she was scared of him, a month before she died. Look, I'll show you…"

Emma scrolls on her phone again, this time in her messages. She pulls up a conversation four years past—almost exactly four years, dated October 10.

Something terrible is about to happen, I can feel it. It's building and building. I'm afraid, and the one person who's supposed to protect me is the person who can't know I've even talked to you because he made me promise I wouldn't tell.

"That was the last message she sent," Emma says.

I read the words over several times.

He made me promise I wouldn't tell…

"The year before, she disappeared for an entire month," Emma says. "I kept texting and calling, no answer… I even went to the house. He wouldn't let me in, wouldn't let me see her. Told me she was 'resting.' I thought he killed her back then. When she finally called, I was crying and freaking out—but she wouldn't tell me what happened. Only that she'd been 'sick.'"

Emma seems so certain. And she's known Dane way longer than I have. She knew his wife, too, intimately…so why am I putting my judgment over hers?

Because you answered the question right, while everyone in town answers it wrong…

It's a hook in my brain, and I can't get it out—the idea of Dane's innocence. It glimmers, thin, sharp, and immovable.

"Are you dating him?" Emma asks, giving me a close look.

"No," I reply with a guilty squirm. I don't know if I feel guilty for denying Dane or for kissing him.

I don't think he killed his wife.

But I also don't think she drowned.

There's more here, I can feel it... I just don't know what the fuck is going on.

"I'm fixing his fence," I say, "in exchange for the use of his road."

"*His* road." Emma scoffs. "Yes, how dare you drive down the royal road..." Her lip curls. "I hate the founding families."

"I take it the Turners weren't one?"

"Not even close. We're only second generation."

"That doesn't count around here?"

"Joey Vega's been 'the new barber' for about twenty-two years. You're not a local unless you were born in Grimstone—and even then, it's better if your great-grandpa was, too."

"That's too bad." I smile. "I'm starting to like it here."

"Maybe you should keep your house after all that work," Emma says, smiling back at me.

"I wish—I can barely afford to fix it, let alone keep it."

"How are the renos going?"

"Better than I deserve, probably. Your cousin's a big help." I check the time on my phone. "Actually, I should head back—he's coming over around noon."

"So, two thirty?"

"Exactly." I laugh.

"Mind if I tag along?" Emma asks. "I've never been inside Blackleaf—I'd love to see it."

"Be my guest. But be warned, it still looks like shit inside. I don't have a single room completely fixed."

"Perfect." Emma grins. "I'll take some before-and-after shots for you."

She ducks out of the booth to leave instructions for the other waitress and probably to tell her to give it a rest with the line cook, because the girl abandons her flirting and starts sulkily rolling cutlery into napkins instead.

"Ready!" Emma says cheerily, slinging her purse over her arm.

"You gonna wear that out?"

She looks down at her spiderweb apron. "Oh, shit! No, I'll leave that here." She tosses it over the back of a chair.

The air is beautifully crisp as we leave the diner, a cool wind blowing off the ocean directly into our faces. Emma's curls look impossibly bright against the slate-gray sky.

"Nippy, isn't it?" She buttons her jacket.

"I like it," I say, not mentioning that it was stuffy in the diner with all the heat from the grill.

"Where did you park?" Emma scans for the Bronco.

"Up by the hotel."

"There it is!" She spots my rusty old car and makes a beeline until shouts break out on the hotel steps.

"Is that Tom?" Emma cries, already running.

CHAPTER 18
DANE

WHEN I WAKE TO A SKY THICKLY BLANKETED IN CLOUD, I FEEL THE opposite of most people—excited instead of oppressed.

The sun is my enemy, my jailor. It's the dividing line between me and everyone else, trapping me in the darkest, loneliest hours.

I didn't mind so much, the past few years. The dark was where I wanted to be.

But now I'm watching Remi rattle past in her old Bronco, heading in the direction of town, and the thought of not seeing her for at least seven more hours sets my teeth on edge.

No, fuck, it'll be a lot longer than that—I'm supposed to work tonight.

That decides it.

I apply my prescription-grade sunscreen and dress in a dark suit, then grab my UV umbrella out of the stand by the door. It looks like a normal black umbrella and won't draw much attention on a day like today, though it would be better if it were actually raining.

I haven't driven into Grimstone during daylight hours in months. The streets and buildings look bleached and faded in the dull gray light. Only the flame-toned leaves burn brighter than ever.

Heads turn as my car drives past. The old anger rises in my chest like a snake. I see the looks, the judgment, and I hate them back with ten times the bitterness.

I could happily watch this town burn, every last building. I've known nothing but misery here. But I don't leave because I earned this hell, and there's no escaping it.

Remi's orange Bronco is easy to find; it's parked right in front of the Monarch. Where Remi herself might have gone is another question—her car is equidistant from the hardware store and Emma's Diner, and not far from the grocery store either.

I try Lou's Hardware first, which turns out to be wishful thinking—no Remi, only a redheaded woman in cat-eye glasses who gives me a filthy glare.

I could check the grocery store, but really Remi's car is a hell of a lot closer to the diner. I start walking in that direction at a slug's pace, asking myself if I'm willing to risk Emma spitting in my coffee and rubbing my pancakes all over her ass before she sets them on the plate—if she'll serve me at all.

I'm looking out for one carrottop, but it's the cousin I see, with his hands cupped around his face, peering through the window of Remi's Bronco.

"Looking for something?"

Tom whips around, the surprise and guilt on his face flipping to aggression when he sees who's asking. "What are *you* doing here?"

"Not breaking into cars."

"I'm not breaking in. I'm looking for Remi."

"I don't think she's in there," I say blandly. The car is obviously empty—whatever he was looking for, it wasn't her.

Tom knows he's caught red-handed, and he responds with exactly the dynamism I would expect from someone who carries a cooler of beer with him everywhere he goes—he scowls and jabs a finger at my chest. "What are you poking around for? Don't you know you're not wanted here?"

"By you? I hope I can contain my disappointment."

"And what's up with you making Remi work on your property?" Tom snarls, stepping even closer, so I can smell that he's definitely sampled that beer already this morning. "Can't you see she's got enough to deal with without putting in slave hours for some rich boy?"

"Your concern is touching. I'm sure it has nothing to do with the fact that you want her at Blackleaf with you."

Tom flushes. "She'd be a hell of a lot safer."

Now it's me who steps closer, the shadow of the umbrella enveloping us both. Tom's right eye ticks, but he doesn't back down, both fists clenched, his face as red as his hair.

"What do you mean by that, exactly?" I say, low and soft.

Tom's throat jerks as he swallows. "You know what I mean."

"I'm wondering if you have the balls to say it."

His glance darts left and right. There's no one around, not even on the steps of the Monarch.

"I'm saying you're a fucking murderer," he hisses. "And if you come near Remi again—"

"I've come a hell of a lot closer than *near*, and I'll do it any time I please." I take one last step so I'm well inside Tom's space, practically nose to nose, reminding him that I'm the one person in town taller than him. "Remi would beg on her knees for me to touch her before she'd let your disgusting mitts—"

I don't even get to finish insulting Tom before he launches himself at me with a roar. I'm anticipating the blows of his fists, looking forward to it with sick recklessness, because it means I'll get to beat the ever-loving shit out of him.

Sadly, the punch never lands. A beefy arm loops around Tom's neck and drags him backward as my brother puts the drunken electrician in a headlock, and not a gentle one. Tom's face swiftly changes from scarlet to eggplant as Atlas applies the full force of a biceps the size of a ham hock. Atlas may be my little brother, but that's the one and only way you could call him *little*.

I'm fucking pissed that he's the one who gets to throttle this idiot. "I had it covered."

"You're not getting in a fight in the middle of the street," my brother growls. "Especially not in front of my hotel."

"Stop it!" a girl shrieks. "You're going to kill him!"

Emma Turner leaps on my brother, pummeling with both fists. Since Emma is about a foot and a half shorter, she can only pound the middle of his back. Atlas hardly seems to notice as he continues asphyxiating her cousin.

"You probably should let him go," I remark as Tom's eyes roll back and his legs go limp.

"Glad to," Atlas says. "He's getting dust on my suit."

He drops Tom on the cement. Only Remi's sneaker prevents Tom's skull from hitting the curb—she catches his head on the top of her shoe like a soccer ball, helping to slow his fall.

"What the fuck?" Emma shrieks.

"He attacked me," I say, holding the umbrella overhead like that proves it. "And he tried to break into Remi's car."

I wink at Remi on that last part to let her know I'm full of shit.

"Wish he would have taken it," Remi says, trying to hide her smile.

Guilt overcomes her amusement, and she kneels by Tom's limp body. "Is he okay?"

I kneel beside her, mostly to get closer. She smells like soap and cinnamon and her own bright scent, orange juice and firecrackers.

"Get away from him!" Emma snaps as I lift Tom's eyelid with my thumb.

"I am a doctor," I remind her.

Emma seems torn. "Well…is he okay?"

"Completely fine," I say as Tom rolls over and vomits into the gutter. "That's good for him."

It probably is since the vomit looks like a six-pack and not much else.

"You're cleaning that up," Atlas informs the lot of us, turning to ascend the grand stone steps of the hotel.

"Don't you want to meet Remi?" I stand and thrust her forward. "She's new to Grimstone."

"Saw her from a block away." Atlas casts a disdainful look backward at her violet hair.

"Nice to meet you!" Remi calls up to him.

"Hm." Atlas grunts before disappearing inside.

"Wow," Remi says, amused. "So you're actually the *nice* brother."

"Atlas makes it pretty much assured."

"Are you going to help me or not?" Emma says waspishly as she tries to hoist her dazed and vomit-spattered cousin.

"Not," I say, at the same time as Remi chirps, "Of course!"

Remi gets under one of Tom's freckled arms, and I grudgingly take the other, though this is far more intimate contact with his armpit than I ever hoped to achieve. I wish I'd at least had the pleasure of knocking him out if I have to haul him back to his truck.

As I shove him into the back seat, he groans and his eyes open halfway.

I lean over to murmur into his ear, "If you think I'm capable of slaughtering my own family, you should be a fuck of a lot more afraid of what I'll do to you if you so much as breathe on Remi again."

Then I close the truck door in his face.

Emma retrieves Tom's ball cap, which rolled away into the street.

"I guess I'll drive him home," she says sulkily. "I wanted to see your place…"

"Come over later," Remi says. "You can bring Tom if he's feeling better."

She casts a quick guilty glance in my direction like she's hoping I won't take that the wrong way.

There's no right way to take it. I don't want Tom Turner near her, ever. Or anyone else with a dick and a pulse. Or a pussy and a pulse, actually. Emma may be a foot shorter than Tom, but she's a hell of a lot sneakier and just as interested in Remi.

And much more interested in fucking me over. She gives me

a malicious little smirk over Remi's shoulder as she hugs her. "See you soon."

Once I've gotten rid of the cousins, the day looks a whole lot brighter. Or pleasantly overcast, depending on your point of view.

"It's funny being out in the real world with you." Remi takes my arm so we can walk comfortably together beneath the umbrella.

"Where are we usually?" I say, smiling slightly.

"Your world. That's why you like it, isn't it? Alone at your house, everything exactly how you want it... That's why you didn't want me driving up your road. But you don't mind so much now..." She tilts her head, half teasing, half asking.

"It's definitely gotten more interesting."

"Is that what I am to you? Interesting?"

"Yes." I look down into her face. "That's exactly what you are."

"I'll take it," Remi says, amused. "Better than being boring."

We've started walking in the direction of the hardware store.

"Is that what you're here for?" I nod toward the flat green awning.

"Yup," Remi says. "Finally making some progress on the main level."

"Is Emma the only one who gets a tour?"

"You want to come see the house?" Remi's eyes flash up at me, brighter than ever against the gray sky.

She's checking my face, wondering if I've already been inside. I haven't forgotten her accusation at 7:00 a.m. on my doorstep, and clearly, neither has she.

"I've seen the house a million times," I remind her. "Ernie wasn't exactly making the trip to my place."

"You were more than just his doctor."

"Yeah," I admit. And then, "I miss him," slips out.

"Me, too," Remi says with strong and simple emotion.

In the silence that follows, I'm sure we're both sifting through memories in which Ernie burns brightly and vividly.

"He wasn't really my uncle," Remi tells me. "He was my dad's uncle. My great-uncle, I guess? He was some of our only family—my dad was an only child. My mom had a sister, but they loathed each other. She didn't even call after the funeral, didn't send flowers. Ernie said we could come stay with him, but he was so sick by then, and Jude didn't want to leave his school…" Remi sighs, her arm heavy as it hangs on my elbow. "Maybe that was the wrong choice. I thought I could take care of Jude, but I don't know how good a job I did."

"Better than most kids could have done. That's all you were: a kid."

"I had to be an adult too soon, and now I feel like I was never an adult at all. I missed a lot of things, normal things… Never went to college. Never traveled on my own. Never had a job in an office…" She laughs. "But I'd hate that."

A flood of all the things I've never done washes over me. At first it was the sun, the hateful sun, and then I found myself in a new kind of prison…chains I chose willingly, gratefully, until they began to choke and strangle and finally dragged me down to a hell that still feels like a ragged, dark hole in my brain, a place beyond memory…

"What are you thinking about?"

Remi startles me with her presence, solid and warm on my arm. Fuck, I'm not used to company. I'm still disappearing inside my own head.

"There were a lot of things I thought I'd do… I haven't done any of them either."

"It's not too late," Remi says. "How old are you anyway?"

"Forty-one."

"There you go—you're not even halfway dead."

"Assuming I live till eighty-two."

"Seems like a safe bet." Remi grins. "I'm sure you're tracking your blood pressure."

"I'm not *that* old," I say, though I do track my blood pressure weekly.

"Aren't you going to ask my age?"

"I can already guess it—twenty-seven."

"How did you know?" she cries.

"Simple deduction—you said Jude was ten when your parents passed. You were eighteen then, and now he's two years out of school…"

"Has it really been two years?" Remi says in wonder. "Time flies."

"You really think you're going to bully him into going to college?"

"It's not bullying." Remi scowls. "He needs to go."

"Because you didn't?"

"Touché." She sighs. "That's not why, though."

"Sure it isn't."

"It isn't! He's never had a chance to really use that brain of his—"

"And why is that going to change at college?"

"Because it'll be an actual challenge! He was bored in school. That was the problem…" She squints up at me. "What are you smiling about?"

"The way you defend him."

"I'm not! Jude's incredible when you get to know him—he's prickly, but he's the smartest person I've ever met, and he's funny and a sweetheart at his core. You'll see."

What I actually see is the love in Remi's face—that crazy, all-consuming love that shapes everything she sees and everything she does.

It was that capacity for love that made me want her so badly. I saw it burning in her face. And I thought, *No one's ever loved me like that. Like they'd love me in spite of anything.*

I wanted it.

I coveted Remi.

And now here she is, on my arm.

Looking up at me not quite with love, but with a brightness that eclipses any sun I've seen.

"What?" She grins.

"I love how much you love him."

She beams at me. "You always know what to say to make me feel so good. Some people talk shit about Jude, and it really upsets me. I know he has his flaws, but he's like my kid as much as my brother. Gideon never really got that."

"What's Gideon like?"

"Oh, you don't want to hear about that." She ducks her head. "I already talked too much about my ex."

"I told you, I'm obnoxiously curious. All the way to nosy, really."

At least, when it comes to Remi—I want to know everything about her.

She takes a deep breath.

"Well, I guess Gideon is the definition of good on paper—handsome, great job, remembers anniversaries, nice to his mom..."

"What does he do for a living?"

"Commercial real estate, and he's really good at it. But that was part of the problem. I never made half as much money as him, and with everything with Jude...Gideon was always saying I should get a better job. I don't think he liked that most of the people I work around are men. Or that my go-to uniform is jean shorts." She gives an unhappy sort of laugh. "He really didn't like how I dress. And I get it, I look like the youngest drug dealer at the skate park—"

"How you dress is sexy."

Remi raises an eyebrow.

"It is," I insist. "The way you dress is *you*, and *you're* fucking sexy."

It doesn't matter that I hated her clothes less than a week ago.

That's all the time it took for me to catch enough glimpses of Remi's strong and capable body, that bronze skin and those tight little tits, her androgyny and femininity a potent combination in the package of her ragged boyish clothes.

Gideon has terrible taste.

I bet the girls he cheated with are bland as Wonder Bread.

Remi is blushing like a sunset, which makes her look the prettiest I've seen.

After a moment, in a guilty little voice, she admits, "I asked Emma about Lila. She showed me a picture."

My heart goes cold, and I have to resist the urge to pull back my arm.

Even hearing her name is enough to make me spiral.

"I'm sorry..." Remi murmurs, watching my face.

I force myself to speak. "What did Emma say?"

"Not much." Now Remi can't meet my eyes. "She showed me the picture of when Lila was Pumpkin Princess. She was so incredibly beautiful..."

I hear the wistful regret in her voice, and I see that look of helpless sorrow, the look of any girl who ever had to stand next to Lila.

"Can't accuse you of having a type," Remi says, her head hanging.

"You're not like...Lila." I make myself say her name out loud. "But that's a good thing."

There was only one Lila.

And there's only one Remi. That's what's beautiful and tragic about human beings—for better or for worse, not a single one can be replaced.

"And it's nothing to do with looks," I add. "Didn't I just tell you how sexy you are? Can't you feel it every time we kiss?"

I kiss her now, deep and warm. I let her feel my attraction to her in the way I pull her against my body, in the way I breathe her breath and taste her mouth.

When I let go, Remi's eyes slowly open.

"Wow..." she breathes, and her smile flickers back. "I must be sexy, because that was the hottest fucking kiss."

I laugh. "I told you."

We've reached the hardware store.

"Are you coming in?" Remi asks, a little edgy.

"Worried about being seen with me?"

"No! Only..." She flushes. "Rhonda's not exactly a fan. But I don't care. I want you to come in! And anyway, I know you can handle yourself."

"I'm used to it."

I push open the door, the bell jingling overhead.

Cat-Eye Lady looks even more irritated at my second appearance, especially when she sees that Remi and I are together. I close the umbrella and hang it over my arm, following Remi down the aisles as she fills a cart with supplies.

"What's that for?" I ask when she pauses at a selection of long, thin teak slats.

"This?" She looks slightly embarrassed. "Just a little side project. If I ever have time."

"Good idea." I nod solemnly. "You should try to keep busy."

Remi laughs. "Sometimes I'm not too tired in the evenings."

"To do what?" I press.

"I…like to build furniture," Remi says, as if it's something shameful.

"What kind of furniture?"

"Whatever comes in my head… Sometimes it's for myself, like a huge cushy chair for reading, with a bookshelf built into the side… Sometimes it's something crazy: a table that looks like a sculpture or a desk with a bunch of secret drawers… I don't make any money," she hastens to add.

"I want to see it when you're done."

"I don't even know what this will be yet." Remi strokes her fingers down the dark grain. "I just like the color of the wood."

"That's why I said 'I want to see it when you're done.' I can see you haven't gotten far yet."

Remi snorts, piling the slats into the cart.

When she can't fit anything else, I wheel the lot up to the register.

"Oh, shit," Remi says. "I forgot painting tape."

"Run back and grab it," I say as Cat-Eye Lady starts scanning. According to her name tag, Cat-Eye Lady is the infamous Rhonda. I could have guessed from the stink eye.

When Remi disappears amid the aisles, the frostiness at the register reaches subzero temperatures. I'm hoping Rhonda will keep her lip zipped, but she doesn't look the type to stick to the silent treatment.

Sure enough, before she's halfway through scanning items, she barks out a highly unfriendly "haven't seen *you* in here before."

"I've been missing out," I say, averting my eyes from a display of FRESH, RAW BAIT! right next to the till.

"Humph!" Rhonda snatches up her scanner so she can laser the barcodes with maximum aggression. She's firing that thing like a Taser gun, glaring at me over the rim of her glasses.

"Four hundred and twenty-eight dollars and sixty-four cents," she snaps at last.

It felt like it took about four hundred and twenty-eight minutes and sixty-four seconds. Remi still hasn't returned, so I swipe my card.

When she comes jogging up a moment later, tape in hand, Rhonda only charges her $4.78.

"What about—?"

"Already got it." I push the cart toward the exit.

Remi chases after me, red-faced. "How much was it? I'll Venmo you."

"It was a couple of hundred bucks, so don't worry about it. Here, take the cart so I can open the umbrella."

Remi steers the cart, frowning. I shake open the umbrella and take the cart back again, passing her the umbrella to hold over us both. The clouds are thicker and darker than ever—it might actually rain.

A few drops spit down by the time we're levering open the ancient hatch of the Bronco. Remi hasn't said a word on the short walk back to the car. It's only after everything is loaded into the trunk that she turns on me, flustered and stammering.

"Don't—don't do that again, please."

"What?"

"Pay for me."

"Why not?"

"Because I don't want you to—I can pay for myself."

"Barely."

Her flush deepens, and now she's angry as well as embarrassed. "I can take care of myself just fine."

"'Fine' doesn't sound that enjoyable. 'Fine' is barely scraping by. Why don't you want me to help you?"

"Because."

I stare at her, waiting for more.

"I don't like being in anyone's debt!" she bursts out. "When my parents died, they owed money to everyone. It was a fucking mess and humiliating, begging our landlady to give us another month when they already owed her for three, when Jude was wetting the bed again at fucking ten years old, when I was sleeping three hours a night, when the only food in our fridge was condiments—"

She stops and takes several breaths, her chest heaving.

"I dug us out of that hole; I got us stable. I've never owed anyone since, and I don't intend to. I haven't even fixed your fence yet, so don't go adding anything else on my debt."

"You don't owe me any fence; I was just being an asshole. I wanted to make you come over."

"What?" Remi cries, genuinely shocked. "I thought you hated me when we met."

I shrug. "I still wanted to see you again."

Her mouth falls open, and then she laughs that loud, raucous laugh of hers that makes me smile, too, whether I want to or not. "You're so fucking weird."

"Yeah, I know."

Remi grins. "Better than being boring."

"So you say—I'm still waiting for it to pay off."

Remi's supposed to head back to her house to tackle her endless list of projects, but since it appears Tom is still recuperating and hasn't texted that he's on his way, we end up loafing around Grimstone for the rest of the afternoon.

We visit Selina at the tattoo shop, then her sister, Helena, two doors down because Selina insists she'll be jealous if we don't, though Remi is much more interested in tattoos than tarot. Selina seems slightly disappointed to see Remi and me strolling around together, while Helena looks like she can't wait to blab it all over town. I try not to care either way.

We stop in at the bookstore/tea shop, where Remi purchases two paperbacks and a pound of loose-leaf chai, then go to a haberdashery, where she pressures me into buying a peacoat.

"You have to get it; it looks incredible on you!"

"Everything looks good on me."

"That's true, and go fuck yourself."

I grab a handful of her ass, growling in her ear, "You're the one managing to make those Dickies look hot…"

She shivers and leans back against my chest, turning her head and tilting up her chin so her lips brush the side of my neck. "You've never been attracted to cargo pants and steel-toed boots before?"

"I'm starting to think it's all I'm attracted to…" I grab her by the hips and pull her even closer so our bodies touch all the way down. I can see her nipples getting hard through her shirt. If she ever tries to wear a bra, I'm going to cut it off her and burn it with fire.

"What are you doing tonight?" Remi asks, her voice husky and low.

"Working," I say with extreme regret.

Remi's phone buzzes. She checks the text.

"Tom?"

"Yeah," she says. "But he's not coming till tomorrow. Says he has a headache."

"I bet he does."

Remi shrugs, smiling. "Means we have a little more time. When do you start work?"

"Not until nine."

"That's practically forever." She says it with so much pleasure that warmth spreads through my chest, sudden and unnerving. "What should we do?"

I'm torn because I'd like to get her back to my house in the few hours we have remaining, but days of impenetrable cloud only roll around so often. Walking around in the open air with Remi is intoxicating. The current daylight may barely seem like light at all to her, but to me it's like bathing in transparent cool silver.

"Do you want to come down to the beach with me?"

Remi slips her hand in mine. "I'd love to."

I can't believe she's walking like this with me, right down Main Street where anyone can see. Her hand is small and firm and warm. The sea breeze swirls her violet hair around her face, tangled with bits of bright leaves.

We take the stairs down to the beach, crisscrossing back and forth down the steep black cliffs. The sand is damp, but the rain never properly fell, and now the wind is dying down, the clouds thinning. A faint pink flush has come into my skin despite the umbrella, but I don't give a fuck; I'm not scuttling back into my hole.

"Come on," I say, pulling Remi along. "I want to show you something."

CHAPTER 19

REMI

"WHERE ARE WE GOING?" I ASK DANE.

He's leading me down the beach, apparently with some destination in mind, though all I see is the long expanse of glittering black sand that eventually leads to the sprawling Onyx Resort.

The bay is shaped like a waxing crescent moon, the town of Grimstone on its southern tip and the resort on its northernmost point. Dane takes me to a spot about halfway in between.

"Do you trust me?" he says.

"More than I should."

"Good. Leave your shoes."

We've already stripped off our shoes and socks to walk on the damp dark sand, carrying them along tucked under our arms. I abandon mine a little farther up the slope, in case the tide is coming in.

Dane takes my hand and begins to walk out into the water. The waves wash around our ankles, cold and foamy.

"Where are you taking me?" I ask a little nervously. "I don't want to swim."

I doubt the bay is warm in July, let alone October, and I'm still fully dressed, my jeans rolled up to the knees.

"We won't be swimming," Dane says, confidently striding deeper.

Only the water's not actually getting deeper—as we walk out

into the bay, the sand beneath my feet remains level and the waves hit no higher than my shins.

"What is this?"

"A sandspit," he says. "The locals call it 'Hellsbench.'"

"How come?"

"You'll see."

We progress into the bay until all that surrounds us is flat dark water. From the beach, it must look as if Dane and I are walking across the waves. I can imagine our silhouettes from the shore, Dane still holding his black umbrella over our heads, as if the umbrella is the mechanism for the miracle.

"This is crazy," I murmur, gazing at the expanse of water all around.

I'm clinging to Dane's arm, enthralled and a little terrified. The largest waves hit my knees, nearly knocking me off the spit. It's narrower the farther out we get, now barely wide enough for us to walk side by side.

"This is why you can't boat in the bay," Dane says. "There are sandbars all over."

This is the closest I've been to the resort. From here, I can see black-and-gray-striped lounge chairs laid out on the neatly groomed sand and several tentlike cabanas with gauzy black canopies. The Onyx is a modern building made almost entirely of glossy dark glass. To me, it looks like a villain's lair, but its cheapest room is twelve hundred dollars a night, so I guess I'm not fancy enough to get it.

"You ever stay there?" I ask Dane.

He glances over, uninterested. "I've been inside. Never stayed the night."

That gives me a bite of jealousy and a strange flush of arousal, too.

I sneak a glance at Dane. "Have you been fucking tourists?"

He shrugs. "Keeps things simple."

I imagine him in one of those posh rooms with some gorgeous

wealthy woman, and my whole body gets hot like I swallowed a burning coal.

Everything about Dane is expensive and refined—his cashmere V-neck, his wool trousers…even the bone-handled umbrella looks like it belongs to an oil tycoon.

I'd barely feel comfortable walking down that end of the beach. I grew up around wealth, but I haven't tasted it in a decade. I only know enough to know how much I don't belong.

"What's wrong?" Dane says.

"Oh…" I give a little laugh directed at myself. "I was thinking you should be lying on one of those loungers with some heiress."

"Why?" Dane frowns.

"Because look at you…" I glance up at his impossibly beautiful face, his wind-tossed hair with its streaks of silver, his elegant hand gripping the umbrella.

Dane takes my chin between his forefinger and thumb and holds me there so I have to look in his eyes and can't turn away. "What have I told you about talking down on yourself?"

"I'm not."

"Yes, you are." His fingers dig into my jaw, and his amber eyes bore into mine. "If I wanted to fuck some heiress, I would. I'm right where I want to be." He dips his head to kiss me firmly on the mouth. "So shut up and watch."

The wind is shifting, dying down. The waves flatten and alter their angle. The blanket of cloud darkens from gray to a deep bruised purple, while the light changes from silver to scarlet.

We can't actually see the sun, but it must be setting. The light becomes deeply saturated, the shining flat surface of the bay as brightly crimson as a lake of blood. Dane and I stand on the spit, steep black cliffs on either side of us, flaming water all around.

"My god…" I turn slowly on the spot. "It's like standing inside a volcano…"

Dane's hand slips under the waistband of my jeans to rest on my bare hip. He pulls me close against his side so the cold water around our feet is nothing compared to the heat of his body. "I thought you'd like it."

I don't just like it—I'm drunk on the rich red light and the ink-black beach and the mind-bending experience of standing in the middle of the bay.

I turn and kiss Dane, feeling the firmness of his lips against mine, the delicious taste of his mouth, the hard swells of muscle beneath his clothes…

Kissing Dane is nothing like kissing Gideon or Tom. With Gideon it felt perfunctory, something we'd do before we had sex. With Tom it was like being attacked by a wet and rubbery squid.

Kissing Dane is like huffing the air out of his lungs—an instant high that fills my body with his scent and his taste. My head spins, and my limbs get warm and heavy.

It's like he's tasting me, testing me… His tongue touches my lips, my tongue, the inside of my mouth… His hand moves through my hair and down my back until my whole body is wrapped up in this kiss, every part of me except my frozen feet.

"Why were you arguing with Tom?" I murmur against his neck.

"You know why."

"I want to hear you say it."

"You want to hear me say we were fighting over you?" His smile flashes as he grabs a handful of my hair and tilts my head back, kissing my mouth, my jaw, and all down my neck…

"Yes," I say, like a whisper, like a plea.

"All right… I saw him looking through your car window, and I provoked him on purpose because I'm jealous. I'm jealous that he gets to come to your house, and I'm jealous that he's fixing your lights. I'm jealous that he talks to you, and I'm fucking enraged that he dared try to kiss you the moment I left the party. I want you all to myself, and I don't care if I have to fight every person in this whole damn town."

That feels so fucking good, I could come just from his voice in my ear.

I've never been pursued by a man like Dane. Guys like Tom, yes, plenty of times, but never by someone who makes me feel like I can barely breathe when he's in the room, like I'll do anything to get him to look in my direction, like I'd give up an hour with anybody else for a minute with him.

His kiss is better than any sex I've ever had.

I kiss him and kiss him in the bloodred water until the wind begins to blow again and the waves shift, rising past our knees.

I kiss him until I feel both his hands on my body, his arms wrapped around me, crushing me close. We kiss as the water rises up our thighs and the light changes from red to violet. His lips devour mine; his taste is sky and ocean.

"You lost your umbrella," I say when we finally break apart. I can just see it floating away until it tips and sinks beneath the water.

"Doesn't matter," Dane says. "Sun's almost down anyway. But the tide is rising."

The next wave nearly knocks us over. We slosh back to shore, struggling to follow the sandspit with our numb toes. The light is fading fast, and the wind is picking up, cold spatters of rain coming in little bursts.

♫ *"Fire"—Two Feet*

We're soaked practically to the waist, sandy and shivering, but as soon as my feet are on land again, I reach for Dane, and he reaches for me. We lock together, our mouths ravenous, our hands tearing at each other's clothes.

Each inch of his skin I uncover is smooth and clean, while I'm tanned, bruised, scratched, calloused, and tattooed everywhere else. Dane and I are nothing alike, or at least that's what I thought—but the more time we spend together, the less opposite we seem.

We're more like two halves of a chemical reaction. Whatever we are apart, together we're electric.

I want to connect with him. I want to understand him. I know the story I've heard from everyone else isn't quite right, but I don't think he's told me the truth either. Grimstone is a honeycomb of secrets, like those black caves in the cliffs: too dark to see, but you can hear the ocean rushing through...

I want to know him—I crave it. All day long while I'm working, I'm thinking of Dane, wondering if he's awake or still sleeping, if he's thinking of me, too. Wondering what thoughts flicker behind those amber eyes when he looks at me a certain kind of way...

It's not like me to fall this hard; I never did before. Jude was my focus. And now I may be falling for the worst possible person, but it's not a choice—every time Dane touches me, it's like a food that only makes you hungrier the more you eat. It's maddening and intoxicating, and I don't want it to stop.

He pulls my shirt over my head and ravages my breasts, pressing his hand into my back to arch my spine and tilt my tits up directly into his mouth. His stubble rasps against my tender flesh while his warm, wet tongue laps at my nipples. He can fit almost my entire breast in his mouth, and he sucks hard while kneading and squeezing the other in his hand.

Gently, gently, he tugs on my piercing, sliding the circlet of silver back and forth through my tight, throbbing nipple. A wave washes far up the shore, hitting my feet with cold foam while his hot mouth makes my blood bubble like soda pop.

The light is fading fast. Dane's pale flesh is luminescent against the black sand and the deep twilit sky. I don't know if there's anyone else on the beach, and I don't care. Nothing seems to exist beyond his warmth and his breath and his hands all over me.

He moves down my body, from my breasts to my belly, licking and kissing, making all of me warm.

My jeans are wet and sticking to me—he only gets them halfway down before burying his face between my thighs. He takes a deep breath, pressing his nose against my pussy and inhaling, filling his lungs, his eyes closed.

"That makes my mouth water…"

He licks me, and his mouth is more than watering: it's warm and melting like butter. And all of me is melting, too, sinking into the heat and softness of Dane that feels otherworldly against the cold grit of sand and the biting waves hitting our bare feet.

My ankles are bound by my jeans behind his back, my thighs shaking around his ears. He lifts my hips in his hands and licks my pussy like a dinner plate, like he'll never get enough to eat.

He watches my face, those golden eyes glimmering in the dark, his eyebrows dark and wicked. I've never had my pussy eaten by someone so good-looking—every time I glance down at him, it makes me shiver.

His mouth makes me moan, and his hands on my skin… I knew from the first time he touched me that those hands would be trouble. He already knows my body like he studied it in a textbook.

He spreads my pussy lips with his thumb and forefinger, his eyes alight with fiendish triumph when he sees the piercing through my clit. "I've been waiting for this…"

He teases his tongue against the stud, flicking lightly until my knees shiver. Then he closes his lips around my clit and gently sucks while my eyes roll back and my toes point, and the clouds overhead crackle with purple lightning.

I come and I come, both my hands thrust in his hair, humping his face like an animal. Thank god the wind has picked up because I'm making sounds so wild that I need a storm to drown them.

I kick off my jeans and straddle Dane's face from the opposite direction so I can undo his pants. His cock springs out like a white cobra, thick with veins.

"Holy shit!"

Dane laughs.

"It's huge," I say defensively. "I was surprised."

"You were surprised?" I can't see Dane's expression since I'm face-to-face with his cock, but there's something in his tone I don't quite understand.

He's obviously not bothered because he buries his face in my pussy again, making me yelp and grab hold of his cock for support. It's so thick, my fingers can't close all the way around it. I can barely fit it in my mouth.

The head of his cock is heavy and warm and slightly salty from the seawater. I pull it down instead of up so I can get a better angle, and Dane lets out a groan that sends shivers from my scalp down my spine.

I grip the base of his cock and bob my head up and down as far as it can go, which isn't very far—his cock rams into the back of my throat before my lips get anywhere close to my fingers.

Meanwhile, his tongue delves inside me, his hands locked so tightly on my hips, there's no wiggling, let alone escaping.

It's like no sixty-nine I've known because I'm halfway choking as I come, his wet mouth devouring my pussy, his cock gagging my throat. In the strangest way, the slight strangulation is what makes it feel so good, all the blood rushing to my brain and staying there.

Lightning cracks and the rain crashes down, lashing our bare skin. My body's so hot, even the rain is orgasmic, the shivers of cold and the shivers from coming running up and down my limbs in indistinguishable waves.

I spread my legs, sinking down on Dane's mouth, my knees digging in the sand as I fuck against his tongue. I gag myself on his cock again and again, the thick saliva from my throat coating the head until it slips an inch deeper…

Dane moans directly into my pussy, smothered by my weight. His hips buck upward, and he drives deep into my throat, letting out a roar that vibrates through my body. I pull back slightly, and he bursts on my tongue, pulse after pulse of thick, creamy come, so much that it overflows my mouth and runs down his shaft, dripping pale pearls on the black sand.

I roll off him and turn myself around again so we're lying side by side on the beach. The next wave washes all the way up to our waists, which is actually useful as a form of instant cleanup.

Dane finds my wet sandy hand and links our fingers.

We gaze up at a sky of boiling purple, enlivened here and there with flashes of lightning that illuminate the clouds, as thunder rolls across the bay.

"Should we move?" I say. "In case we get struck?"

"A month ago, I would have wished for it."

I turn my head to look at his face. "Not anymore?"

"No," Dane says, looking at me and smiling slightly. "Not when things just got interesting..."

He rolls on his side and touches my cheek, kissing me more gently than he ever has before.

The fluttering in my chest and the anxiousness in my stomach are very bad signs.

Never once did I feel like this for Gideon. Or anybody else.

"What's wrong?" Dane says, pulling back slightly.

"I'm scared of how much I like you."

"Ah." He nods like he understands. "Me, too."

Now that Dane has gotten scratched from the sand, I'm noticing his sunburn.

"Fuck, I shouldn't have kept you outside for so long..."

He shakes his head, pushing me down and kissing me again. "I'd do the whole day over again, starting this minute, and I wouldn't change a thing."

CHAPTER 20
DANE

PARTING WAYS WITH REMI BY OUR RESPECTIVE CARS IS TORTUROUS.
I want to take her back to my house and do so much more than we managed on the beach, but I'm on call all night.

I think about her all through my shift, and maybe that's why, when I return home at last, the scent of pear and bergamot assails me the moment I open the door. A single dusty bottle sits on Lila's vanity table, yet the smell seems to spread through the house.

The same parts of the brain that process memory and emotion also process odors. That's why nothing brings back memories more strongly than a particular scent.

The moment I walk through the door, thoughts of Remi are forced from my mind by images of Lila.

Lila in a flurry in the kitchen, cooking up enough dinner for ten people, laughing and singing and twirling around in her apron, steam in the air...

Then Lila sobbing on the floor of the bathroom, curled on her side, her dark hair spread across the tiles, mascara smeared down her face...

Will you love me forever, no matter what?
Promise me...promise me...
The guilt is overwhelming.

All the memories of today, the bright and cheerful moments, swirl like leaves, then wither and crumble.

Who said I could smile? Who said I could laugh? Who said I could feel happiness?

Not Lila.

I climb the steps to the main suite, trying not to notice the art we chose together, the painting Lila found in an antique shop that we didn't realize was abominably heavy until we had to carry it almost a mile back down the promenade to our car.

I thought I'd never redecorate. Now everywhere I look, I'm racked with shame.

I shower quickly because I'm fucking exhausted. I've been awake for nearly twenty-four hours, and the night shift wasn't nearly as dead as I'd hoped.

When I wipe the fog from the bathroom mirror, Lila stands behind me, gazing at me reproachfully with those huge dark eyes.

You promised. You swore.

"I haven't broken my promise."

Liar. LIAR!

The mirror shatters.

I whip around.

There's no one behind me.

Blood drips down on the tiles. I lift my hand, gazing at my own split knuckles. I punched the mirror without realizing.

Liar...

The guilt is like sickness, like food poisoning. I wish I could vomit it out.

I lie down in my bed, trying to push her from my head. The sound of her voice...the first time we kissed...

After a moment, I feel something like cold hands on my bare chest...

Then frozen lips against my ear...

I close my eyes and give in.

CHAPTER 21
REMI

THE NEXT WEEK, DANE TEXTS TO CANCEL MY FENCE-FIXING appointment. I don't want to take it personally, but it's hard not to when he doesn't set a different time for me to swing around. The cancellation feels linked to what we did on the beach, and I spend the whole week worrying if I fucked up somehow, pent up and irritable because my vibrator is a lot less satisfying compared to his mouth.

Emma visits three times in the same period, to admire my progress on the house and drop off fresh muffins. The first time, they're raspberry crumble, but after Jude says something snarky about Emma's coat, the next two batches are blueberry.

"Why does she keep coming around?" Jude complains. "It's bad enough the other one is always here."

"The other one almost has our lights running," I remind him. "And shouldn't you be glad I finally have a friend? Weren't you nagging me about that just the other day?"

"I regret it." Jude scowls. "She's slowing you down, yakking at you while you're trying to work."

"That's not even true! She helped me paint the whole ballroom."

I give Jude a pointed look because he hasn't even finished with the workshop yet.

Jude is impervious to looks and to most of the words that come out of my mouth. "She's not even that good a cook."

"You should give her lessons: one hundred different meals made mostly of peanut butter."

"Cooking's for plebs." Jude tosses his hair.

"Don't talk like one of those idiots from your old school."

"I am one of those idiots," Jude says sullenly. "Or I was."

"You could be a Harvard idiot—your SATs are high enough."

"This again."

"Yes, this. If you would just—"

But Jude is already out the back door, fleeing from my nagging.

The rest of the day passes slowly. I'm still working on the ballroom, refinishing the parquet floors. Luckily, I didn't have to replace them entirely, just sand them down to within an inch of their life and restain.

I can hear Tom overhead, rewiring the opulent old chandeliers. He's been surprisingly subdued since being throttled unconscious by Dane's brother. But I think he's getting his moxie back because the past two days, he's been pushing hard to take me to dinner.

I told him no the first three times, but now I'm staring at my blank phone screen, feeling real frustration. Dane still hasn't responded to my last text.

So, when Tom comes into the ballroom ten minutes later, sweaty and dirty and grinning, to tell me he's almost done, I say recklessly and a little spitefully, "That calls for celebration."

"Hell yes, it does… You finally going to let me buy you a pizza?"

"I think I should buy *you* one."

"Won't argue with that. I'll go home and shower, then I'll meet you there."

"Great." Already regretting it, I give him a queasy smile back.

I don't owe Dane anything. We aren't in a relationship, and it really fucking hurts my feelings that he hasn't spoken to me since our incredible all-day date and beach hookup.

On the other hand, it's shitty to let Tom take me out just to make myself feel better.

But now I'm stuck. *Fuck.*

The only thing cheering me up is the progress I'm making on the house. I've been working from the moment I wake up until I roll into bed, sometimes so exhausted that I almost fall asleep in the shower.

Either I'm too tired to hear it or the ghostly piano player has been as absent as Dane. I've been sleeping peacefully all week.

I meet Tom at The Slice Factory, which looks pleasingly industrial inside, with bare brick walls and gleaming copper pipes.

"It used to be a chocolate factory," Tom tells me. "The Archer family were chocolatiers."

"Archer as in Aldous and Amy Archer?"

"That's right—they're a founding family."

"I thought the founding families were rich?"

"The Archers were—until someone poisoned a batch of their mint truffles. Eight people died, and the company was ruined. They never found out who did it. Some people thought it must have been a disgruntled employee, but Emma has a different theory."

I bet she does.

"Tell me," I say, stuffing down cheesy bread sticks as fast as I can. They're unlimited, and I haven't eaten yet today 'cause we're out of groceries.

Tom is happy to oblige now that he has my interest.

"Well, Old Archer, that was their grandpa, he was about the meanest man in town. He had sixteen kids, and he worked every one of them at the factory like a fuckin' Oompa Loompa. And even though he was too stingy to give birthday presents, he expected every one of those kids to marry according to their stature. But there was hardly anybody else in Grimstone that he thought measured up. So, when his youngest daughter fell for the local mechanic, he wasn't having it."

The waiter interrupts, carrying out our extra-large pepperoni, jalapeño, bacon, and pineapple pizza. I made the order, and I don't want to hear a fucking thing about the pineapple 'cause spicy and sweet were meant to be together.

I take a huge bite, scalding the skin off the roof of my mouth.

"Go on," I mumble to Tom. "Gimmie the dirt."

"Well, the mechanic gets beaten to a pulp by 'unknown assailants,' and the youngest daughter just disappears—gone for months. Or else, like some people said, kept prisoner in the Archer mansion. Then, a year later, she's back working at the chocolate factory, but people only see her in glimpses; she doesn't work the counter anymore, only the factory floor. And a couple of months after that, she's married to one of her father's friends in some quickie ceremony. But she keeps working at the factory. And finally, six months after that…the poisonings. The family's ruined, factory closes, Old Archer has a stroke."

"Did anybody suspect the daughter?"

"Nope. The cops didn't even interview her because she was pretty heavily pregnant by then, with twins."

"No…" I say softly.

"That's right." Tom grins. "Aldous and Amy."

"And what about the mechanic?"

"Well…that's the fun part. The mechanic had a surprise of his own—a black-haired toddler who seemed to come out of nowhere."

"Corbin," I say, piecing it all together.

Tom smiles and shrugs. "There's definitely a resemblance."

"So, the twins and Corbin are…half siblings?"

"Not according to them." Tom takes an enormous bite of his own pizza after picking off all the pineapple and jalapeños. "But that's Emma's theory."

"Shit…this town really is fucked up."

"I don't know…" Tom gives me a sly look. "I think it's getting better all the time."

That would be a whole lot sexier if he didn't have tomato sauce on his chin.

I pass him a napkin, hoping he'll take the hint.

He ignores the napkin, distracted by the jingling of the pizza shop door.

Tom's face slackens and goes several shades paler.

I don't have time to turn before someone drops into the booth next to me. He brings in the nighttime chill on his coat, with the scent of forest and earth and his own warm spice. And just the slightest hint of antiseptic.

"Tom." Dane slings his arm around my shoulders. "How nice of you to buy my girl dinner."

"I'm not your girl." I attempt to shove off his arm. "And *I'm* the one buying dinner."

"No, you're not," Tom and Dane simultaneously say before turning to glare at each other.

Dane only locks his arm tighter around my shoulders, yanking me against his side. "Then I guess *I'm* buying," he says. "And driving you home."

"We're on a date," Tom informs him, but without much oomph. In fact, he's kind of edging toward the end of the booth.

"No, you're not." Dane sounds completely certain and entirely in charge. "Now get the fuck out of here before I show you just how much Atlas is the nicer brother after all."

"Whatever." Tom shoves out of the booth without so much as a glance in my direction.

"What the fuck?" I turn on Dane. "Who do you think you are, ignoring me all week and then crashing my date?"

"That wasn't a date," Dane says disdainfully. "It was a fucking tragedy."

"You don't give orders! I don't belong to you!"

"Wrong with conviction." Dane seizes me by the jaw and kisses me on the mouth.

I'd like to say that his kiss enrages me, but my body and brain have never agreed where Dane is concerned. While I'm telling myself to shove him off and maybe slap his face for good measure, my hands go from gripping the front of his shirt to caressing the back of his neck while the kiss deepens and my spine turns to noodle.

How does his mouth taste so fucking good?

It's like the week apart was a year. I'm ravenous, my hands all over his body, even groaning a little in the confines of the booth.

He's twice as ferocious, kissing and groping until the teenagers sitting across from us look both intrigued and alarmed.

"Why the fuck didn't you text me back?" I snarl as I kiss his mouth, his jaw, and bite the lobe of his ear.

"Because I'm an idiot," he says. "And fucked in the head."

"That works for me."

I lose myself in Dane's unholy heat, in the rabid taste of his mouth and his desperate longing that makes me feel wanted, desired, needed, like I never have before.

The waitress clears her throat. "Do you need a to-go box?"

Dane throws cash on the table. "Nope."

"Actually, yes," I say. "But hurry."

🎵 *"Yellow Flicker Beat"—Lorde*

Dane drives me back to his house, not mine. That suits me just fine because I want what I haven't gotten yet, and I want it loud and rough, somewhere far away from my brother's earshot.

We're ripping at each other's clothes before we've crossed the threshold, which is on par with the groping, handsy shit we were doing the whole car ride home until Dane almost ran us off the road. Twice.

I had his cock in my mouth the second time. He ran onto the

gravel shoulder so hard that I almost bit off the very thing I'm determined to experience in more than just my mouth...though I certainly wouldn't say no to another round of that either.

I leap on Dane as soon as we enter the living room, wrapping my legs around his waist, grabbing his face in both hands so I can kiss him. He locks his hands under my ass and carries me, not just to the couch—all the way up the stairs to his bedroom.

I hadn't been here yet. His scent overwhelms me, that scent of his sheets and sleeping that made my heart gallop that first morning I banged on his door, but that was a light rainfall compared to jumping into a pool—now I'm submerged in it.

His room is as dark as the inside of a cave, with heavy blinds to block out the sun when he's day sleeping and no mirrors nor photographs anywhere. The only object I can see that doesn't obviously belong to him is an old-fashioned perfume bottle sitting on a low table that might once have been a vanity, if it still possessed its mirror.

It's the bed I'm interested in.

Dane throws me down on the mattress, sending up another puff of his rich, masculine scent.

I'm attracted to him in an animal way that warps the very fiber of my soul. I'm like those animations of sharks where they sniff the smallest drop of blood, and their eyes go black and they turn into killing machines. I want to devour Dane—and anything that gets in my way.

But barely has my back touched the bed before something padded but immovable closes around my wrist with a soft *snick*. As I'm looking at one wrist, Dane is cuffing the other.

I get a thrill that's part terror and part exhilaration. Now the look on Dane's face is 100 percent shark as his eyes crawl down my prone and helpless body.

"Remi, Remi, Remi..." He shakes his head. "I tried to warn you." He closes another manacle around my ankle, this one attached to a long strap.

"You ignored me first!" I cry, outraged at the injustice of it all.

"I know," Dane says implacably. "But I still have to punish you."

"Like last time?"

"No, not like last time." Dane cuffs my last limb, then hoists the straps upward to tie to the same bedposts as my wrists, yanking my legs into the splits. "This time, let's make sure the message sticks."

This is not a position I've found myself in before. I'm not that flexible, and my thighs are already starting to tremble.

Dane takes a pair of shears out of a drawer and deftly slices up the leg of my jeans.

"Hey! You know, you've cut off half the pants I own!"

"Can't really blame me for the first pair," Dane says without an ounce of repentance.

The cool air hits my skin. Dane has eyes only for the part of me still covered in a strip of cotton. His tongue wets his lips, and he smiles with anticipation.

He cuts off my undershirt in two quick snaps, the steel blades kissing my skin. All I can think is I'm glad I already dropped my plaid shirt on the floor before we started because that one belonged to my dad, and I'd hate to see it in shreds.

Dane pulls the remnants of my clothes away from my body. All that endures is my white cotton underwear, the kind that comes six in a pack from Fruit of the Loom. It's probably for the best that Dane cuts it to bits next.

But now there's nothing between me and him, not even a millimeter of fabric, and I'm on full display. The sense of exposure is unbearable, particularly as Dane takes his time examining my spread-open pussy.

He cocks his head in that way I'm coming to know so well—his look when something interests him. His eyes gleam their darkest coppery color, and his beautiful pale hand floats out to part my pussy lips.

Just the sensation of spreading sends shivers running up my legs.

Gently, he stretches me apart to the farthest limit, slowly, but with firm, even pressure until my clit is completely exposed. Then, lightly, lightly, he tugs on my piercing, running the silver ring back and forth in a short half-moon shape, making it feel as if every nerve in my body connects in that one place.

I'm shaking and begging and groaning, and we've hardly begun.

"You're going to have to get a lot tougher than that," Dane says, and he shoves a gag in my mouth.

The gag is made of leather but padded inside so I can bite down on it. And bite down I do when Dane slaps my bare pussy with the flat of his hand.

SMACK!

"*Ugrhhhhhhhh!*" I scream through the gag.

The sensation is sudden, sharp, and blinding. My pussy is completely exposed, my legs tied so tightly in the splits, I have no hope of closing them. My thighs jerk with the impact, so hard that the bed frame hits the wall. After the quick blast of pain comes intense heat and throbbing.

"Apologize," Dane says.

"*Ahmsrrrry!*"

"Hm." He shakes his head. "I can't hear you."

Dane strips off his thin charcoal sweater, revealing the hard planes of muscle beneath. He's a statue come to life, as beautiful and terrible as a marble-made man. My eyes follow the deep cuts from his hips down into his trousers. Behind the gag, my mouth begins to water.

Dane opens the chest at the foot of his bed and pulls out a riding crop, long and flexible, black as jet. He bends it lightly, testing the tress.

He touches its flat head to my exposed and throbbing clit, resting it there so I can feel the supple leather. I feel everything like I never have before—the trembling muscles of my thighs, the hard points of my nipples with my arms wrenched back tight, Dane's eyes burning over my exposed flesh, and most of all, the throbbing heat of my poor little pussy that's already turned a dusky pink.

Dane lifts the crop and, with a flick of his wrist, brings it down directly on my clit.

SMACK!

I shriek around the gag as my legs jerk, the jolt running all the way down to the tips of my toes.

SMACK!

SMACK!

SMACK!

He does it three more times, and each time I give a muffled scream as the headboard hits the wall and my entire body jolts. The impact is electric, the current blasting through my body, leaving an intense, throbbing heat in its wake. The heat spreads from my swollen red pussy all the way up to my belly and breasts.

SMACK!

SMACK!

SMACK!

Each strike is a little harder than the last, gradually increasing the impact from barely tolerable to something that might blast me out of my own body.

"*Ahmsrrrry! Ahmsrrrry! Ahmsrrrry!*" I cry in muffled delirium.

SMACK!

He finishes with one last strike that draws a long, shrill scream out of me, strangled by the gag.

Dane lowers the riding crop, his eyes dark and satisfied. "Now you're sorry."

He unbuttons his trousers with one deft flick of his thumb. His pants drop, showing an erection that could be used to drill to the center of the earth. His cock isn't pale at all right now; it's engorged with dark, dusky blood, heavy as a bludgeon.

If there ever was proof that Dane really is fucked in the head, it's his intense arousal at the sight of my pain.

But if so, I must be just as fucked up, because when he lightly runs his fingers from the base of my slit up my pussy lips, they come away dripping with thin, clear fluid.

"I knew you were meant for me," he says, raising his fingers to his lips.

I glow like he gave me the compliment I've always wanted to hear—because he really fucking did.

My pussy is on fire. It throbs with each beat of my heart, puffy, swollen, and exquisitely sensitive. His breath whispers across my raw red flesh. The piercing glints in my erect little clit.

Dane positions himself on the bed, upright on his knees, gripping my ankles in his hands. His body takes my breath away, his muscles swollen and gleaming with exertion, veins running down his forearms and the backs of those beautiful hands.

His cock points straight ahead and doesn't look as if it would fit inside an elephant, let alone my small frame.

But he grips my ankles and rams it right in.

Now I'm screaming around the gag in an entirely new way—the way of someone being hollowed out from the inside. His cock rearranges my organs, shoving everything aside to make room. He burrows all the way back, hitting a place that's never been touched, that never existed before this moment.

He carves a new pathway until his hips meet my body, and the front of my belly bulges like an alien birth.

This would already have been intolerable under normal circumstances. With my legs yanked in the splits and my pussy swollen practically shut, the noises I'm making could be heard all the way down in Grimstone if not for the gag.

Dane looks down into my face, his brows black as the devil, his eyes full of wicked orange light. He fucks me and fucks me, my legs pulled back, no way to protect myself, no way to resist. That huge cock reams me out until I don't know where I am or who I am or what I ever wanted—all I know is that I'm completely in his power, and each slam of the headboard is the tolling of a bell, marking the end of everything I knew before.

My eyes roll back, and what was pain and intensity beyond imagining slowly begins to become something else—something that builds like a hurricane, beginning at some tiny interior point, then whirling outward, gaining in power and speed.

What was pain becomes heat, and what was heat becomes pleasure, but a wild, dark, electric pleasure that grows and grows without breaking. Each thrust of his cock, each slam of the headboard, cranks the fury until it seems it has to burst or else tear me apart.

I'm biting down on the gag, my back arched, my fists clenched, my wrists trembling in the restraints. I can't even feel my legs anymore, but that doesn't matter because I feel each stroke of Dane's cock like it's going all the way through me up to my chin. My whole body rocks, the bed slamming the wall while the storm builds and rages.

Then, with one last thrust, Dane rams himself all the way back in this pocket he's dug, his arms turned outward, every muscle on his frame rigid like he's being electrocuted, his head thrown back in a roar.

And I'm shrieking, blasting, exploding outward, every bit of me clamped around every bit of him.

CHAPTER 22
REMI

I FIND MY DAD'S SHIRT ON THE FLOOR, AND DANE LENDS ME A PAIR of his pants even though I never returned the others.

Dane pulls the soft plaid shirt up on my shoulders, buttoning the buttons for me. He does it carefully and gently, like I'm an invalid, and it's such a contrast to how he behaved ten minutes ago that I'd laugh if I could do anything but sway on my feet.

He kisses me softly on the mouth, then looks into my eyes like he's checking for concussion. "Are you okay?"

I kiss him back, deep and not at all soft. "I'm way better than okay."

"Thank god," he says in relief. "Jesus, Remi, I don't know what got into me; I'm like a fucking animal around you. I don't want you to think that's what I was like with Lila because I wasn't. I've never gone to that extreme before."

In the strangest way, that pleases me. I don't want Dane to be like that with anyone but me.

"I don't think anyone's done that before." I laugh. "Or at least they didn't come as hard as me."

"If they did, they're too dead to tell us." Dane grabs a hand towel from the bathroom to mop down his neck and chest. "I barely survived."

"You should try being on the receiving end."

"Is that what you're into?" Dane gives me a naughty look as he tosses me a fresh towel.

I laugh. "It wasn't before, but now I feel like you kind of deserve it."

He shrugs. "I'll try anything if it involves you naked."

My face colors all over again, and I can't seem to find a response.

"What's wrong? Was that too much?"

"No." I shake my head. "It's just…"

"What?"

"Sometimes I can't quite get it in my head that you're attracted to me."

Dane frowns, the towel pressed against his chest. "Remi, do you really not think you're beautiful?"

"Beautiful!" I snort. "Cute, sure. But also, a fucking mess and a broke-ass bitch and a B+ student. While you're some gorgeous doctor who probably doesn't even need to work 'cause it looks like your parents were a hell of a lot better than mine at financial planning."

"There's more than one kind of intelligence," Dane says. "Watch me try to build a piece of furniture or even put one together from IKEA, and we'll see who looks like a fucking idiot. The money shit— who cares. That's luck of the draw. And as for you being 'cute'…"

He crosses the room and takes me in his arms, pulling me against his bare chest. "I haven't been able to take my eyes off you since you stepped out of your car."

He kisses me until my body gets warm and heavy, and I go limp in his arms.

"That's not the kiss of someone 'cute,'" Dane says. "That's the kiss of a fucking stunning woman who impresses me, who makes me laugh, who's got more grit in her little finger than most people will show in their whole damn lives."

I'm blushing and hot all over, and I never want him to stop.

But Dane isn't content with compliments alone.

"Who tells you these lies?" he says, looking into my eyes. "Is it you or somebody else?"

"I dunno." I drop his gaze. "I've always had this feeling like I'm not quite right or I just don't belong. It got worse when I lost my parents. I wasn't ready to be on my own. And I definitely wasn't ready to be responsible for someone else."

"But you made it work anyway. And that's why I admire you."

My chest burns. "Really?"

"Yeah. When my life went to shit, I fell apart. I barely left this house for a year. If Atlas didn't bring me food and make me eat, I probably would have starved. I couldn't have taken care of some little brother. Definitely couldn't have held down a job."

"Well…" I say softly. "What happened to you was worse."

"There is no 'worse' when it comes to losing the people you love." Dane wraps his arms around me and gives me the kind of hug that could prevent a war if all the right people could get it. The kind that makes you feel comforted from head to toe. "Come on, let's get you something to eat."

———

We pad downstairs, both of us dressed in Dane's clothes with the addition of my dad's shirt.

Dane heats up the pizza in his air fryer, which makes it even crispier than when it was fresh out of the oven at The Slice Factory. I'm pleased to see Dane does *not* pick off his toppings but has the bravery to sample my slightly unorthodox combination.

"Know what I'd add to this?" he says, taking another huge bite. "Roasted red pepper."

"God, you just can't help being fancy."

He laughs. "It'd be good, though."

"Sounds fucking delicious," I admit.

By the time we're done eating, it's past midnight.

Dane tucks a piece of hair behind my ear. "Are you tired?"

"Surprisingly, no… I think I'm adjusting to your clock."

"Good," he says, smiling a little. "There's something I've been wanting to show you."

We leave the bits of leftover crust on the table, and Dane takes my hand, leading me out through the kitchen door to the back garden.

♪ *"Aurora"*—*Snow in April*

I've seen his garden before, from a distance, and thought it rather drab. But that's because I'd only seen it in the daytime.

As soon as we walk out into the cool, damp air, I'm surrounded by the pale blossoms of moonflower and night-blooming jasmine. As we walk deeper into the garden, into the parts overhung by heavy mossy trees, I see the spectral glow of bioluminescence. On the broken stumps, growing up the trunks of the trees, and on the hanging branches, thick clusters of mushrooms and toadstools give off the faint glow of purple, orange, and turquoise. Tiny fireflies float in the air like flecks of gold.

It's eerie and ethereal, beautiful and haunting, like Dane himself. A night garden for the night doctor.

I spin in place in this midnight wonderland of glowing light and deepest shadow, in this world that feels separate from any other because it was made by Dane.

"It's magical," I say, turning to take his hand.

"You like it?" He's nervous, only half believing.

I pull down my plaid shirt off my shoulder to show him the tattoo of moths and mushrooms running down my arm. "I've always liked fungi better than flowers."

Dane kisses me softly, the cool scent of Japanese wistaria and Queen of the Night filling my lungs.

"I saw that tattoo the very first day you were here. From the moment you stepped out of that hideous orange car, everything about you was so electric—it's like you jolted me and restarted my heart."

"Then why didn't you text me?" I ask because I need to know. "And why wouldn't you dance with me on the beach?"

"I'll tell you," Dane says. "But first, can I fix my mistake?"

I nod, though I don't quite know what he means.

"Wait here…"

He reenters the house, then returns with a portable speaker, which he sets on a stump, careful not to crush the frilly chanterelles growing from the old dead wood.

The music that plays is soft and lilting but melancholy, too. In Dane's eyes, I see the sadness that's always there, though he tries to hide it with anger and arrogance.

I understand because I'm sad, too, but I hide it for Jude's sake. Pretending to be yellow sunshine when my heart is heavy with dark blue ocean.

I work and I work like that will fix my problems. And maybe it will, but it never fixes how I feel.

Dane takes me in his arms, his hands on my waist, while mine link behind his neck. He looks down into my face, and I look up into his, and in this otherworldly light, there's no barrier between us. There's only him and me and the gently bobbing fireflies.

"I wanted to dance with you," Dane says. "I was aching to take you in my arms…but Lila was the first person I ever danced with. The only person until now. After she died, I swore I'd never dance again."

Unconsciously, his eyes flit to the house, then back to me again. Guilt weighs him down like chains draped over every limb.

"Who did you promise?"

"I promised *her*," Dane says miserably. "I swore it."

"But Dane…you can't live your life like that forever. I don't think that's what she'd want."

He laughs bitterly. "You don't know Lila—that's exactly what she'd want."

"What was she like?" I say softly, though I know I'm asking for trouble. Whatever Dane tells me will gnaw at my brain.

"Gorgeous, charming, witty," he says, and each word is a bite. "But also wild and reckless, with a horrible temper. We fought constantly. I thought that was passion—it was passion. But it was anger and resentment, too. We hurt each other again and again. But we loved each other so hard, I never would have— I never wanted it to stop."

I don't want to push, but I have to know the truth. We can't be together otherwise.

"What happened?"

Dane swallows, his throat jerking.

"We were kids when we met. Barely teenagers when we started dating. I was angry about my condition and jealous when she'd go anywhere without me. Lila was faithful, but she was also a flirt. And me..." He makes a disgusted sound and shakes his head. "I'm a shitty person, Remi. I always have been. But I'm not a murderer, I swear to you."

I believe him. I've believed him from the beginning, before I had any reason to. Maybe I still don't have a reason, except what I feel.

"Everyone's shitty sometimes," I say. "I wouldn't want you to see the worst and stupidest things I've done."

"You're too forgiving."

"That's what Jude says."

"Maybe he's trying to tell you something."

"About twenty times a day—but I'm a slow learner."

"That's not true."

"Oh, trust me, it is."

Dane lets that pass, though I can tell from the tension in his jaw, he's holding something back. But he presses on, wanting to finish his story because it probably hurts like fuck to get it all out.

"Lila was the darling of this town. Her father was the mayor; her mother ran the historical foundation. They were Grimstone's Kennedys, and they weren't at all happy when their only child became infatuated with the town freak."

"Don't call yourself that," I say, as fierce as Dane when I talk shit about myself.

"Everyone else does."

"I don't give a shit—you and I aren't going to agree with them."

"Lila could have had anyone. She could go anywhere, do anything she liked, but she chose me. And at first, she seemed happy with her choice. But it started to wear on her, like it would wear on anyone. And for Lila, it was worse because freedom was everything to her. She hated restraint. And that's what I am—a ball and chain in the daylight hours."

I can see it now—the deep root of the self-loathing Dane tries so hard to hide. Just like Dane sees himself in me, I see myself in him—the part of me that fears I'm just not good enough. Not good enough to get what I so desperately long for. Not good enough to deserve to be loved.

"Our fighting got worse and uglier. And then it stopped because Lila was depressed. She'd been depressed before, but never like this. Never so dark or so long. And then…she told me she was pregnant."

I remember what Rhonda told me: *He never wanted that baby.*

Unbidden, I ask, "Were you excited?"

"No." Dane shakes his head. "I was terrified."

"Why?"

He hesitates, and again his eyes flick back to the house.

"Because we weren't in a good place," he says at last. "And most of all, because I worried our son would be like me. I didn't want to put that curse on a child."

"And…was he?"

Dane drops my gaze, staring down at the ground. "We never found out. He died of meningitis." His head hangs. He's not touching me anymore, his hands limp at his sides.

"I'm so sorry."

His exhale is like a last breath. "I never want that pain again. I thought it would kill me. It should have."

I don't say it out loud, but I don't see a future with kids either. I feel like I already raised one with Jude. But that doesn't mean my heart isn't ripping for Dane. I've loved Jude like a son and a brother and the only person I've had for half my life—I think I can imagine what it would feel like to lose him.

And for a doctor to lose a child to an illness—no wonder Dane feels so much guilt.

"Then a month later…Lila drowned."

Now Dane's voice is more than miserable. Each syllable weighs like a stone on my chest.

"And the whole town decided I killed her. Every day I wanted to join her and my son… The only reason I didn't is because I knew everyone else would take it as proof of my guilt." He gives a hollow laugh. "I stayed alive out of spite."

I take his hand. For the first time, it's cold in mine. I lift it to my lips to warm it. "I'm glad you did."

Dane looks at me. There's so much pain in his face.

God, he was right. We are the same.

"I never thought I'd be happy again," he says. "I didn't want to be. All I felt was anger and bitterness. Guilt and regret. I think I stayed alive to punish myself as much as everyone else. But then you showed up, and I started to feel other things again. To tell the truth, pretty shitty things, at first… I wanted to take advantage of you. I wanted to use you and fuck you."

That should probably make me mad, but in a weird way, it just turns me on. Being used by Dane is pretty fucking fun.

"But once the dam broke…" Dane sighs. "I started to feel more and more. And the guilt was overwhelming. I wanted to dance with you that night, Remi—I've never wanted anything so badly. And I hated myself as soon as I left. But I don't know how to make it okay in my head for me to enjoy you…or anything else."

I don't know how to answer that. I don't know what to say at all.

So I say possibly the stupidest thing: "Maybe I should hypnotize you."

Dane gives a hollow laugh. "Remember when I told you I'd done it once before?"

I nod.

"I did it to myself, hypnotized myself. I told my mind not to feel anything anymore, to keep it all locked inside. And I thought it worked…until you came along."

Again, I feel that nagging urge to ask Dane what suggestion he made to my mind, but opposite that urge lurks an intense panic that I don't want to examine—that I can't even fully admit.

Instead, I say, "Emotion can't be banished. It can only be stuffed down inside to fester."

"And what happens when it festers?" Dane asks.

"It rots you from the inside out."

CHAPTER 23
DANE

AFTER REMI GOES HOME, MY HOUSE FEELS EMPTY IN A WAY IT never used to.

If anything, it used to feel too full—full of memories, full of spirits. Not just Lila and James but my ghost, too—the ghost of who I used to be. And sometimes, the ghosts of what could have been. I'd hear us laughing, running through the halls…little feet that I never actually heard pattering across the floorboards because my son never had a chance to crawl, let alone walk.

Sometimes I did everything I could to feed the memories, to feed my hopeless longing.

And once, I smashed every mirror in the house.

That day I swore I'd sell this place and move away.

But I never did because I couldn't bear to leave them.

And I knew I deserved this torture.

Maybe I still do.

Fucking tourists is one thing, but Remi is different. She's making me feel happiness again.

Who said I could feel happiness? Who said I was forgiven?

Definitely not Lila.

Lila would hold a grudge until Judgment Day and beyond; I know that about her like I know her favorite songs and her favorite cereal.

If I go back up to the bedroom, she might be waiting for me. Raging for what I dared do in our old bed.

Maybe I meant it to be an exorcism. Remi's screams could clear the house.

But I know the truth… Lila's here because I keep her here.

I can't let go. Letting go means acceptance, forgiveness… She's not here to give them to me, so I'd have to forgive myself. And that I'll never do.

So instead, in the cool pale hours of the early morning, I go for a walk in the woods. I don't walk toward Remi's house but deeper into the forest.

I walk until I come to something strange…a hole in the ground. Maybe seven feet long, four feet deep, and about as wide. The earth is piled up in a heap, with no one in sight of this lonesome place.

I stand and stare at the fresh-turned earth and the blank black hole.

I've had a suspicion for quite some time now, built from a succession of hints that have been piling up in my brain.

It's all whispers and vapors, nothing I'd call actual evidence.

In fact, I could just be flat-out wrong…and I definitely can't tell Remi.

But maybe I could show her…

I didn't want to do this, but I think it might be time.

I reach into my pocket, touching the key to Blackleaf that Ernie gave me six years ago.

CHAPTER 24
REMI

"WHERE WERE YOU?" JUDE ASKS, LOOKING AT MY WILD HAIR AND swollen lips.

"Uh…I went for pizza with Tom." I hold up the mostly empty box. "It's really good, actually, you want the last piece?"

Jude makes a face. "Not until we've got a microwave. Or better yet, an air fryer."

"That would make it better," I say, struggling to keep a straight face. I did not expect to find my brother in the kitchen when I came home at 2:00 a.m. "What are you doing up so late?"

"I've been clearing out the workshop," Jude says. "I'm almost done."

"Wow, Jude, thank you!" I really wasn't sure if he was actually doing anything in there—I hadn't seen much evidence. "I can't wait to see."

"Well, don't come in yet—I want it to be a surprise."

"I won't."

"How's the rest of the house coming along?"

"Surprisingly well. Tom said we'll have full power by tomorrow."

"Assuming he can sleep off whatever the fuck you two were doing."

"Uh-huh." I can't look at Jude, or he'll know I'm lying.

I hate misleading my brother, but he'll lose his shit if he knows

I've been hooking up with Dane. He's on Rhonda's side, and I'm not sure how to convince him otherwise.

"How much longer do you think it will take till we can sell this place?" Jude asks, yawning and getting up from the kitchen table.

"I don't know—maybe another couple of months?"

"That long?"

"It's a fuck ton of work! And I'm mostly doing it myself."

I don't think I need to point out that while I've almost completed the dining room, ballroom, and library and made headway on the two upstairs bedrooms, Jude hasn't finished one measly barn. But maybe I should if he's going to get snippy.

But he doesn't give me any more shit—he's probably too tired.

"Whatever," Jude says. "Good night."

I listen to him climb the stairs, and then I pull out my laptop.

I've been working on his college applications.

It feels a little sneaky or boundary crossing in some way, but all I want to do is show him that he'll be accepted. I'm starting to think it's nerves keeping him away—his fear of failure or embarrassment if he gets rejected. An acceptance letter could be exactly what he needs to get excited.

I spend an hour filling out his info until my eyelids get heavy. Then I push the laptop aside, pleased that I completed two more.

Jude doesn't have to go to any of these schools, but it's good to have options.

I haul my own exhausted ass up the stairs so I can catch a few hours' sleep, just in case Tom actually does manage to make it to my house by noon.

Assuming he's coming at all after that send-off from Dane.

Tom arrives at a shockingly prompt hour, probably because Emma is driving. She honks the horn, grinning and waving when I come out into the yard.

"I brought you muffins!" she calls.

"What kind?"

"Blueberry!"

I guess she and Jude are still in a fight.

Grinning right back, I grab the bag of muffins and devour one before Tom has even stepped out of the truck.

He looks around nervously, like he thinks Dane might be lurking in the bushes.

"Sorry about last night," I say, trying to break the ice.

"He's the one who should be sorry!" Emma interrupts. "Leaving you alone with that psychopath."

She gives her cousin a dirty glare.

Tom is unnecessarily shamefaced.

"She's okay," he says defensively, like they both thought there was a good chance I ended the night in a body bag.

"Dane's not like that," I tell them, wondering how in the hell I can clarify this mess.

Emma shakes her head, giving me a sympathetic look. "Remi, sweetie, you don't know what he's like. You've been here a month. We've known him our entire lives. He's always been fucking weird, and that brother of his is almost as bad—you saw what he did to Tom!"

Tom actually does have some pretty impressive bruises on his neck. I would not want to fuck with Atlas—or Dane either, if I'm being honest.

God, I wish my only friends in this place would get along.

I made it worse by letting Tom take me on a date.

I need to come clean, though that's hard to do when I can hardly explain what Dane and I are, even to myself.

"We're...sort of seeing each other," I mumble.

Strangely, that doesn't seem to surprise or upset Emma—if anything, she only looks more intrigued.

"Oh, you sweet summer child...don't say I didn't warn you."

Tom is disappointed but far from devastated.

"Is it 'cause he's so rich?" He sighs. "I never get anybody worth getting."

"Well, you could try showering more often," Emma remarks. "And cleaning out your truck."

"Women don't care what's in my truck."

"A little bit, they might," I say gently. The back seat of Tom's truck is full of crushed beer cans, sandy blankets, and several bags' worth of crumbled Doritos.

"Well, guess I better get to work." Tom heaves his tool bag out of the truck bed.

"Can I grab you a glass of water or something?" I ask, feeling like an asshole.

"Nah, I already had a drink."

"Of coffee," Emma assures me, though I don't believe her.

"How about you?" I ask.

"I brought my own." She holds up a thermos. "And I'm here to work! What can I help with?"

"You don't have to do that. You've got your own business to run—"

"It's dead till Halloween. And if I go in, Mandy will be lazier than ever. I don't know what I'm paying her for; she doesn't even wipe down the tables."

"I'll come wipe 'em for you—fair's fair: you helped me paint the ballroom. I'd offer to carry some trays, too, but I have to admit I got fired from my one and only waitressing job after a single shift."

Emma laughs. "Let's keep you right where you belong."

We spend the afternoon replacing smashed windows on the upper levels. Emma isn't quite as good at holding the heavy panes steady as she was at painting, but she keeps me entertained with a string of anecdotes about the craziest customers she's gotten at the diner and more local gossip.

She's just finished filling me in on all the gory details of Corbin and Helena's doomed love affair when a splintering crash and a horrible thud send us running downstairs.

We find Tom on the floor of the ballroom, covered in cobwebs and plaster dust, his leg at a disturbing angle. His face is white as chalk, and I can't tell if he's breathing. A tendril of blood leaks out of his ear.

The hole in the ballroom ceiling, twenty feet overhead, shows where he fell through.

Emma starts screaming, her hands at her mouth.

"JUDE!" I bellow. "Call 911!"

My brother doesn't emerge, so I'm the one who scrambles to find my phone.

The ambulance takes an agonizing forty-two minutes to arrive.

In that time, Tom begins to stir enough that we know he isn't dead. That's about all we know because he can't do more than groan after his second concussion in a week.

Emma lays a blanket over him while I hunt for Jude. His moped is missing from the yard. In fact, I haven't seen him since our 2:00 a.m. chat. I glance at the barn, starting to feel seriously annoyed with my neglectful brother.

Still, it's probably for the best that he isn't home—he'd never stop puking if he saw Tom's leg.

I can't stop apologizing, though I don't know if Tom can even understand me.

Emma prefers chastisement. "I told you this would happen!" she shouts at poor groaning Tom. "You never wear your goddamn safety harness!"

The paramedics won't let us in the ambulance, so we follow in Emma's car and spend several hours in the waiting room at the hospital in Hickima.

By the time I'm back home, it's almost eleven o'clock at night.

Jude's moped has returned, but he's already in bed, oblivious to the entire debacle.

Even though it's late and dark as hell in the house, I grab my lantern and climb up to the crawl space above the ballroom. I shimmy across the groaning beams, cognizant that this is exactly what Tom was doing when he fell through. But I'm a lot lighter than him…I hope.

I don't know what, exactly, I'm doing up here. It's impulse more than conscious thought that drives me. But the impulse is strong enough to push me through feet of dust, cobwebs, and dangling wires.

Then I see it ahead—a gaping hole, darker than dark. The place where Tom fell. At the edge of the gap, I spy several of his tools and meters. And then, the place where the ceiling joist broke…

Only…I don't think it broke at all.

At least, not all on its own.

The edges should be ragged if the beam simply snapped.

Instead, the first three-quarters of the joist looks smooth, like someone sawed it. Only the last inch or two show broken splinters.

I don't think Tom fell through on his own.

I think he was booby-trapped.

And I only know one person with the motive to do it.

CHAPTER 25
DANE

It's midnight when Remi comes pounding on my door, which is a hell of a lot better than 7:00 a.m. But I can't say I'm pleased to find us in the exact same position we were in a month ago, accusations hurled in my face the moment I open the door.

"Tom Turner's in the hospital with a broken leg and four broken ribs," Remi informs me. "Oh, and a dislocated shoulder."

"DUI?"

"Very funny," she says, stone-faced.

It's not hard to guess what the attitude's about. "I take it you think I had something to do with it..."

"Are you going to pretend you didn't?"

A dark mood settles over me. I've seen the look on Remi's face many times before on a hundred faces in town. Maybe I deserve it. But it fucking hurts coming from her.

"You've already made up your mind, so what does it matter what I say?"

"Maybe it doesn't—maybe I shouldn't even be here asking." Her cheeks are flushed, her eyes bright with tears. "You've lied to me before."

"I never lied."

"You acted like you barely knew my uncle. You made me feel like an idiot. Do you have a key or don't you?"

Fuck.

This seems like the worst possible time to make an admission, but I really don't want to lie to her.

Too late...she sees the truth.

"My god, you had one the whole time..." She covers her face with her hands and takes several steps away before turning back again in fresh outrage. "That was you looking in my window that night, wasn't it? The night of the storm. The night I dreamed—"

She stops herself, clapping her hand over her mouth, shaking her head at me.

"I'm so fucking stupid. Jude was right—I do the same thing again and again. Has this been a game to you the whole time? Breaking into my house, making me think I'm crazy?"

"That wasn't— I didn't—"

It's hard to defend myself when some of what she's saying is absolutely true, but not in the way she thinks.

Remi won't let me get a word in anyway. "You tried to tell me, didn't you? *'I'm not a good person, Remi...'* and I tried to convince you that you were! Because that's how desperate I am to ignore what's right in front of my face."

My temper snaps. "That's the one part you got right—you are fucking oblivious."

"Well, not anymore!" she bellows. "You stay away from me!"

"Gladly!" I shout back. "Enjoy cooking up bullshit with your new friend Emma; she dishes it out with every fucking pancake. And don't worry about the fence—it never really needed fixing anyway."

I close the door in her face.

Then I wait on the other side of it, trapped in the sick sinking feeling that my own entryway has become a quagmire. Already I regret everything I said and everything I've done.

But that's an old feeling, one I'm damn sure used to.

I can hear that Remi hasn't moved either. I feel her on the other side of the door, hesitant, confused…

After a minute, she turns and slowly tramps back across the yard to her car.

CHAPTER 26
REMI

THE REST OF OCTOBER PASSES IN GLOOMY MISERY. THE DAYS ARE darkly overcast, which makes me unhappy in the most perverse sort of way because I keep thinking of all the fun things Dane and I could have done beneath the blanket of cloud.

I work every waking moment to distract myself from the incessant back-and-forth of my brain.

What if you're wrong?

I'm not.

But what if you are?

I'm not!

You accused him, like everyone else...

Because he's fucking guilty! Where there's smoke, there's fire, and there's always smoke around Dane...

But what if—

JUST SHUT UP ALREADY!

The only thing cheering me up is how epic Grimstone is starting to look as the town gears up for the Reaper's Revenge.

Regardless of what Emma says, I'm looking forward to it. I fucking love Halloween, and it'll be nice to take a night off after weeks of working myself to the bone.

Even Jude is getting in the spirit. He's been working on a costume, a skeleton suit made with glow-in-the-dark fluorescent paint.

Tom Turner comes to the house on crutches to walk me through connecting the last few elements on the electrical panel. The moment of truth when we can finally throw the switch and watch the chandeliers in the ballroom light up is nothing short of exhilarating. For the first time, Blackleaf is starting to look like a real house and not just a mausoleum.

Tom shares the celebration with Jude, Emma, and me but doesn't partake in our champagne toast.

"I've been cutting back," he says, leaning awkwardly on his left leg.

"You have?" Emma says, pleased and surprised.

"Yeah." Tom shrugs. "Thought I might as well—they made me detox in the hospital anyway."

I thank him about a million times for all his hard work and apologize again for the accident.

"Hazard of the job," Tom says, but I notice he doesn't stay any longer than he has to, and he doesn't come within ten feet of me throughout his visit.

It's like he's scared of me.

Which makes me think Tom suspects Dane had a hand in his accident just as much as I do.

The night before Halloween, I head into Grimstone for more supplies, stopping at the hardware store first to buy more teak slats. I've been working on my little side project in stolen minutes here and there.

When I finish shopping, it's only eight o'clock, and I've got nowhere to be. I head to The Fog Cutter for a drink, hoping to sketch out the next stage of my project in the little notebook where I keep all my design ideas.

One drink turns into six as I struggle with the exact dimensions of my design. Customers come and go along the bar, and I barely notice when a pretty redheaded woman takes a seat beside me until she peeks over my shoulder at the sketch.

"Are you an artist?"

"No…" I resist the urge to close the notebook in embarrassment. "It's a design for a gazebo."

"Oh, okay…" She tilts her head to get the full view. "Are you going to build it?"

"That's the plan, but it's a bit trickier than I expected. I'm trying to interweave the slats to make a pattern…"

I turn the book to show her, thinking that she looks familiar, though I'm not sure how—I don't think we've met before.

"Well, that'll be real pretty when it's done," the woman says kindly. "I should hire you to make one for my place."

"At the rate this one's going, I should be free next Christmas."

She laughs. "That's probably when I could afford it. I'm Annie, by the way."

She holds out her hand. I shake it, noticing her extremely chapped knuckles.

"Don't mind that," she says. "It's not contagious. I work at the coroner's office, and I'm allergic to some of the chemicals we use. I slather my hands in protective cream all day long, but still—"

"You're Rhonda's cousin!" I cry, startling her.

"Well, yeah," she says, her smile slowly returning. "But how'd you know?"

"She mentioned you once." My mind works madly. "I go in there all the time—to the hardware store, I mean."

"Poor Rhonda." Annie chuckles. "Lou made her open that place, and she's never forgiven him. She wanted to run a flower shop. Wouldn't have mattered to me 'cause I'm allergic to flowers, too. Men are always giving them to me anyway; it's like a compulsion. Sometimes I—"

She goes on in that vein for a minute, chatting in a friendly way.

From the empty wineglasses in front of her, I'd guess Annie's been unwinding from work for a couple of hours already.

I'm barely breathing because I just realized this is the sister who showed Lila Covett's coroner report to Rhonda and put the idea in her head that Dane falsified the ruling.

I badly want to ask her about it, but I don't want to scare her off—I'm pretty sure she'd lose her job if anybody at HIPPA knew what she shared with her sister.

So how can I get her to spill the dirt all over again?

"Let me buy you a drink," I say, motioning to the bartender for another round.

"I don't know if I should." Annie giggles. "I've had a few already. Ah, well, twist my arm…"

Three more chardonnays later, she's singing like a bird, so bleary-eyed that she can barely stay up on her barstool.

"Well," she whispers, her breath tickling my ear, "the first thing I noticed in the report was that it only had two pages, which was weird 'cause usually a case like that would be a lot thicker. There were things missing, forms and tests and a full formal write-up. The coroner told me not to worry about it. But I could see, too, the file had the wrong color sticker on the spine. We use color codes for type of death, and this one had a blue sticker when it should have been pink."

"So, what really happened?" I ask, leaning in close, my heart throbbing in a sick, uneven sort of way. "How did his wife actually die?"

"Oh, it wasn't the wife, honey." Annie takes a large gulp of her wine and blinks slowly like that will help everything blurry come back into view. "The report they changed was the one for his baby son."

"Oh." It feels like the floor beneath my stool has dropped several feet. "What happened to him?"

"Well, I don't know for sure…" Annie hiccups softly. "But here's what I'll tell you—if that baby really had meningitis, there would have been a viral sample in the file and a pink sticker on the spine. But since they used blue...I'm guessing he drowned."

"Drowned?"

"That's right." She nods firmly. "Just like the wife."

My head's spinning when I leave the bar, and not just because I joined Annie for one too many drinks.

I'm trying to decide what to make of what she just told me and if I should believe her.

And if I *do* believe her, what the fuck does it mean?

If Dane's baby drowned, why did he tell me he died of meningitis?

Maybe because both of them drowning sounds a fuck of a lot more suspicious...

Is it really possible that Dane is just some cold-blooded killer who held his wife and son under the water with his bare hands? Those same gorgeous hands I was so grateful to have all over my body?

The idea makes me sweaty and nauseous, so much so that I stop walking and lean against an iron lamppost. Grimstone looks more old-fashioned than ever with hay bales stacked up against the buildings, fake cobwebs strung everywhere, scarecrows menacing the pigeons, and witches' brooms propped in doorways.

It's all the trappings of a pretend horror in a place that Dane says is an epicenter for the real thing.

I'm not a good person, Remi...

That's what everyone here says—that Dane Covett is a killer.

So why did he look so hurt when I accused him of attacking Tom? It was like I stabbed him in the chest.

Jude's voice whispers in my ear.

You're not a good judge of character, Remi.

You only see what you want to see...

I shake my head hard.

That's not true anymore.

I'm going to see what's right in front of me. I'm going to figure this out. There has to be a way to know what's going on here, to really know, not just guess...

The light's still burning at Lou's Hardware. On impulse, I cross the street and tap lightly on the glass.

Lou answers the door, Rhonda nowhere to be seen.

"Well, hey there, stranger. Haven't seen you in two whole hours."

Lou, I have found out, is an absolute sweetheart—every time I visit, he shows me his favorite putty compounds. And Rhonda's not so bad either, when Dane's not around.

"Lou," I say hesitantly. "Do you happen to have any security cameras?"

CHAPTER 27
DANE

THE KNOCK ON MY DOOR AT EIGHT O'CLOCK IN THE MORNING makes my heart leap. I'm thinking it has to be Remi because Atlas wouldn't come at this time of day, and nobody else comes here at all.

It's embarrassing how quickly I roll out of bed and pull on my pants and hustle down the stairs.

I pause briefly in the living room, smoothing back my hair, taking a few breaths so it's not as obvious how I ran.

I try to tell myself she better be ready with an apology, but I already know I'm going to kiss her the minute she opens her mouth.

The weeks since we last talked have been fucking miserable, and each glimpse of her roaring past on the road in her rickety Bronco have been nothing less than torture. She won't even look in my direction as she passes, her eyes glued firmly ahead on the road.

My only solace has been that nobody's been going the other way up to her place except Emma and sometimes Jude on his moped at odd hours of the day and night.

If I thought I was lonely before, it's nothing compared to how I've been feeling now that I've tasted something else. God damn Remi for waking me up in my coffin just so she could stake me in the heart.

I'm bitter and resentful, but I'll forgive her everything if she'll just give me one hopeful look. Fuck, I'll forgive her just for being here...

But when I open the door, instead of Remi, I'm met with a tall, blond, disgruntled-looking man.

"Hey," he says, with a glance at my bare chest, "sorry to bother you, but I can't seem to find a thing on these goddamn back roads. Do you know where I can find Remi Hayes?"

"Maybe." I take in every detail of this dude, from his too-tight joggers to his shiny new truck. "Depends on who's asking."

"Gideon Price," he says, puffing up his chest like he's trying to match mine. "Her fiancé."

"Huh. Kinda funny you don't know where your fiancée lives."

Gideon flushes.

"I know where she lives," he says belligerently. "She's at her uncle's old place. I just don't know how to find it in these shithole backwoods."

"And you thought I could help since I live in these shithole backwoods."

"Yeah," Gideon says flatly, without the grace to look embarrassed.

"Gideon...Gideon..." I say, like I'm struggling to remember. Then I snap my fingers. "Oh, right, you're the one who cheated on her."

Gideon jerks like I slapped him. "Sorry, who the fuck are you exactly?"

I'd like to say, *Remi's new boyfriend*, but even I can't make that bullshit sing. Not even to annoy this also-ran.

"Don't worry about that—worry about why the fuck I would ever show you where she lives."

"How about 'cause I never fucking cheated, for a start?" Gideon shouts. "Not that it's any of your business!"

Even though he reeks of douchebag, there's something righteously offended in his tone that makes me pause for half a second.

My brain is ticking, considering several different scenarios.

What I'd really like is a little more information.

So I soften my tone, dialing back the aggression, even pretending a note of apology.

"You're right, that was out of line." I step out of my house, gently closing the front door behind me. "Why don't you come with me...? I can show you where to go."

CHAPTER 28
REMI

POUNDING ON THE FRONT DOOR STARTLES ME AWAKE. I'M USUALLY up early, but last night I tossed and turned through a series of nightmares so grueling that I practically had to wring the sweat out of my sheets.

Even though it's well past noon, it feels like I didn't sleep at all. My skull is throbbing, and I'm seriously regretting how much chardonnay I had to drink with Annie to get her to spill her guts.

The knock comes again, louder and more insistent.

"Okay, okay," I grumble, rolling out of bed onto the floor so I can crawl around and look for my pants.

I haven't actually considered who might be at the door, and when I see a tall masculine shape through the glass, my heart skips a beat. I shouldn't want it to be Dane, but that's exactly what I'm hoping for even though nothing's changed—it's still his word against everyone else's and how I feel against how everything looks.

When I open the door, I get the nasty surprise of Sheriff Shane's pissed-off face. I'm guessing he's grumpy because something made him miss his triple stack of waffles with his two best deputies, not to mention the pleasure he gets from annoying the hell out of Emma by scattering sugar packets all over the table every time he doctors up a fresh cup of coffee.

"How can I help you, Sheriff?" I say in the same tone of voice

I'd use to tell him to take a long walk off the edge of the Grand Canyon.

"You recognize this car?" He holds up his phone to show me an image of a shiny blue truck.

"I don't think so..." It kind of looks like Gideon's truck, but it can't be because Gideon's truck is back in New Orleans.

"How about the driver?" He swipes his thumb to switch to the next image, a grainy snapshot of a driver's license. This time, it's impossible to deny Gideon's face or his full name and birth date printed below.

"That's Gideon..." I'm starting to get a very bad feeling. "My ex. Why are you—?"

"I'll ask the questions." Sheriff Shane cuts me off. "When's the last time you spoke to him?"

"A month or so ago—he texted me, but I didn't answer."

"Why not?"

"Because we broke up." My anxiety is mounting. I wrap my arms around myself to try to hold still. "Can you just tell me—?"

"Sure." The sheriff smiles in a way I don't like one bit. "Why don't I come inside so we can chat?"

That's not what I want at all, but it's pretty obvious the sheriff isn't going to tell me shit while he's standing on my porch.

I step aside to make way for his broad frame to pass. From the moment he steps through the door, he's looking around in a very different manner than his last visit. Then, he could barely be bothered to look where I pointed. Now his eyes crawl across the floor, the walls, even the ceilings, looking for something...

Looking for evidence.

My spine goes cold. "Is Gideon okay?"

The sheriff points at my couch. "Take a seat."

I sink onto cushions composed mostly of dust and springs.

The sheriff takes a position in the chair opposite. "So, you didn't see or speak to Gideon at all yesterday?"

"No." I shake my head firmly. "I haven't seen him in months."

"Well, that's interesting." The sheriff licks his finger and turns a page in his notebook without taking his eyes off me. "Because we found his truck abandoned about two miles from here. People in town said he was looking for you. You're *sure* he didn't pop by, even for a minute?"

"No! I didn't even know he was coming! We broke up, and I blocked him."

The sheriff's eyes gleam, and he scribbles something down.

"What was the reason for the breakup?"

"He"—*don't tell him he cheated*—"snored."

"He snored?" The sheriff raises an eyebrow.

"Like a pig," I say firmly.

"And was it an amicable breakup?"

"Extremely," I lie.

"Uh-huh." The sheriff writes something down that looks nothing like what I said.

"What was he doing here?" My heart rate keeps climbing without any end in sight. "You said he was looking for me?"

"Apparently so." The sheriff stands, hitching his belt. "How's about I take a look around the property? Just in case he got lost…"

The easy thing would be to say yes, to prove I've got nothing to hide. But I've seen too many episodes of Law & Order to let a cop search my house—not without a warrant. Especially a cop who hates me as much as this one.

"I don't think so."

"Why not?" The sheriff's lip curls like Elvis. "You got something to hide?"

Yeah—the edibles, underwear, and vibrator scattered around my bed.

"Nope." I stuff my hands in my pockets as I stand. "I just know my rights."

"Your *rights*." The sheriff scoffs like that's a dirty word. It probably is, to him. "Let me tell you about your rights, little missy. From the moment you strolled into town, you've been nothing but trouble to me. And now it sounds like your ex-boyfriend is missing...so what you got a *right* to do is rot in a jail cell for the rest of your natural life if he doesn't show up safe and sound by tomorrow."

"Who needs a judge, jury, or trial, right?"

The sheriff sets his hat a little straighter on his sweaty head. "I'm sure I'll be seein' you real soon."

CHAPTER 29
REMI

♫ *"Fangs"—Younger Hunger*

DOWNTOWN GRIMSTONE LOOKS LIKE THE INSIDE OF A HAUNTED house—bedsheet ghosts float from lampposts, drifts of leaves have been allowed to pile up in the streets, and hundreds of jack-o'-lanterns flicker from every window frame and doorway along Main Street.

Most of the shops have brought their wares out onto the sidewalks, so the sweet scents of caramel apples and fudge mingle with popcorn and grilled franks and the pumpkin cider pumped fresh from kegs stacked up outside the brewhouse.

The streets are packed with people in costumes, including dozens of variations of the town mascot, Mr. Bones. A twenty-foot-tall papier-mâché Mr. Bones towers at the end of Main Street, his skeletal arms outstretched and his jaw hanging open to show all his bone teeth.

Emma's dressed like sexy Pennywise, and I'm the Scarlett Witch, after spending most of the day making my own headdress. I search for Jude among the many Mr. Boneses, but I don't see his glow-in-the-dark paint.

Tom came as a lumberjack, probably so he can wear one of his innumerable plaid shirts. He's glued a paper axe to the side of one of his crutches and a paper pine tree to the other.

Aldous and Amy are dressed as the twins from *The Shining*.

"How come you've got better legs than me?" Amy demands, scowling at her brother's shapely calves.

"'Cause I go for a walk once in a while," Aldous says.

"I walk all over that damn resort! Lugging a mop, too."

"Then I guess it's just better genetics." He blows her a kiss.

I've got an apple doughnut in one hand and a scalding cup of hot cocoa in the other, so I'm the happiest I've been in ages, even after a pack of three Mr. Boneses almost runs me off the sidewalk. Hot cocoa sloshes on my sneakers.

"Watch it!" Emma snaps.

The Mr. Boneses turn and stare at us silently through the dark holes in their skeleton masks.

"Creeps." Emma passes me a wad of napkins to wipe my shoes.

The three skeletons mutter to one another, one of them giving an ugly, low laugh as they carry on down the sidewalk.

Across the street, a plague doctor watches the entire encounter, his black, raven-like beak turned in my direction, his long cloak sweeping the ground.

It occurs to me that anybody could be walking around inside these costumes—Dane, or maybe even Gideon...

It's kind of freaking me out that Gideon found me here in Grimstone. I didn't tell anyone where we were going. How long has he been looking for me?

Gideon never seemed like the unstable type—if anything, his need to overplan everything used to drive me crazy. He didn't even like to buy movie tickets at the last minute.

But I wouldn't have expected him to cheat on me either. And he never actually admitted it—he kept lying to my face like a psychopath even when there was no denying it anymore.

Did he really drive all the way out here to try to convince me to take him back?

Or is he here for an even more fucked-up reason...

What if he's been in Grimstone longer than I think?

What if he followed me out here weeks ago...?

"What's wrong?" Emma says.

My mind is racing with wild theories: What if Gideon's the one who's been messing with me? What if he's not missing at all but just waiting, watching, biding his time?

"The sheriff knocked on my door this morning," I tell her. "He said he found my ex-boyfriend's truck."

"Here?"

"Yeah, like two miles from my house."

"Did you know he was coming?"

I shake my head. "Maybe he tried to call me, but I still have him blocked."

I told Emma all about Gideon, so I don't have to fill in the backstory again.

"Where'd they find his car?" Emma says with a sly look. "Anywhere close to Dane's house?"

"Don't start that again."

"Why not?"

"Because for one thing, we're not even dating anymore." Just saying it out loud makes my stomach clench. I don't feel good about the things I said to Dane, and I feel even worse when I remember the look on his face.

But he lied to me. Annie told me his baby didn't die of meningitis.

I don't know why he lied, but I'm tired of being with someone I can't trust.

Love, trust, and respect—you can't have one without the others.

"I'm just saying, people have a hell of a lot of accidents around Dane Covett..." Emma glances over at her cousin. "Including Tom."

My stomach gives another guilty squirm. I never told Emma that it looked like the ceiling joists had been sawed through. I told myself I wasn't sure; it's an old house...they might have just snapped that way...

You're afraid of the truth.

I can feel it, every time I try to fit the pieces together...the anxious panic that builds and builds until I stuff it all down and slam the door shut in my mind.

What am I so afraid of?

I don't know.

I don't understand it.

I don't understand myself.

"Oh, there's Helena!" Emma points. "Let's get our tarot read."

Helena's sitting outside her shop, dressed like a fortune teller, dripping shawls and gold jewelry. Last time I visited her, she was just wearing yoga pants.

"Sit down, sit down!" she calls.

"You first." Emma shoves me forward.

"Where's your date?" Helena asks as I take a seat at her small round table draped with purple cloth.

"They split up," Emma says with an annoying level of cheerfulness.

"Shouldn't you know that already?" I tease Helena.

"I haven't laid the cards out yet," she says with great dignity. "Give the spirits time to do their work."

She passes me her deck of cards, beautifully decorated on their backs with silver stars and moons.

"While you shuffle, try to hold your problem in your mind..."

I do as she bids, clumsily cutting the cards and shuffling them several times, while trying to decide which single problem I'd like to fix.

Unfortunately, there's about a dozen different issues jostling around in my head...

How to get Jude to go to college...

How to finish this renovation on time and on budget...

How to avoid getting arrested by our gestapo sheriff...

How to stop thinking about Dane every minute of the day...

How to learn to trust myself so I know who else I can trust...

"Ready?" Helena asks.

"I guess so..."

She deals out seven cards.

"The first three represent your current state," she says as she flips them over.

The names of the cards are written across the bottom in silver script.

The Fool.

The Queen of Cups.

The Devil.

I stare at the last card: a winged beast with horns and hooves.

"Interesting..." Helena tilts her head, scanning the images.

"That doesn't look good." I'm already regretting participating in this.

"No, no, it's not bad..." Helena says in a completely unconvincing way. "The Fool represents a potential misstep, a tumble into the unknown..."

Sure enough, the Fool is perched right on the edge of a cliff, looking like he'll step off any moment as he gazes into nothingness.

"That's my current state?"

"Well, let's keep going," she says hastily. "The Queen of Cups offers unconditional love. She's extremely empathetic—sometimes to a fault."

Emma raises an orange eyebrow and mouths "Dane" at me, like I need the reminder.

"And what does this mean?" I tap the goat-headed Devil.

"The Devil is the shadow side of all of us," Helena says gravely. "The darkness we carry in our core."

I don't feel like any of this is helping. In fact, I'd rather stop, but there are still four more cards to turn over.

"This card represents your problem..." Helena flips the center card, revealing the image of a man dangling upside down from one foot. "The Hanged Man…that means you're unable to help yourself."

My stomach sinks. That's exactly how I feel—like I'm dangling by my ankle over an abyss, and no matter what I do, no matter how hard I work, it never seems to get better…

"So, what am I supposed to do?"

Helena flips the last three cards.

Three swords stabbed into a bloody heart.

Two lovers wrapped in an embrace.

And finally…a grim reaper in a dark cloak, riding on a skeletal horse.

"These represent your future," she says.

"My future is death?"

Helena gives a slightly nervous laugh. "Not always. Not usually! The Three of Swords means a separation or the breakup of a significant relationship. The Lovers represent choice as well as romance. And Death…that could mean the death of a project, plan, or relationship, not always physical death! The reaper's scythe cuts the cord to the past, allowing us to move forward because we have nothing else to lose…"

I really don't see how any of this is supposed to help. I'm more confused than ever and more depressed.

Emma sees my gloomy expression and tugs me up from the table. "Come on! Let's go dance!"

"Don't you want your cards read?"

"Helena's done mine a million times."

I let Emma pull me along. By the time we've split a bag of kettle corn and danced for an hour in the city square, I'm starting to feel a little better.

♬ *"Hush"—The Marías*

Selina joins us, dressed as Ursula in a strapless gown with a tentacle hem that shows off the impressive sleeves of tattoos running down both her arms. Tom tries to dance, but his crutches get in the way, and he ends up sitting on the sidelines, sulky until I buy him an orange-and-black snow cone.

"Sorry about your leg." I apologize for the hundredth time, steeped in guilt.

"Ah, it's not so bad…only two more weeks of these things." He kicks at one of his crutches, knocking it over. I pick it up for him and rest it against the pile of hay bales he's using as a chair.

Across the square, the plague doctor watches me again.

The party's getting crazy, people packing into the square until there's barely room to move, let alone dance. The smell of pumpkin cider is thick in the air. The whoops and shouts from the park have become wild as a pack of wolves.

Someone slaps me hard on the ass.

"*What the fuck!*" I whip around and see a Mr. Bones grinning at me.

I'm considering punching his creepy skeleton face until he pulls up his mask and I realize it's only Jude.

"I almost decked you, you idiot!"

"Then you wouldn't get your drink." He passes me a bottle of cider with the cap already popped.

"Where have you been?"

"Getting into trouble."

"What kind of trouble?" I ask nervously. "'Cause the sheriff was already up my ass this morning…"

Jude shows zero concern as he swigs his own cider. "What for?"

I fill him in, glancing back at the plague doctor, who's still standing at the edge of the square, his beak pointed right at me. I can't help thinking that might be Dane.

Or Gideon…

When did he get to Grimstone? And where is he now? Could Dane really have hurt him?

Yes, of course he *could*. The question is…*would* he?

Emma's right—there are too many coincidences, too many accidents...

Somewhere deep inside my brain, a ghostly piano plays...

"I'm really starting to freak out," I whisper to Jude.

"Ah, Gideon'll turn up. He's probably drunk in some bar, boo-hooing 'cause you won't take him back."

"But what if someone hurt him?"

"Who?" Jude says, and I remember that I never even told him I was dating Dane. God, I'm such an asshole. Jude wouldn't keep something like that from me.

If it turns out Dane really is dangerous, then that means I've put Jude at risk, too. And maybe Tom and Gideon as well... Everything that's happened would be my fault.

I gulp down my cider, my anxiety rising.

"Want to dance?" Selina asks Jude.

"Maybe later." He pulls his mask down and disappears into the crowd.

"Sorry," I apologize to Selina on his behalf. "He's not really into dancing."

"Your brother's cute," Emma says. "Too bad he's a little shit."

"Tell me about it." I force a smile even though I don't like Emma talking about Jude that way. He may be a shit, but he's *my* little shit—me and Jude against the world.

My chest burns, and I feel a little unsteady on my feet—I must have drunk that cider too fast. Or the two drinks I had before.

"I better sit down for a bit," I tell Emma.

"Sure." She turns and dances closer to Selina instead.

I head to the side where Tom was sitting, but his hay bales are now occupied by four girls dressed as Ninja Turtles, with colored headbands, plastic weapons, and green miniskirts. Tom and his crutches are nowhere to be seen.

I stumble a little. A Mr. Bones in a glow-in-the-dark suit grabs my arm, helping to steady me.

"Thanks, Jude," I mumble. "I'm not feeling too good…"

He helps pull me out of the suffocating press of people, into fresher air.

My legs are wobbly, and my feet seem encased in wet cement. Each step takes all my energy and focus until I can hardly see anything but the path a few inches in front of me.

The streetlights are fading. I'm walking through crunching leaves, over ground that's no longer paved.

"Hey…" My voice comes out mushy. "Where are you—?"

A second Mr. Bones appears at my other elbow, pulling me along with surprising strength. Each has a painful grip on my arm, and each, I realize with a sickening lurch, is a hell of a lot bigger than Jude.

"Who—? What are you—?"

I try to dig my heels into the earth, to pull my arms free, but they're dragging me along at double speed, deeper into the park, where the trees grow close together and there are no streetlamps at all.

One of them flings me down beneath an oak tree. The back of my head smacks against the base of the trunk, and suddenly three Mr. Boneses crowd around me, their painted skull masks tilting, the black holes of their eyes staring down at me.

"Looky what you found…" the third and largest Mr. Bones says, his voice horribly familiar. "The little troublemaker…"

He bends, reaching for me. I kick up with both feet as hard as I can, booting him in the center of his ugly grinning mask. His nose makes a nauseating cracking sound, and blood bursts from under the hand he claps to his face as he howls, "*You little bitch!*"

One of his friends kicks me hard in the back, and the other seizes my arms. I'm shouting and thrashing with all my might, but it takes about two seconds for them to subdue me. I couldn't fight off one of these guys, let alone all three of them.

"*You're gonna regret that, you filthy fucking cunt,*" the biggest one snarls.

Even when he's choking and snuffling on his own blood, I recognize his voice, which means I have a pretty good idea who his buddies are, too.

He grabs my knees, wrenching them apart, ripping at my scarlet-colored leggings. It takes a man really unleashing his force on you for you to realize how much stronger they are—even if he's panting and puffing 'cause he's not in that great of shape.

His buddies yank so hard on my arms, it feels like they're about to pull out of their sockets.

Thick, prodding fingers grope my body, pinching bruises everywhere they touch, while the man's weight crushes me into the dirt. He fumbles with his buckle, that hideous cowboy belt I recognize all too well...

I can't stop him. Can't even slow him down.

All I can do is say, "I guess you did try to warn me...didn't you, Sheriff?"

He freezes in the act of tearing off my underwear.

"How does she—?" one of his friends mutters.

"*Shut up*," Sheriff Shane snarls. "It doesn't matter—she's not walking out of here."

His meaty hand closes around my throat.

Fucking brilliant, Remi. When will you learn to keep your mouth shut?

I guess right now...

He squeezes until my eyes water and the trees spin like a carousel. The glow-in-the-dark Mr. Bones masks whirl around me, grinning, cackling...only now there seem to be four of them, one crouched low and watching from the bushes...

I can't shout, can't scream, can't breathe...the carousel spins faster and faster...

"Fucking take it, bitch." The sheriff grunts, pulling his cock free of his pants at last.

It flops against my thigh, moist like a slug.

Then several things happen at once.

A figure in black swings a branch like a baseball club, slamming it into the side of the sheriff's head. The guy holding my right arm turns to see what the fuck is going on, and I take the opportunity to kick him in the jaw. I kind of miss with the first kick, but the second hits just right, sending him tumbling backward.

The guy on my left retaliates with a sucker punch to the side of my skull. Stars explode across my vision, and now I'm not sure how many Mr. Boneses are around because I'm seeing double of everything.

While it was a pretty good punch, it was a very bad idea because the plague doctor throws his branch aside and tackles my assailant with a roar, slamming him onto his back and pounding his face again and again with both fists.

The beaked mask slips, and I see part of Dane's face, his expression contorted in rage as he hits the prone Mr. Bones over and over.

Dazed, I roll over and vomit across the roots of the oak tree. My head is spinning, and I can barely lift myself up on all fours.

Images leap around me like phosphorescent flames: Dane pounding the guy who punched me, blood all over his fists. The smallest Mr. Bones darts forward to attack the sheriff, hitting him five or six times in the chest, almost faster than I can see, then rolling away. The one I kicked in the jaw fumbles in his pocket.

I puke again. Crawl a few more feet.

One of the Mr. Boneses staggers up, something bright and glittering in his hand.

"*Dane!*" I shriek.

Dane turns and catches the knife as it swings down, its blade biting into his forearm. He lets out a strangled yell.

I've picked up Dane's branch, but it's a fuck of a lot heavier than a baseball bat. When I swing it at the last Mr. Bones, I don't even get close—the branch arcs through empty air, its weight pulling me all the way around, so I fall on my ass.

The guy laughs and then makes a startled grunting sound.

He looks down. His own knife is buried in his stomach.

"Shit…" he says, dropping to his knees.

Hands lift me up—hands that feel nothing like the ones that were ripping and tugging at me before.

These hands are warm and careful… They lift me until I'm cradled in Dane's arms, my cheek against his chest. I smell his scent, which is everything safe, everything I need right now to still the helpless shaking in my legs.

"Are you okay?" He pulls his mask all the way off so I can see the concern in his face. I could already hear it, plain as day in his voice.

"You saved me." I'm staring up at him, shocked and a little awed.

Nobody's ever saved me before.

I've always had to save myself.

"Those fucks," Dane says bitterly. "No wonder they never caught the people doing this."

"Wait!" I cry, making Dane set me down, though I'd much rather stay in his arms. "We need to take a picture…"

I grab my phone and yank the mask off the guy Dane was pummeling—the one who sucker punched me. Just as I expected, it's one of the sheriff's deputies—the one who whispered and laughed at me that day in the café. His face looks like hamburger, but I snap a pic anyway as he groans.

I pull off Sherriff Shane's mask, too, planning to snap a pic of his stupid passed-out mug. But the blank eyes staring up at me are much more than unconscious.

"He's dead," Dane says unnecessarily.

"But how…"

I lift my hand off the sheriff's chest, my palm soaked in bright-red blood.

"Come on…" Dane tugs my arm. "We should get out of here."

CHAPTER 30
DANE

REMI LETS ME LEAD HER OUT OF THE PARK. REALLY, I'M HALF carrying her—she's wobbly on her legs from shock and fear or from drinking too much.

"How did you find me?" she mumbles.

"I've been watching you all night. I thought Jude was taking you home, and by the time I realized it wasn't him, I'd lost you in the park. Then I heard the sheriff shrieking like a little girl…"

Remi gives a slightly loopy laugh. "I kicked him in the nose… been wanting to do that for a while."

"Well, he got his…"

I'm thinking about the blood soaking the front of his robe. The sheriff was stabbed multiple times—way more than was necessary.

"I didn't do that," Remi says at once. "I think… I think one of his guys did it."

"One of the deputies?"

"I—yes. Maybe. I don't know, everything was spinning; I hit my head on the tree, and then that guy punched me…"

"I saw that." That's all I saw of the fight because as soon as he hit Remi, my vision went black, and I leaped on him and punched him until it felt like my fists would break.

I've never known anything like the rage that consumed me when

I found those fuckers swarming on top of her, the sheriff unbuckling his pants…

I'd have torn apart all three of them.

Instantly, cheerfully, with no remorse.

Which is a little bit fucking scary because I've never even been in a fight before.

But there I was, ready to hurt and even to kill.

Except…I don't think I actually did kill anyone.

And Remi's saying she didn't either.

She clings to my arm. "Do you think the cops are the ones who've been breaking into my house? The sheriff gave me a speeding ticket the first day I was in town. It could have been him fucking with me all along…"

"Maybe."

I feel like I need to come clean about something, and now's the time to do it.

I look Remi in the eye and tell her the truth. "I never played your piano. I didn't come inside your house, not at first…but I did watch you through the windows. That was me, looking down at you the night of the storm."

Remi pauses at the edge of the park, turning to stare at me. "You didn't come inside my house…at first?"

I swallow hard. "I do have a key. Ernie gave it to me years ago. But I never used it to come inside, not until recently. And then, I only broke in once…to set up a camera."

Remi looks fucking pissed, and I can't blame her. "You put a camera in my house?"

"Yes."

"Where is it?"

"Inside the grandfather clock in the entryway."

She presses her fists against her eye sockets and shakes her head, making a sound almost like a laugh.

"What?"

"I almost put my camera in the exact same place."

"You put up a camera, too? Have you seen anything?" I can't help my eagerness.

"No." Her hands drop and her shoulders sink. "I haven't caught anything. Which makes me think…"

But she doesn't finish that sentence.

Instead, her eyes dart over to me. "What about you? Have you seen…anything?"

I swallow, forcing myself to tell the truth and the whole truth. "Once, I saw you running downstairs for a glass of water…without any clothes."

Remi's eyes widen by a few degrees. She breathes slowly through her nose.

"And…I waited and watched you go upstairs again," I admit. "And then jerked off afterward."

Remi takes steady breaths, her face deeply pink.

I can't gauge her exact level of rage. All I can hope is that she'll forgive me.

At last, with steely calm, she says, "What gives you the right to put a camera in my house?"

"I have no right. And no excuse. All I can say is I'm sorry."

Remi sways slightly on her feet. She's pale as chalk, and there's a nasty scrape across her forehead. I'd like to kill that sheriff all over again—and his buddies, too.

Low and quiet, she asks, "Why did you do it?"

"Because I'm worried about you."

That's the plain and simple truth. And I'm praying she can see it, or feel it, or simply know it to be true.

"I care about you, Remi. I think someone's trying to hurt you, and I'll do whatever I have to do to protect you."

Her butterfly eyes search my face. She wants to believe me, but I haven't given her enough consistency. I haven't earned her trust.

She looks at me with so much longing, but her eyes fill with tears. "How can I believe anything you say when you've lied to me?"

That fucking cuts me, but it's true. I have lied to her.

"You're right," I spread my hands, wishing with all my heart I could take back every shitty thing I've done to Remi since the moment I met her. "I was an asshole when we met. I fucked with you and misled you. I didn't expect to develop feelings for you. I sure as hell didn't expect you to develop feelings for me. If I could go back and do it all from the beginning, you'd see how differently I'd treat you. But I can't. So let me tell you again, *I'm sorry*. I'll never lie to you again. And I'm not asking you to believe me—I'll prove it to you. Watch how I treat you today and every day moving forward…let me prove that I can love you like you deserve."

I hadn't meant to use that word at the end, but when it comes out, it feels exactly right…

I love her.

I knew it when I followed her around all night, watching the funny expressions on her face, hearing that loud, cackling laugh, observing her terrible dancing… I knew that I was watching my most precious, favorite person—the only person who's brought me happiness in years…my perfectly imperfect Remi.

And I knew it for certain when I saw her lying on the ground, bloodied and outnumbered but still fighting. That was the first time in my life I've felt the urge not just to fight but to kill. Because I knew I'd do anything to save her.

"I love you," I say to Remi.

Her mouth opens in shock.

"I love your work drive and your stubbornness. I love how you understand me and how hard you work to understand yourself. I love that you're brave, and you're bold, and you want the truth…"

I take her hand and link my fingers with hers.

"The truth fucking hurts sometimes, and it's scary… I don't want to admit to you the shitty things I've done, the ways I've fucked up…

because I worry you can't love me back if you know who I really am. But you can't love me at all if you don't."

Remi blinks, and two tears run down either side of her face until they join together beneath her chin.

"Ask me anything, Remi. I'll tell you the truth."

Her lashes are wet and black around clear blue-green eyes the color of a sunlit sea. A sea I could float in forever.

She whispers, "What happened to Tom?"

"I was a jealous ass," I say at once. "I picked a fight with him; I would have fought him."

"I'm talking about the ceiling in the ballroom. Someone sawed through the joists."

"I didn't do that. I've never been inside your attic."

Remi chews her lip, her expression troubled. "What about Gideon?" she blurts.

"What about him?"

"Where is he?"

I pause, sensing that we've stepped onto shaky ground.

Remi sees my hesitation, and her expression sinks. She takes a half step back from me.

"You saw him, didn't you?"

"I—"

"The truth, Dane. You promised."

I close my eyes and take several deep breaths.

I won't lie to Remi. Not anymore.

"Yes," I admit. "I saw him."

"*Oh my god…*" she whispers.

"But I didn't hurt him! Fuck, Remi, I even showed him where you lived…and I was extremely tempted not to. I wanted to tell him to go back to New Orleans and stay the hell off my road, but I was trying not to be such a piece of shit anymore."

She doesn't believe me. I can see it in her face, confusion and fear…fear of me.

I take a step toward her, and she flinches. I stop and stand still instead.

"I didn't hurt him," I repeat. "I haven't hurt anyone." I jerk my head in the direction of the sheriff and his fallen deputies. "Except those assholes back there."

"I need to ask you one last question…" Remi's lips tremble.

I don't know what she's going to ask, but I'm determined to answer honestly, no matter what it costs me. There's no other chance for trust between us.

"How did your son die?"

The pressure on my chest is instant and crushing, and the temptation to lie is a black wind howling in my ears. I don't want to speak that truth—I don't even want to remember it.

It's the truth I fear most of all because the guilt could kill me. It could rip me apart.

But keeping it inside is killing me every day.

"He drowned," I choke out. "In our bathtub."

Remi lets out her breath, and her shoulders sink. Her whole body deflates, and instead of fear and anger, all that's left is sadness.

"I'm sorry," she says.

Tears flow down my cheeks, hot and burning. "Don't give me sympathy…it was my fault."

The words are so painful, I can barely get them out, but they're true and I mean it—I deserve this misery and so much more.

The bitter blackness inside me is an ice storm that cuts everywhere it swirls, freezing and slicing my guts—numbness, then pain, then more numbness in a never-ending cycle.

I'm ready to sink into it, ready to lose myself in the storm like I have so many times before…until Remi wraps her arms around me. She hugs me and holds me, all her heat pouring into me from her arms around my body and her head against my chest.

At first, I just stand there, still numb and unbelieving. But the longer she holds me, the more her calm and her strength overpower the raging blackness inside me.

At last, my arms wrap around her, too, and then the circuit is twice as strong, her heat flowing into me and mine into her until our bodies relax and we're not clinging to each other like survivors anymore—we're just hugging, breathing deeply in rhythm.

"Tell me what really happened," Remi begs.

And for the very first time, I tell it all.

♫ *"Love Story"—Sarah Cothran*

"I loved Lila, and she loved me. But we were young and immature and made constant mistakes. It all felt so intense and romantic when we were thumbing our noses at our parents, eloping when she was only nineteen and I was twenty...but we were kids, stupid fucking kids, making stupid-kid decisions.

"We'd always had fights, but the fights got so much worse once we were living in the same house, constantly in each other's orbit. I was jealous when she'd go out in the day without me; she hated that I kept working nights when neither of us really needed the money.

"She'd scream and smash things, and I'd get cold and critical and shut myself away in my study or pick up extra shifts so I'd be gone all night long and then sleep in the day..."

I swallow hard, remembering the cycle, how it would repeat again and again...we'd apologize and make up, and then there'd be a week or sometimes only a couple of days of reconnected bliss until something would trigger one of us, and in an instant, we'd be tossed back into the hurricane, like it was raging right behind a door, never calming, always howling worse than the time before...

"Lila had always been...volatile. Her wildness and passion were what drew me to her. But once we were living together, I saw the uglier side of her and began to realize how little control she had over that part of herself. Once, she smashed a clock that had belonged to my grandfather, the most sentimental thing I owned...

"It really hurt me. I couldn't believe she'd do that, knowing what it meant to me. Afterward, she bawled and begged my forgiveness, and I gave it to her like I always did, but the amount of time that other Lila was in control began to increase, and the things she would do got worse and worse...

"When she was herself, she'd cry and beg me to help her, but that other part of her, that part that's inside all of us, that irrational mind, was on *fire*. And like a fire, it raged and spread because she couldn't control it—she'd never controlled it.

"Then she stopped taking her medication. And I realized things weren't even close to as bad as they could get."

I remember the day I found her pill bottles in the trash. She'd always kept them hidden from me. That was the first time I read the labels and understood what a cocktail she'd been taking all that time—uppers, downers, painkillers, antianxiety meds...

"Without the medication, she went into a deep depression—stopped talking to her mom, her sister, her friends. Then it was Lila who wouldn't leave the house. She started talking about how life is a cruise ship, and whether you're up on the lido deck by the pool or down in the boilers shoveling coal, eventually you get sick of the cruise and you want to get off...

"I didn't know what to do. Some days she'd seem happy again, manic, even—she'd clean the whole house and cook enough food for an army. But then an hour later, she'd be sobbing and crying on the floor because the steak burned or the soufflé fell...

"I tried to get her to go to therapy. I said we could go together. Lila hated therapists because her parents used to make her see a shrink who would tell them everything she said. Things got so bad between us, I said she had to do something, or I was leaving—and that's when she told me she was pregnant."

I hear Remi's soft intake of breath. She still has her arms wrapped around me, and I'm grateful that I don't have to look into her face. It makes it easier to get this all out while I can.

"I wanted to be happy...but I was fucking terrified. She was getting more unstable by the day—doing things she never used to do before. She wanted all the windows open in the house, all the time, even when it was raining, because she said she couldn't breathe without the fresh air... She painted the nursery pink before we knew if it was a boy or a girl because she said she knew she was having a daughter, that she could feel it..."

I try to swallow again, but my throat is too dry; my Adam's apple only jerks.

"That was the last fight we had. I told her we should wait to paint, and she got so upset, screaming at the top of the stairs, clutching at her belly... I was scared she might fall. Scared she might get so upset, it would hurt the baby somehow... After that, I let her do whatever she wanted.

"We stopped fighting, but the connection between us only deteriorated. She was trying to hide some of her strangest behavior from me, and I was trying to hide it from everyone else. I thought everything would be okay once the baby was born..."

I choke on my own bitter laugh.

"What a lie I told myself. When James was born, it got a thousand times worse. Lila's mother and sister visited—she was talking a mile a minute, full of energy like she hadn't just given birth. She wouldn't let anyone else hold the baby and kept pacing the room with James in her arms.

"Her mom pulled me aside, tried to talk to me in the kitchen. I said Lila was fine, just excited. After they left, she demanded to know what we talked about. I tried to explain without getting anyone in trouble, but she was furious, and after that, she wouldn't let anyone visit. She said they were trying to take James away from her..."

"Was she upset that he was a boy?" Remi asks.

"I'm not sure… She was quiet after the ultrasound, and she never repainted the nursery, she left it pink…but she seemed happy, and she started buying boy's clothes…"

My guts feel like bricks. That time is a cold black well in my mind—no matter what direction I tried to swim, I only kept sinking…

"She was fixated on James; she'd barely let him out of her sight… She'd feed him and diaper him and bathe him and change his clothes, sometimes several times a day—different outfits for breakfast, lunch, and dinner… But other times, she'd stand over his crib and stare at him while he slept, and her face would get blank… I'd say, 'What are you thinking about?' And one time she said…she said, 'Sometimes when I'm standing at the top of the stairs, I'm scared he's going to slip over the railing…like my arms will just let go…' and I knew, I fucking knew, Remi, that something was wrong."

Remi's round blue-green eyes gaze up at me, full of sadness and sympathy.

Sympathy I don't deserve.

I put my hands on her shoulders like I'll push her away, but I can't quite seem to do it. I'm so fucking weak.

"My son lived for thirty-two days, and every single one of those days, I was terrified for him. I stopped going to work. I stopped going anywhere… I'd wake up again and again through the day and the night. Every time Lila got up to feed him, I'd creep out of bed, too, and wait just around the corner, listening, sometimes peeking in…and she'd always just be sitting there, rocking him, nursing him, taking care of him like the best possible mom. But I knew, I fucking knew he wasn't safe…"

Remi's arms tighten around my waist. She's trembling slightly, but she doesn't let go.

I close my eyes and force myself to finish.

"One afternoon, she was nursing him, reading a book. I was reading on the other couch. The next thing I heard was screaming, and my head jerked up…

"Lila came running out of the bathroom naked, dripping water on the floor, saying, 'He drowned—he drowned in the bath...'"

Remi holds me so tightly, it's like her arms are the only things keeping me together against the maelstrom in my chest that wants to tear me apart—guilt and regret and the bitter black anger against myself...

"He drowned," I repeat. I make myself say it out loud. "My son drowned, and it was my fault because I fell asleep. And even more my fault because I didn't pick him up and carry him out of that house the instant I saw Lila staring down at him with emptiness in her eyes."

"You think she hurt him?" Remi whispers.

"I don't know!" I howl, clutching at my own face, my nails digging into my cheeks. "I don't know, and I'll never fucking know. She said she fell asleep, too; she said it was an accident. But when she looked at me, all I could see in her eyes was guilt. I couldn't know what really happened...because I didn't trust her anymore."

"I'm so sorry, Dane—"

"Don't apologize!" I bellow. "Don't give me sympathy! It's all my fault, every lie I told myself, every cruel thing I said to her...it's my fault she got so fucked up in the first place. It's my fault she had a baby to try to set things right between us. And it's my fault I didn't protect him—that was my one job, to keep him safe, and I failed. I fucking failed him..."

Remi shakes her head silently, tears running down her cheeks. I am trying to push her away now because I can't stand her sympathy, I don't deserve it, but she clings to me, stronger than she looks.

"And I failed Lila worst of all." My voice is hoarse, tears dripping off my jaw onto Remi's hair. "Because it really might have been an accident, a fucking horrible accident...but I blamed her. When she looked to me for comfort, all she found was judgment."

I have to tell Remi this last part even though it twists like a knife in my guts.

"I falsified the death certificate—got an old friend to help me out. He wrote that James died of meningitis. I didn't want anyone to know what really happened. But when I told Lila…it was like admitting I thought she did it on purpose. The look on her face—it was pure betrayal. She stopped talking about James. She stopped talking to me about anything. Stopped eating. Stopped going for walks…"

Lila pulled away from me, and I let her go. Instead of turning to each other in our greatest pain, we closed up like clams and isolated in our hollowed-out house.

I'd never heard silence like when James was gone. He'd only been there a month, but my ears were already tuned to his little gurgles and cries. The emptiness without him was like the barrenness of outer space.

"On the last day, Lila asked me to go for a walk. I agreed because it had been so long since she asked me to do anything. Since we'd even spoken to each other. As we walked along the river, she kept stopping to pick up stones. I thought that was a good sign…she used to collect flowers and shells and pretty stones to fill jars to decorate our house.

"When we got back to our yard, she said, 'I'm going to walk a little longer…'

"I let her go and went back inside the house. An hour later, I started to get worried. I went looking for her…"

I can't finish. My head hangs down. All I can see is Lila, facedown in the river, her dark hair tangled with weeds and branches, her pockets full of stones…

"It's my fault," I repeat. "All my fault. And that's why I don't care that everybody thinks I killed her. I did fucking kill her. I fucked up our relationship, and then I fucked up again when she needed me most. And I didn't keep James safe, which means I'm no kind of father at all. He deserved better. They both did."

"Maybe they did," Remi says, lifting her head, looking into my eyes. "But so do you, Dane. You deserve better, too."

"Why?" I cry, my voice cracking. "How could I deserve anything good after what I did?"

"Because you're human." Her eyes fix on mine, clear as the sea. "And humans make mistakes. Every single one of us. Isn't that what you told me? How many waves are in the ocean?"

"Infinite," I murmur.

"And how many mistakes will we make?"

"Infinite."

"We can't change the past," Remi says, calm and clear. "We can only change what we do now."

Her arms are wrapped tightly around me still. She hasn't let go.

I told her the truth, and she hasn't let go.

She's still here with me, holding me, accepting me, in spite of it all.

And maybe I don't deserve this comfort...

But I need it so fucking badly.

I need it so much, I almost don't tell her the last thing, the thing that matters most of all...

But like I told Remi, I'm trying not to be such a piece of shit anymore.

"I was afraid," I tell her. "Afraid to admit that Lila and I were hurting each other. Afraid to see how bad it was getting. Paralyzed from acting until it was too late... I said you were like me, Remi, but *don't* be like me—do you understand?"

I hold her by the shoulders, looking into her eyes. Looking at the real, essential part of Remi, the part that sees me, too.

She gazes back at me, nodding slowly. "You're saying...don't be afraid of the truth."

"No matter how ugly it might be."

CHAPTER 31
REMI

I EXPECT THE SHERIFF'S DEATH TO ROCK GRIMSTONE—AND IT certainly is the topic of gossip with the townies everywhere I go. But I underestimated how much power the hoteliers have and how good they are at hushing up anything that might turn away tourists.

The speed at which they install a new sheriff and send him around to have a "chat" with me is nothing less than spectacular. By two days after Halloween, they've made it perfectly clear that they'll ignore the shady circumstances of Sheriff Shane's stabbing and the disappearance of my ex-boyfriend as long as I keep my mouth shut about any "unpleasant interactions" I might have had with local law enforcement.

I can't tell if I'm getting a good deal or completely fucked.

"And either way, this is so messed up!" I tell Dane. "What about Gideon?"

He shrugs. "I told you, this place is rotten to the core."

"Then why do you stay here?"

Dane sighs. "Because it feels like home even when I don't want it to. I've always lived here. I've always been a part of it, rooted to the bone. I told myself I stay here as a punishment, but there's no lock on my chains. I'm here because I choose to be."

In a strange way, I understand.

I think about staying in Grimstone more often than I think of leaving.

But maybe that's only because of Dane.

He grows here, and only here, like one of his phosphorescent mushrooms, eerie and rare.

And maybe he's poisonous...but he lights up my night.

"How bad a thing would you forgive?" I ask him.

"I don't know." He looks at me, stroking his fingers through my hair. "Pretty bad."

"Me, too. Probably too bad. Way over the line."

"What line?" Dane says. "Who's drawing it? All I know is how I feel."

He puts his arm around me and draws me close. We're swinging lazily in his hammock, with a blanket over us because the nights are getting colder.

Dane's hammock swings in a rare space without tree cover so he can use it for stargazing. Tonight, the stars are thick as sand on the beach.

He's been helping me finish the gazebo. I brought it over to complete at his house before it gets too big to fit in the back of my Bronco.

Even when I was the most frustrated with Dane and didn't expect to speak to him again, I never could picture the gazebo anywhere but inside his garden, draped in gently glowing lichen.

It was a little tricky to finish without my sketch. My notebook went missing, and I haven't been able to find it anywhere, which really bums me out—it had the designs for all the furniture I built before, as well as sketches for a dozen different projects I haven't even started yet.

I'd really like to stop losing my shit. Get organized and stay that way.

But that really would be a different Remi—someone I'd barely recognize.

I yawn and ask Dane, "How do you know if someone's past changing?"

He considers.

At last, he says, "Everybody fucks up. And everyone can change. But real change is painful, and for some, it might just kill 'em."

"*Kill* them?"

"Yes," he says seriously. "Because you have to kill the part of yourself you don't like. And for some people…that's almost all of them."

He brushes his lips lightly against mine, smiling. "Why? Are you talking about me?"

I laugh. "No. I'm thinking about myself. Wondering what flaws I really could change."

"Anything," Dane says at once.

"You really believe that?"

"I do. The mind creates itself. And sometimes it must tear itself down again."

I kiss him on all the parts of his face: his forehead, his cheekbones, the side of his mouth, the edge of his jaw.

"Sometimes you sound so crazy. But then, you convince me."

"Crazy isn't an on-off switch. Everyone's crazy…when they're being irrational."

"And everyone's irrational."

He nods, lips pressed together. "And what will the irrational mind do?"

"I don't know."

"Anything," Dane says at once. "The irrational mind will do *anything* and justify it to itself."

That's an awful thought. But the sinking in my chest tells me it's true. I've done things I never thought I would do. *Often.*

Dane makes me feel wild and untethered but also like I don't have to be afraid of the worst parts of myself. Like I could at least throw a leash over the monsters—and maybe even tame them.

"Do you trust me?" he says.

The answer comes easily, so easily that I'm surprised.

"Yes. You came clean with me, and I'm clear with you. I think you want good things for me, and you're showing me that every day."

Dane gives me a wicked look. "I think I was pretty soft on you all along."

I laugh. "I can't say I *hated* anything you did…"

"And some things became quite a favorite…" He slips his fingers down the front of my shirt and pinches my nipple, gently tugging at the ring.

Dane is a master at linking sensations in my body. The way he plays with my nipples and my clit makes it a near certainty that when he touches one, the other instantly awakens.

I squeeze my thighs together around his leg, my shorts riding up so his jeans rub against my pussy lips.

He turns me on so fast, it's embarrassing. I'd like to have a little dignity, but it feels so good to sink into the feel and the smell of him. There's something so pleasing about the texture of his skin under my hands, I'm always reaching under his clothes to touch his body.

"I want to show you that video," Dane says. "From when I hypnotized you."

I want to keep kissing his neck and maybe pull down my shorts, so we're not on quite the same wavelength.

I try not to pout as I lie back in the hammock, saying, "Okay…"

My heart rate is already increasing. I don't know why I freaked out so badly the day Dane tried to show me the video of our hypnotism session, but I sure as hell didn't want to see it then, and right now, my body's sending the same message.

"Maybe we could watch it later…"

"Relax." Dane puts his arm around me, pulling me against his warm chest. "I promise, you had fun."

That intrigues me enough that I sink into Dane's incredibly calming body heat and let the hammock sway.

He pulls up the video from our second session. It seems so long ago, even though it's only been a few weeks. The on-screen version of myself looks tense and nervous, especially when Dane gets close. That Remi wasn't as comfortable with that Dane.

But as he goes through the visualization portion of the session, I watch my shoulders loosen and my head droop and my breath become slow and steady.

"*How do you feel?*" Dane asks in that smooth, low voice of his.

"*Good...*" the on-screen Remi says. "*Relaxed.*"

It sounds like me, but also...it doesn't. My voice is softer and lower and looser. Like I surf for a living. Like I know what I'm doing.

I stare at this new version of myself on the screen, who sits calm and still, who doesn't fidget or wince. No, this Remi is smiling slightly, her eyes closed without the slightest concern for what Dane might be doing or how she might look to him.

"*How does your body feel?*"

On-screen Remi stretches her arms over her head and points her toes, uncurling like a cat. "*Fucking fantastic, actually. I think it's all the orgasms you've been giving me...it causes this chemical reaction that lasts for hours...*"

I clap my hand over my mouth, making an embarrassed squeak. On-screen Remi doesn't hesitate to spill my most intimate secrets to Dane as casually as if we're discussing the weather. "*I've never thought about sex this often... I'm really starting to get concerned. The number of times I've fantasized about you in pajama pants—it's border-ing on a fetish.*"

On-screen Dane gives a delighted laugh, and the one lying next to me smirks. He was waiting for that part.

"Oh, you're loving this..." I cover my face.

"Shh," Dane says. "Just watch."

"*What do you fantasize about?*" on-screen Dane inquires.

"Shut up!" I hiss at myself. "Don't tell him!"

But on-screen Remi has no intention of shutting up—she's here to destroy me.

She says, "*I'm obsessed with your hands... They're the nicest ones I've ever seen. And you can do all this clever, intricate stuff with them, but they're so strong, too... When they touch me, it's like magic. This sooth-ing, calming feeling spreads everywhere from your palms, all through my body... And the rest of your skin feels so good, too, on your back, your arms... I can't stop touching you, can't stop looking at you, can't stop thinking about you..."*

She pauses and at least has the good grace to seem embarrassed for half a second. But then she plunges on: *"You even have the most beautiful feet, and I never thought I'd say that about a man...They're so clean and smooth. You walk around barefoot in your house with your pajama pants kind of hanging low on your hips, that soft, dark material that makes you look like a ninja..."*

Her voice goes softer still, and she licks her lips. *"You're so scary and intimidating and capable...it makes me want to just...kneel down in front of you... It turns me on when you boss me around... It's like, every man I've ever met, I want to punch him in the nose when he tells me what to do, but when it's you, I want to give you everything, especially the things that embarrass me most...because it feels so damn good just to be near you..."*

I'm praying this is the worst of it. I'm already scarlet with humil-iation, my hands clapped over my face, peeking through the gaps in my fingers...

Dane's hand slips beneath the waistband of my shorts and touches my pussy lips. He presses softly, parting them just enough to rest his middle finger against my clit. His pressure is perfection. His touch works the buttons of my body and my brain, effortlessly informing me that I'm very, very fucking turned on.

Everything the on-screen Remi is telling Dane is true. That's exactly how I picture him, how he makes me think and feel... My brain associates him with marble and velvet, samurai and watch-makers, everything that fascinates and stimulates...

Dane's fingers slip inside me, and his palm grinds lightly in my favorite place. He rocks the hammock with his foot, timing the motion to the waves of pleasure radiating out from under his hand…

On the phone screen, I watch myself crawl across the floor. As I move, I'm stripping off my top and shorts and underwear, littering a trail, until I reach Dane's feet, naked and kneeling.

He's already barefoot.

I watch myself lie down on my back and spread my legs.

On-screen Dane gently steps on my pussy with the ball of his foot.

Real-life Dane rubs harder on my clit, fucking his fingers in and out of me.

My pussy spasms around his fingers as my eyes lock on the screen, fixated on what I'm watching myself do.

On-screen Remi moans the moment his smooth, pale toes touch her clit. All he's doing is stepping and pressing, and already she's coming, her eyes closed, her mouth open, her head thrown back.

In some ghost memory, I remember the exact texture of the sole of his foot, smooth and clean like his hand but firm and power-ful and so deeply degrading that I detonated like a land mine the moment he stepped on me.

I do it again right now under Dane's hand, exploding instantly at the filthy, erotic sight of myself doing what I *never* would have believed I would do.

If Dane would have described this video to me, I would have laughed in his face. I would have said, *There's no fucking way…*

But here it is, right in front of my eyes—the evidence that I don't know myself at all.

On-screen Remi bends her back, thrusting up her hips, fitting the mound of her pussy into the arch of his foot. She humps her hips, fucking the bottom of his foot like an absolute demon, mouth open as she comes like the choirs of hell…

I'm coming right now just from watching, just from the pressure of Dane's hand mimicking what I'm watching on-screen…

I'm remembering how it felt, and I'm feeling it all over again now, the embarrassment and titillation, the naughtiness of doing something so dirty and depraved, and the strange, reverse arousal of being turned on by the very extremism of what I'm willing to do...

Witnessing what I'll do for Dane proves to my brain how much I like him. My wild orgasms against the sole of his foot are the video evidence of how much he attracts me...

The Dane of real life rubs my pussy with his hand, his face flushed and triumphant, his eyes fixed on the screen.

When I touch his cock, I'm shocked by its hardness... It feels painful under my palm, stretched and hot and raging stiff. Dane makes a deep groaning sound and rolls his body so we're pressed tighter together in the hammock.

I grip his cock at the base, and he rocks his hips, fucking into my hand. I have to squeeze him *hard* because the texture of his cock is iron under tight, burning skin. His whole body shakes against mine, waves of pleasure rolling down his legs. Every time he thrusts into my hand, another deep groan wrenches from his throat, and another long wave of shivers runs down his limbs.

Dane switches the angle of his hand and pushes deeper inside me, rubbing with two fingers on the soft, swollen, aching place beneath my clit.

"Watch..." he murmurs in my ear. "This is my favorite part..."

"*Splits...*" the on-screen Dane orders.

On-screen Remi spreads her legs in the splits, or at least the best she can do because neither of us is that flexible.

On-screen Dane jerks his cock over her prone body.

I love watching Dane stroke his own cock—his hand is so beautifully shaped and strong. Watching how sensually his fingers move, how thick and straight and hard his cock looks in his hand... this is the porn I would film for myself, just Dane touching himself so I can listen to the fucking sexy gasps and groans he makes...

I try to stroke his cock the same way right now, mimicking the motion of his hand on-screen, bringing my palm all the way over the head of his cock, letting my fingertips drag lightly up the shaft and then swirl under the head...

Dane's fingers plunge in and out of me at the same pace, stroking and stroking at my most swollen, aching spot until my pussy pulses like a heart, until Dane's cock throbs in my hand, until our on-screen selves and our two bodies in the hammock have synced up, all of us controlled by the speed of Dane's hand...

The on-screen Dane erupts, a rope of white come spurting from his cock to splash down on my spread-open pussy.

The Dane in the hammock lets out a deep, guttering groan, his cock pointed at my cunt. The heat and weight of his load splashes down like a bucket of lava poured right on my clit. It's sudden and shocking and perfectly timed, so what I'm watching and what I'm experiencing overlap to blast my fucking brain.

My pussy is so swollen and sensitive, I feel his come on a molecular level. I'm bathed in it, submerged in it, blasted by it... My clit spasms and jerks as Dane rubs his semen in circles, as he gathers it up on his fingers and pushes it inside me...

It's like he's anointing me with it, like he's giving me his most precious gift...

My pussy twitches around his fingers, clenching, squeezing, wanting every last bit as deep inside me as it can possibly get...

The orgasm goes on and on.

Dane fucks me with his fingers as I stroke every last drop out of his cock. He drags it out until I collapse against his chest, shivering and limp, my thighs clamped around his hand. The Remi on the phone flops back on the carpet, her hand cupping her come-soaked pussy, her naked body spattered in white.

Dane's on-screen image picks her up and wraps her in a blanket, while real-life Dane tucks his phone back in his pocket.

"See?" he says. "That wasn't so bad."

I bury my face against his shoulder, shaking my head. My

voice comes out muffled and screechy, nothing like the girl on the screen.

"Oh my god, what the *hell*, Dane!? What was that, like our *second date*?"

"That's just the first part," Dane says. "We did way more than that."

"What?"

"Yeah…" He chuckles. "That's why I laughed when you acted like you'd never seen my cock before."

"Because I hadn't!" I lift my head to shout. "I thought the beach was our first time!"

"Ah, it'll all come back to you when you watch the video," Dane says. "Probably."

"How are you so calm?"

"Well," he says reasonably, "I remembered the whole time. There's nothing new to me on there; I was just surprised how well it worked. You are *quite* the subject—"

"And you're so fucked up!" I smack him on the shoulder. "I can't believe you got me to do that!"

He shrugs, grinning. "You seemed to enjoy it. Or at least, your pussy did…"

My head is reeling. Of all the things I thought I'd find on that tape…that wasn't it. "I don't understand…"

"What?" Dane says, still rocking us.

"I thought people wouldn't do anything they wouldn't usually do when they're hypnotized…"

"That's the point. You *did* do that…you *would*. You just didn't know it."

Dane looks at me like he expects me to understand.

And I'm afraid I'm finally starting to.

CHAPTER 32
REMI

DANE AND I DRIVE UP TO EMMA'S FOR BREAKFAST BECAUSE I'VE made her promise to behave herself, and even Dane can't deny that her pancakes are phenomenal.

Emma's become quite forgiving since I told her what happened on Halloween night. I think she feels guilty because she didn't notice I was missing for about two hours, and only then because she ran out of money and wanted to borrow a drink ticket.

It's funny to see her and Dane laughing and discussing mutual acquaintances—I sometimes forget that pretty much everyone here has known him longer than me.

Neither of them brings up the topic of Lila, and for that I'm grateful. I would really love it if Emma and Dane could at least not hate each other, even if there's too much water under the bridge for them to truly be friends.

While they're chatting, I amuse myself by reading the notice-board over Emma's shoulder. Somebody's already put up an order form for handmade wreaths even though Christmas is almost two months away. There's also a new missing-cat poster and one for a little mutt named Fitzie. That makes four in total—nobody ever took down the posters for the gray Persian or the golden retriever, so I guess they were never found.

"What are you looking at?" Dane asks.

"A lot of pets go missing around here…"

He glances at the board. "They probably got hit by a car. Or eaten by a coyote."

"Yeah." I nod. "Only…the bone the sheriff found in our sink came from a golden retriever. Or so he said at the time."

"How did he know that?" Emma perks up.

"It had a little fur on it."

Dane frowns. "Or he was the one who put it there."

I try to remember if Sheriff Shane seemed extra smug when I showed him the mess in the kitchen. "I thought it was weird at the time how he barely looked around the house."

"That's fucked up…" Emma looks nauseated. "You think he killed Mrs. Beeman's dog?"

"Maybe. I'm more concerned with what happened to Gideon."

I called Gideon's mom and his sister. Neither one had heard from him in almost a week now. It was an awkward phone conversation; Gideon hadn't even told them we'd broken up.

It's pretty obvious the sheriff and his two deputies were into some dark shit together—I don't know why they'd want to break into my house and fuck with me, but I also don't get why they enjoyed pulling girls into parks for Halloween gang bangs.

They could have targeted Gideon because he was from out of town. Or because they planned to pin it on me. The sheriff was over at my house pretty quickly, pointing fingers…

"Maybe one of the deputies will spill his guts," Dane says. "Rat out the other one for a lighter sentence or something…"

They're both sitting in a jail cell at the moment, so it's certainly possible. Sheriff Shane is in the custody of Rhonda's cousin Annie at the morgue.

I'm relieved that the deputies Dane beat to a pulp and stabbed in the stomach are doing okay, though only for Dane's sake—as far as I'm concerned, all three of those rapey bastards can burn in hell.

I took the rap for stabbing the sheriff, though I know I didn't.

I had the better argument for self-defense, and I couldn't risk Dane taking the blame, not with six knife wounds in Sheriff Shane's chest.

But I'd sure like to know who that fourth person was—if they existed at all. My jumbled memories are an exercise in frustration. I was fucked up on a whole new level that night, and I don't think it was just from hitting my head. I could barely stand after only three drinks.

"I better go," I tell Emma and Dane. "I've got a ton of work to do today."

"As opposed to your usual laid-back schedule." Emma laughs.

"I'll drive you." Dane grabs his coat.

Dane drops me off at Blackleaf, pulling up close to the barn because my Bronco and Jude's moped are taking up the better parking spaces. As I cut through the garden, I catch a whiff of a weird smell. It might be our trash heap piling up—I haven't made a run to the dump yet this week.

I head inside through the back kitchen door and find Jude waiting for me, the mail spread out in front of him on the table. I get a bad feeling as soon as I see his face.

"What's up?"

Jude's lips are so pale they've disappeared into the rest of his skin. "What's *up*…is I just received my acceptance letter from Portland State. Which is weird because I don't remember applying to Portland State. Or anywhere else."

Fuck.

"Okay. I can see that you're mad—"

"No, I'm not mad, Remi, I'm fucking *pissed!*"

Jude stands up from the table, and I remember that he's taller than me now.

"Look, I'm sorry…" I hold up my hands. "You don't have to go to Portland State. I just wanted you to have options. I thought if you saw an acceptance—"

"Why are you so desperate to get rid of me?"

Jude's jaw is so stiff, the words come out tight and clipped. His chest rises and falls in short little jerks. His pale hair is messier than usual, hanging down in his face like he was yanking on it while he looked through the mail.

I've really upset him, and I feel like shit about it. I wanted to encourage him, not make things worse.

"I'm not trying to get rid of you, Jude. I'll miss you like crazy when you're—"

"Then why are you always pushing this?" he interrupts, swinging his arms so wide, one of them collides with the pendant light over the table, making it lurch back and forth. "You're constantly bringing it up, putting pressure on me, acting like I have a choice, but there's no fucking choice!"

The kitchen seems tiny and claustrophobic and way too hot. But I can't back down, not on this.

"Because I want something better for you, Jude! I don't want you to end up a broke-ass loser"—I swallow—"like me."

I wince at the look of our dirty, dingy kitchen. I haven't done anything in here yet other than breaking up the old tile. The floor smells like mold from the overflowing sink. Our fridge is mostly empty. The rest of the mail on the table is unpaid bills.

"This isn't what I want for you," I tell Jude. "Not long-term."

"We won't be broke once we sell this place," he argues, disregarding the kitchen. "Then we can move anywhere we want."

I take several slow breaths, lowering my voice to a calmer level.

"I hope we make bank on the reno, Jude—but that's not going to solve all our problems forever. You still need to go to college and figure out a career, and I need to find the next place to flip. Maybe somewhere close, if this one goes well... I kind of like Grimstone."

I hesitate, but it's better to get it all out at once. I never should have hidden this from him in the first place. "Plus, uh, I've kind of been dating our neighbor..."

"*What?*" Jude's eyes narrow.

"Dane didn't kill his wife," I say quickly. "Their relationship was pretty fucked up, but the whole murdering thing was exaggerated."

"Oh, well, everything's cool, then," Jude says in disgust. "I can't fucking believe you, Remi."

"I like him." I'm getting defensive, and I know my face is red. "He's not like you think, and he's the one who saved me from those guys on Halloween night. If Dane hadn't come—"

"*He's* the one—!" Jude starts to shout something, then stops himself, shaking his head at me in outrage. "So, he's your savior now?" he sneers. "The guy threatens and extorts us, you thought he broke into our house, he's the most hated person in town, but you've decided he's perfect boyfriend material. Fucking *typical*, Remi—you're pulling out all your greatest hits."

The anger and disdain on Jude's face makes me feel about two inches tall.

When he says it all like that, it does sound pretty stupid and reckless.

And he's not done yet—Jude points his finger in my face.

"You're off the fucking rails—you have been since we got here. Something's wrong with you, Remi. You're fucked in the head. Quit trying to fix my life when yours is a train wreck."

He shoves the acceptance letter into the rest of the mail, making the whole pile shoot off the end of the table and scatter across the floor. Then he stomps out the back door.

CHAPTER 33
DANE

REMI'S THEORY ABOUT THE SHERIFF MAKES SENSE. HE PULLED HER over coming into town, targeting her pretty much from the moment she got here, and he didn't let up until he lured her into the park on Halloween night and almost succeeded in making her this year's victim of the Reaper's Revenge.

I should feel relieved, knowing that he's dead on a slab in the morgue, and his two buddies are locked up, too.

The only problem is...neither Remi nor I remember stabbing him.

Granted, she was drunk, and I was in a homicidal rage. I certainly *wanted* to kill Sheriff Shane and anybody else who laid a finger on Remi. It's possible I went blitzkrieg on him, or Remi did, or one of his own buddies who might have held a grudge.

But something keeps nagging at me, and around ten o'clock at night, I find myself pulling up the feed to the camera I hid inside Blackleaf.

It hasn't been much use so far, other than I like to open the app and get a peek at Remi whenever I miss her.

I know that's fucked up and inappropriate. That's why I'm glad Remi knows about it now, too—I really don't like lying to her. But she didn't ask me to shut it down. Because, in a weird way, I think she likes knowing I'm watching her.

She likes my attention. And she knows she's safer when I've got my eye on her. Because I won't let anything happen to her—not if I can help it.

I'm the only one who gets to fuck with Remi.

And I'm the one who will keep her safe…from the sheriff, from Gideon, and even from her own damn self.

I'm starting to think that's the real danger…what Remi won't admit to herself.

And maybe that's the reason I installed this camera in the first place.

To prove what I've suspected from the very beginning…

CHAPTER 34
REMI

I COOK A PROPER DINNER, HOPING JUDE WILL BE HOME IN TIME TO join me, but he ignores my texts. I end up sitting down alone to eat in the formal dining room, which is looking pretty damn good now that I've replaced the windows and floors, repainted the walls, and restained the woodwork.

I wonder if anybody could restore the old piano.

It's probably not worth the money to do it, but I couldn't bring myself to haul the thing outside and bust it up with a hatchet. That's why I wheeled it right back into the dining room when I was done refinishing the floors, even though the ancient grand weighs as much as a cruise liner and might possibly be haunted.

I touch one of the keys. The single mournful off-tune note sends a shiver down my spine.

If I chopped up the piano, I wouldn't have to worry about anybody playing it at night.

But I'd rather solve that mystery than eliminate it.

That's why I set my security camera on the mantel, pointed directly at the piano.

If it was our recently deceased sheriff breaking into my house, then those keys will stay quiet all night long.

But if not…the next note played will be caught on film.

After eating, I spend another three hours rebuilding the

bookshelves in the library. I'm getting pretty good at amateur carpentry, enough that I'm considering building the kitchen cabinets myself. It would save a lot of money, and I could stain them some trendy color, though maybe I should stick with something more neutral...

As I'm pondering my options, I hear Jude climbing the stairs.

"Hey!" I call. "I'm in here!"

If he's still mad at me, he'll probably walk right past to his room.

Instead, he pokes his blond head through the doorway and surveys the shelves. "Looks good."

"Thanks," I say, feeling ridiculously relieved. I hate when Jude and I get in a tiff—nothing feels right until it's resolved. "And listen— I'm really sorry about sending in those applications. I shouldn't have done that behind your back."

"It's fine," Jude says curtly. "You're right, it's time for me to be out on my own."

"...Yeah." I nod after a moment's hesitation.

Jude's frame fills the doorway, blocking the light behind him, so it doesn't quite illuminate his face. I can't tell if he's angry.

I mean, he's got to be a little irritated, but he also must know it's for the best, right?

"You won't be completely on your own... I'll still help out with money, and we'll talk all the time on the phone, I'll come see you at school, you'll come home on holidays...wherever home is..." I laugh awkwardly.

"Right."

Jude's tone is flat, and all I can really see is his silhouette. I get the urge to ask him where he went all day, but that would only piss him off more.

Instead, I say, "I left pasta for you in the fridge."

"Thanks."

"Well, good night..."

Jude turns and heads into his room, closing the door. I guess he isn't interested in reheated pasta. He probably already ate.

I work for another hour until my arms feel like liquid lead and my eyelids are drooping. Then I take a blessedly warm long shower and finally roll into bed.

The wind is howling. The ship is rocking. Not rocking in a soothing way like it usually does at night, but in huge uneven rolls that almost toss me out of my bunk. Even so, it takes me a long time to wake. I have to force my eyes open against lids that feel glued shut.

I shriek when a cold hand touches my arm.

It's Jude, his eyes huge in his small face. He sleeps on the top bunk, but he's not on the top bunk right now—he's crouching on the floor, wearing a coat over his pajamas.

"Remi…" he whispers. "Something's wrong. There's water in the hall…"

Jude turns his head and gives a hacking cough into the crook of his arm. His hands are filthy, streaks of grease on his coat.

"Where's Dad?"

He shakes his head. "I don't know."

When I open the door to our tiny room, water sloshes in the hallway. We climb the steep steps to the hatch and look out, but there's no one on the deck, and the ship isn't properly anchored. The wheel turns back and forth as the boat reels. Lightning cracks and rain pours sideways, lashing the sails to ribbons.

We're practically hurled back down the steps; I have to catch Jude to stop him from falling, my shoulder joint screaming.

The water's deeper in the hallway now, up to our ankles, and black smoke billows from the direction of the engine room.

"Get a life jacket!" I tell Jude, rifling through the cabinets. But then I see he's already wearing one under his coat. I pull the life jacket over my own head instead.

We slosh down the hallway to our parents' room. The door is locked.

I knock and then hammer on it with the side of my fist. The seconds drag past with no answer as smoke pours down the hallway, making Jude cough worse than ever.

"DAD!" I bellow, hammering on the door. "MOM! DAD! Wake up!"

At last, after what feels like an eternity, our dad wrenches open the door with a splintering sound. Half the frame rips free, the tips of exposed nails pointing in all directions.

"Remi?" he mumbles.

His eyes look sleepy and dazed. He's still holding the door handle, swaying with each roll of the ship.

"The boat's sinking!" I shout. "The engine's on fire, and there's water everywhere…"

He stares at me like he doesn't understand what I'm saying. His eyes are dull, his expression confused.

"Something's wrong with your mom," he says at last, slow and slightly slurred. "She won't wake up…"

The ship lurches, and a wine bottle rolls across the floor behind my dad. He's drunk, they both must be—that's why he's acting so stupid and slow…

"We have to get out of here!" I shout, trying to wake him up so he'll be himself again, so he'll take action and save us.

He stares between Jude and me, blinking slowly, so fucking painfully slowly. Then he gazes back at the bed, where I can see my mother's hand hanging over the edge of the mattress, her fingers tangled in her blond hair.

The ship rolls the other way, throwing Jude and me against the wall and knocking my dad sideways into the door. This time it stays tilted at a crazy angle, and more water rushes down the hall. Black smoke fills the air, making us hack and choke.

"DAD!" I scream.

He blinks again, shaking his head as if to clear it, but that only makes him more unsteady on his feet. "Get—get Jude in the lifeboat," he mumbles.

"But what about—"

"Get him in the boat." He hangs on the door. "I'll bring your mom."

I don't want to leave him there, but the water is rushing in, flooding down the hall, pouring into my parents' room. The angle of the floor grows steeper. The hallway up to the hatch is like a ramp now.

Jude clings to my hand, terrified.

"Remi!" he squeaks.

I have to get him out of here, but I can't leave our parents.

"Dad—"

"GO!" our father shouts, pushing us.

I slosh back up the hallway, leaning forward against the increasing angle, dragging Jude along with me. It's even more difficult to force the hatch up against the wind.

I know where the lifeboat is; I even know how to launch it because my dad makes sure to show us whenever we take a trip like this, just in case. He's an optimist, a glass-half-full person, but he still reminds us about the life jackets and the raft, every single time.

I help Jude climb into the lifeboat, but I don't pull the lever to lower it down, even though the ship is tilting and it's lifting the raft, too, hoisting us high above the water. The waves are wild enough to splash over the side of the raft, soaking our legs.

The idea of bobbing in this tiny boat on these mountainous waves horrifies me, but the front of the ship is dipping lower, and I don't know if Dad's going to be able to get it straightened out…

Every second is agonizing. I'm watching the hatch, waiting for our parents to emerge.

"Remi!" Jude sobs as the ship makes an awful wrenching sound and the bow sinks.

"It's okay," I tell him. "They're coming…any second…"

"REMI!"

I drag my eyes away from the hatch, toward his terrified pale face.

"It's sinking!" he shrieks. "We have to go!"

The crash of piano keys wakes me.

I lie on my bed, rigid as a board, my heart hammering.

My instinct is to go sprinting out of bed like before, but this time I'm not going to rush around in a panic. I'm going to act with deliberation.

I grab my phone and pull up the app for my security camera, finding the motion notification and scrolling back to watch.

The dining room is dark, only a little moonlight coming through the unshuttered windows, gleaming on the open keys of the piano.

A shadow moves in the corner of the frame, and something hits the camera, knocking it sideways, turning it to face the wall. Then the piano keys crash and boom, while the lens records nothing but plaster.

Someone snuck in from the side and moved the camera.

Like they knew it was there.

And that person is inside my house right now.

A cold, tingly feeling begins at the crown of my head and spreads all the way down my spine…

That feeling is determination.

I slip out from under the covers and pad across the room in my bare feet.

♫ *"Bitter and Sick"—One Two*

I should be terrified as I exit my bedroom and walk down the dark hall. And I *am* terrified, but not with physical fear. It's more like existential dread—the understanding that whatever I thought my life was, it's about to change.

One way or another, this ends tonight.

I descend to the second level and stand outside Jude's door, listening. I don't hear snoring or even heavy breathing. Quietly, I turn the knob and peek inside.

I see his shape, the long line of his back humped beneath the blankets. He's always slept like that, the blankets pulled all the way up with just the tip of his nose poking out so he doesn't smother.

But as I listen, I still hear…nothing.

So I cross the room and yank back the covers.

Underneath, I find four pillows, expertly bunched up to create the exact shape of Jude when he sleeps on his side with his blanket over his head.

I stare at the pillows. Then, slowly, I pull the blankets back over them and shut the door again with the softest of snicks.

When I reach the main level, my toes land in cold water. A fresh lake spreads across the entryway, flat and dark, two inches deep. I slosh across it in my bare feet, headed for the kitchen.

The water is running again, overflowing the sink, flooding the floor. I shut off the faucet, gazing down at the deep, dark basin.

I don't want to put my hand down that drain.

I'm dreading it with a revulsion that makes my stomach roll and all the little hairs stand up on my arms…

But I take a breath and plunge my hand down into the frigid water anyway, reaching through the slime and muck to find what's been jammed inside…

I can feel it, skinnier than before, clogged with mud and leaves and stones, and softer in texture, almost rotting…

I dig out the object and hold it aloft as water glugs down the drain.

A human finger.

There's no mistaking it this time because the finger is only days old, still clad in moldering flesh and somehow horribly familiar to me, even without checking the inscription on the gold class ring…

This is Gideon's finger.

I drop it on the counter, turning my mouth into the crook of my arm to hold back the bile rushing up my throat.

A pair of boots stands by the back door.

My boots. Caked in mud.

A dirt-crusted shovel is propped next to the door.

My stomach rolls over again at the sight of those boots.

I get an even sicker feeling when I try to imagine what that shovel's been burying.

There are two minds in there...two Remis...

All these strange sounds no one heard but me...

All these occurrences inside the house, with the doors and windows locked: piano keys, dishes smashed, kitchen flooded...

I thought maybe you'd been sleepwalking...

I've been feeling like I've been going crazy for almost a year now. No, much longer than that...

The nightmares have been torturing me since the *SeaDreamer* went down, dragging my parents to the depths of the Atlantic.

I woke up groggy that night, confused and disoriented, unable to remember what had happened for hours before...

I don't want to lie to myself anymore...

"No, no, no..." I whisper, covering my hands with my mouth.

It can't be. It's impossible.

Isn't it?

I could stop right now. Call the cops. Call Dane, even.

But I'm not going to do that. The day of reckoning has come... and I'm finally ready to meet it.

Leaving the boots and the shovel, I exit through the back kitchen door.

Chunks of mud trail down the steps and across the garden. A pair of drag marks furrows the dirt, leading into the woods.

I could follow the mud and the drag marks.

It's almost like they were left there on purpose, like breadcrumbs...

I even have a pretty good idea of what I'd find at the end.

Instead, I turn and gaze across the garden at the sagging shape of my uncle's old work shed.

I haven't gone in there once since we came to Grimstone.

At least…not that I remember.

The barn looms up in the dark, weeds choking the path to the entrance, that strange, unsettling smell leaking out from the gaps between the boards.

The wooden doors groan on their hinges, releasing a gust of fetid air as I step inside the stuffy space. Spiderwebs tickle the back of my hand when I grope for the light switch.

The light flickers on, revealing a jumbled space stuffed from floor to ceiling with junk. The towering piles of trash lean against one another: old bicycles and machinery, stacks of books and magazines and newspapers, broken lanterns, rusted saws, camping tents, even a canoe balanced on its nose.

Jude hasn't cleaned this place out at all, not one bit.

And if I'm honest with myself…I knew he wasn't working on it.

Traps dangle from the rafters—coil spring traps, the type you step on that close around your ankle like teeth, raccoon traps that look like a collar and chain, and small cages with doors that slam shut.

The traps are the source of the smell, or part of it, anyway—the clinging bits of bloody fur give me a pretty good idea why so many pets have been disappearing from Grimstone.

And maybe something bigger, too…I stare with horror at a bear trap with dark blood crusted on its teeth.

The far wall is papered with drawings—strange, disturbing scribbles of eyes and mouths, moth wings, and dismembered limbs. Pages of bizarre poetry. And mixed in, my furniture designs, torn from my notebook—pinned up with everything else like the mad ramblings of a seriously fucked-up brain.

"Remi?" a voice says behind me.

My brother steps inside the shed. He's wearing his pajamas, his hair rumpled like he just woke up.

"The kitchen's flooded again…" He looks around the workshop, blinking like he's confused. "What's all this?"

"You tell me."

Jude tilts his head, regarding the drawings on the wall. "What do you mean?" His voice is strangely flat. "That looks like your handwriting to me."

The funny thing is, it *does* look like my handwriting.

I'm having a slow-motion panic attack. Each beat of my heart is a seizure, the muscle squeezing so hard, it feels like it will never relax.

It can't be true, it can't be true, it can't be true...

But is it?

"I didn't do this." My voice comes out croaky and unsure. "I didn't trap any animals. I didn't put those drawings on the wall."

"Just like you didn't flood the kitchen?" Jude shakes his head, his expression pitying.

"I didn't do this," I repeat. "None of this is my fault..."

Isn't it, though? Who else could be responsible...

"Remi..." Jude's voice is silky and soothing. Encouraging, even. "Be serious. It's time to come clean. About everything. There's no ghost playing the piano. There's no one breaking into our house. Gideon didn't go missing..."

"What are you saying?"

"You know what I'm saying."

"No. I don't." I cross my arms stubbornly over my chest. The rotting, coppery scent of the dangling traps makes my stomach churn. I'm surprised Jude can even stand there. He's always been terrified by the sight of blood.

Or at least...he's always had a strong reaction.

You see what you want to see...

"Where were you just now?" I ask my brother.

"What do you mean?" He blinks. "I was in bed. Asleep."

But I already know that isn't true.

Sometimes you need just one more piece of the puzzle for the rest to make sense.

For me, it was remembering the nails in the doorframe of the *SeaDreamer*...

All those little silvery nails, their jagged tips pointing in every direction when my dad ripped open his bedroom door...

Why were they there?

Because his door was nailed shut. Nailed all the way around the frame like a coffin, to take my parents to their watery grave.

Piece after piece clicks into place.

The life jacket under Jude's coat.

The grease on his hands.

My grogginess, when I could barely lift my eyelids...

The glazed look on my dad's face...

"You drugged us," I whisper.

Jude blinks again so fast, it's barely more than a flutter of his pale lashes.

That's always been his tell.

"What do you mean?" he says sharply.

I ignore him, gazing at the scribbles on the wall. The rambling poetry, the fake journal entries...it looks like my handwriting. Sort of. Almost.

Except the loops on the *g*'s and *f*'s aren't quite right.

Just like when Jude used to forge my signature on the notes he'd write to excuse himself from school.

I let out a sigh that comes from the very bottom of my soul.

"You must think I'm so fucking stupid."

Something in my tone tips him off that this time isn't like the other times. The look of innocent confusion falls off Jude's face with unsettling speed, replaced by an even more disturbing blankness.

The hanging light bulb casts deep shadows around his eyes, so they resemble nothing more than holes in his bone-white face.

"Well..." Jude says, "you weren't supposed to come in here yet."

Even his voice sounds different—lower, flatter, missing some softening element.

My scalp prickles, and I want to take a step back, but I force myself to stay right where I am, to pretend like I'm in control of this situation.

"Where did you think I'd go?" I try to sound strong, confident. "Out to the woods to find whatever you buried?"

"What *you* buried," Jude murmurs.

My exposed skin goes clammy as a fish.

My brother's expression contains none of what I would consider characteristically Jude—no mocking humor, no mischievousness, no affection. His face is as tight and smooth and featureless as a skull.

I lick my lips. "I haven't buried anything."

Jude gives the smallest of shrugs. "It's your boots covered in mud. And your fingerprints on the shovel."

"And my ex-boyfriend under the dirt."

Jude's mouth curves into the ugliest of smiles. His hands are tucked in his pajama pockets as he blocks the one and only doorway out of the barn. Coldly, he says, "I never liked Gideon."

"He never liked you either."

It was one of the biggest conflicts in our relationship—Gideon never seemed to have anything nice to say about Jude, which really bothered me at the time. He was always pressuring me to make Jude get a job, stop giving him an allowance, crack down on him about his schoolwork, and tell him in no uncertain terms that Gideon and I were moving in together, that Jude was going to have to move into college dorms or get his own apartment...

Those were the conversations I was supposed to have with Jude once Gideon and I got engaged. But instead, right after Gideon put that ring on my finger, I started to notice the smell of perfume on his coat...and then I found the first bobby pin in his truck, on the floor mat of the passenger side, like it had been left there just for me...

"Gideon never cheated on me," I say out loud. "The hair clips, the lipstick, the perfume...that was you."

Jude smiles, and this smile is the most disturbing one yet because there's so much pleasure in it.

"Baccarat Rouge…" he says. "I'm sure you wondered."

He crosses to the workbench and opens a drawer, pulling out a small glass bottle. He sprays the perfume in the air, instantly filling the barn with the hateful scent of jasmine. It mingles with the sweetly rotting smell of old blood. My stomach heaves, the chicken breast from dinner attempting another appearance.

I remember the hundred times I smelled that perfume on Gideon's clothes, in his car, even on his sheets…

"Did you have his key?" I croak, my throat choked with suffocating sweetness.

"I had copies of all his keys. That wasn't the hard part." Jude frowns. "The hard part was how many times I had to plant evidence on him before you'd actually break up with him. Fucking pathetic, Remi."

That's right. I could never quite seem to do it, no matter how the smell of that perfume tortured me…

Until I found the thing that finally made me dump Gideon for good—a used condom on my side of the bed.

I held it in my hand, lifting it to check if it really had been…*used*.

Now the chicken does come up in a rush of hot vomit, spattering on the filthy floorboards.

I wipe my mouth on the back of my hand, groaning. "You sick fuck—you left a condom in my sheets."

"Yes," Jude says, and something in the way he looks at me makes me want to puke all over again.

It's like the look on his face when he saw the stitches on my thigh.

"You're not afraid of blood," I mutter, another puzzle piece clicking into place. The so-called vegetarianism, the way he'd stare if he saw something violent on TV, then leave the room to go to the bathroom or his own bedroom… "It turns you on."

Jude's lips twitch. "I'm not afraid of anything," he says with chilling calm.

"Why were you fucking with me when we moved into the house? Why did you want me to think it was haunted?"

Jude makes an irritated sound. "At first, I was just annoyed with you for making me sleep in the car. But then you brought that redheaded *amoeba* here, and I could tell it was going to be Gideon all over again…" He pauses, his expression darkening. "I didn't realize you were fucking the wife murderer on the side."

"You sawed through the boards. You made Tom fall through the ceiling."

He smiles, pleased with himself. "That was partly for you and partly to get back at that little Emma cunt—bringing her fucking blueberry muffins over just to spite me."

"You tried to kill Tom over a couple of *muffins?*"

"He didn't die," Jude says, though it's perfectly obvious he wouldn't care if he had.

It's like he's a different person. The expression on his face is like no expression I've seen on him before—flat, devoid of emotion. It really is like a mask. Only, I get the feeling it's the other expressions he wears that are the masks—this is what he actually looks like underneath.

I can't believe it.

And at the same time…I finally do believe. Because I can see what I should have seen all along.

My brother's an asshole.

No, strike that. He's a straight-up psychopath.

Let's call a spade a spade for once in my damn life—it may be the last chance I get to be honest with myself.

"You killed our parents."

I don't expect him to admit it, but in a strange way, my brother almost seems proud to tell me these things. It's like he's been waiting for years to finally brag about how clever he is.

"Ding, ding, ding!" Pinpricks of light glitter in his dark eyes. "Though I guess you could say they got the last laugh."

"I don't think they'd see the humor."

"Why not? Even I had to laugh at myself after I went to all that trouble just to find out they were broke."

That's what he says, but Jude doesn't look amused in the slightest—actually, he seems deeply, bitterly angry. Like it was my parents who fucked him over, and he's the innocent victim.

"You were ten years old," I whisper.

"Yeah, and I wanted to get rid of them since I was six. Especially that bitch."

"Our *mother?*"

"A self-obsessed wannabe–social climber," Jude spits. "But she was only an irritation—*he* was the problem."

My stomach lurches as a thousand forgotten memories flood through my brain. Times my father would watch Jude and then look away, frowning slightly. Times he'd try to talk to my mother, and she'd brush him aside…

He's bored at school. He's acting out…

The other kids pick on him. He's not the problem…

"He knew what you were."

"He suspected." Jude shrugs. "After a couple of little incidents at school, he was on my ass constantly…so he had to go."

The nightmare rushes through my head, each detail flashing like a silver fishhook that snags because none of it ever quite made sense…

Both parents asleep, nobody at the wheel of the ship, the life jacket already on under Jude's coat, the nails in the doorframe, the loopy, slurred way our dad responded…

"You drugged them," I repeat.

"You, too," Jude says casually. "Just not as much. A quarter of Ambien in your drink, and half a bottle in theirs." He snickers softly. "I doubt Marla even woke up."

Marla…like he barely knew her. Like she was just someone to hate.

I wish you were my mother...

My stomach gives another sickening roll.

I'm in a state of slowly mounting hysteria. It's like being inside a fun house with a hundred distorted mirrors. Which one is the real Jude? And which is the real me?

This can't be my actual brother, this creature standing before me with black pits for eyes and a cruel smirk.

"How could you?" I moan. "Our own parents, Jude..."

He takes the question as one of logistics rather than morals.

"The storm was a surprise. But at that point, I'd already drugged their wine, so..." Jude shrugs. "I wouldn't say it was the best plan, but I pulled it off pretty good for a ten-year-old."

"Pretty *well*," I correct him. "You probably should have gone to college."

That pisses him off, as I intended. His face flushes, and his lower lip sticks out, like it always does when he pouts.

"You'd fucking love that, wouldn't you?" he seethes. "You couldn't wait to get rid of me. I heard you plotting with Gideon, trying to shove me off to school so you two could move in together. He never wanted me around."

"Well, I guess he was more perceptive than me."

Jude's lip curls. "Everyone's more perceptive than you."

Don't tell me your stories about your brother...

There's only one way you're stupid...

Your brother's cute... Too bad he's a little shit...

I remember every time I defended Jude against teachers, boyfriends, friends...

I really am so fucking blind.

At least when it comes to him.

I thought of the discrepancies as fishhooks in my brain, but really, there was a poison dagger at the root of my tree. And every day, the poison spread until all the leaves were black with deception.

A relationship is only as strong as its trust.

I loved Jude. But did I ever trust him?

I couldn't trust Gideon, and I was easily fooled.

But Dane and I built trust, slowly and surely, as we learned to be honest with each other. We fucked up, we made mistakes, but we figured it out, we did better… And in the end, we took care of each other.

Jude said he loved me…but where was the proof? What did he ever do to show me? Buy me an ice cream? Set up a movie?

He lied to me. He didn't keep his commitments. He didn't help me when I needed him. He let me do all the work.

I didn't see it because I didn't want to see it—my brother never loved me at all.

Love is action.

Love is trust.

It's not words…because words can be lies.

My brother doesn't love me.

After everything I did for him, all the times I put him first…

He still doesn't love me.

The truth fucking hurts.

I feel it now, the pain of that truth rolling over me like a tsunami—cold, black, and crushing.

I let it hit me, again and again and again, not fighting it, not drowning in it…simply waiting for it to settle.

Because I've finally learned…

The truth hurts, but it won't harm you.

It's lies that injure and destroy.

Jude's hand shifts slightly within his pocket. "I was counting on you staying oblivious a little longer," he says. "At least until the renovations were finished. But you've done enough for me to make some money, I bet—god knows I won't be wasting it on college."

"So you don't need me anymore."

"I guess not," Jude says, and he pulls a pistol from his pocket and points it at my face.

CHAPTER 35

DANE

AT ONE O'CLOCK IN THE MORNING, WATER BEGINS TO SPREAD across the entryway of Blackleaf. I watch on my phone screen as Remi's barefooted figure comes hurrying down the stairs, turning into the dining room, and then reemerging a few minutes later, splashing across the shallow lake toward the kitchen.

I'm already standing and pulling on my shoes when I see something that makes my blood run cold: a second figure melting out of the shadowy entry to the ballroom.

From the blond hair and the pajamas, I know it's Jude, but from the way he follows Remi, I know that doesn't mean she's safe. Not even a little bit.

I never trusted that sneaky bastard.

Not from the moment I saw how he looked at Remi when her back was turned. It's like he had two completely different sets of expressions—the smiles when she's watching and the smiles when she's not.

Of course, Remi wouldn't hear a word against him.

That's why I never said anything even when I suspected exactly who was the "mouse" running across the piano keys.

But now I'm getting a very bad feeling that there might be more at stake here than a pissed-off girlfriend or a brother pulling pranks. Because the last time I saw Gideon, I pointed him in the direction of Blackleaf.

And if he never talked to Remi...

I'm guessing it's because Jude answered the door.

I grab my coat and my car keys and then hesitate, glancing at the black doctor's bag by the door.

Slipping my hand inside, I take my scalpel, too.

Blackleaf is dark and quiet, no lights burning at the house. I run in through the kitchen door anyway, shouting for Remi. When the heavy silence makes me certain there's no one inside, I dash back outside to the pumpkin-filled garden.

Mud crusts the back steps. I follow the mud to the two deep grooves cutting across the garden and leading into the woods...

I think of the hole I found in the forest, and my heart stops beating, and my vision goes black.

Those grooves better not be from Remi's heels.

They just better not be, because if that motherfucker hurt one single hair on her head...

I'm already running, branches whipping at my face.

If I didn't know where I was going, I never would have found the spot. Not in the dark, not without a flashlight.

But I know these woods like I know my own backyard. They *are* my backyard—and I remember exactly where I saw that shallow grave.

I slow my pace as I get close, my ears straining... My knees go weak with relief when I hear Remi's voice.

"Are you really going to do this, Jude?"

"You're the one who did this," Jude replies coldly. "I got us a fresh start, away from Gideon, just the two of us, the way it's supposed to be...and as soon as we got here, you were already ruining it all over again."

"Because I tried to make you go to school?"

"Because you're a traitor!" Jude shrieks.

Now I'm close enough to make out his pale figure in the gloom, his white-blond hair and the dark pits of his eyes in his narrow face—and most of all, the black barrel of the gun he has trained on Remi's chest.

Remi has a shovel in her hands, and she's re-digging the grave, uncovering the sickly rotting scent of what I assume is her ex-boyfriend.

Her brother watches her work, in a bizarre recreation of the first time I saw the two of them together. In fact, I'd wager it's their most characteristic dynamic.

"It was supposed to be you and me!" Jude cries, his finger twitching against the trigger. "That's what you said, Jude and Remi against the world—but as soon as Gideon came along, or Emma, or that fucking doctor..."

Remi scoops up another shovelful of earth, tears running down both sides of her face and dripping onto the dirt.

"I always put you first," she says bitterly. "Even when I shouldn't. That's why it never worked out with Gideon—because he was second place, and he knew it."

"He should be second!" Jude shrieks. As his thin shoulders shake, he looks both childlike and oddly ancient, deep lines of fury etched into his face. "I'm the one you're supposed to love! I'm the one you're supposed to take care of!"

Remi stabs the shovel down in the dirt, her hand clenched around the handle. She glares at Jude, her blue-green eyes bright and burning.

"Love goes both ways. You lied to me, Jude. You used me. You manipulated me."

"Pick that up!" He jerks the gun at her.

"No." Remi shakes her head. "If you're going to shoot me, you're going to have to shoot me here and now, face-to-face. I won't make it easy on you."

"You already have," Jude says, and he cocks the safety with his thumb.

There's no time for thought or planning. I launch myself out of the darkness, stabbing the scalpel straight down into his arm. The gun goes flying into the bushes. Jude and I roll around on the ground, kicking, punching, biting, clawing. It's a fight where I have all the advantage in height and strength, but Jude has become some kind of unholy animal, powered by desperation and rage.

I've lost the scalpel, but I manage to get my hands around his throat. I throttle him until the blood vessels begin to burst in his eyes, ignoring the punches he rains on my face and the deep gouges in my arms from his fingernails.

At last, he weakens, his pale face turning a dusky purple, until Remi screams, "STOP IT! BOTH OF YOU STOP!" and I realize she's recovered the gun and pointed it at us both.

I relax my hands on Jude's throat, but I don't let him up, pinning him in the dirt with my knees.

His face is filthy, blood in his teeth. The burst vessels in his eyes make him look nothing short of demonic.

Still, he softens his voice and tries to plead with his sister.

"It's not too late, Remi…" His tone is high and wheedling. "It can still be you and me. We don't need *him*. We can pin it all on Dane—Gideon, the sheriff—everyone already knows he's a killer. We'll be heroes. Or we can just bury him right here next to your ex. Nobody's going to look."

Remi's eyes meet mine, and I can see that hers are filled with tears—tears of pain and anguish and even love because love doesn't die so easily. No matter what Jude has done or how he's hurt her, she loves him still and probably always will.

"What are you waiting for?" Jude cries, his voice cracking. "You barely know him. I'm your brother! *I'm* the one who saved you from those cops, not him—"

"You're the one who drugged me in the first place," Remi says. "You gave me that drink with the lid already off."

"Only so you'd get sleepy and come home!" Jude howls. "I was looking out for you! I protected you! I love you, Remi—*I'm* the one who loves you, not him!"

Remi's head hangs. Her lips barely move as she whispers, "Then why do I always feel so alone?"

She turns to look at me. The sadness on her face could fill an ocean with her tears. "I'm sorry," she says. "I'm sorry I ever thought it was you…"

I shrug. "It's okay. How many mistakes do we make?"

Remi sighs. "Infinite."

"I forgive you. I'm always going to forgive you. I love you, Remi. I love you, and I trust you."

You can't have one without the other.

Remi and I have both.

"That's twice you saved me," she says. "Three times, if you count helping me to see the truth… Thank you for helping me to do better. Thank you for helping me to *be* better. I love you, Dane."

Jude shrieks in rage.

Remi still loves her brother, but she doesn't trust him anymore—which is why when he lunges at me, stabbing the scalpel upward at my neck, Remi is ready.

She shoots him in the chest.

Jude falls backward, blood bubbling from his mouth. His lips move silently as he curses the empty sky.

Remi throws the gun away and runs to her brother's side, lifting his head, her tears spilling down on his face.

But Jude is gone, beyond the reach of apology or regret.

EPILOGUE
REMI

I GUESS I FINALLY KNOW HOW DANE FEELS.

I was acquitted of murdering my brother and Gideon, but I don't think most people in town believe it.

Everywhere I go, they whisper and mutter behind my back.

Even Rhonda seems a little scared of me now—Emma says she's started calling me *the Black Widow*.

I can't say it doesn't upset me, but I've still got my true friends. Emma only finds me more interesting now that she thinks I've got a dark side, and I've started having lunch with Amy Archer, who has some pretty crazy stories of her own about her murderess mother.

The truth is, in Grimstone, everyone's got a dark side…

The question is, how tight a leash do you keep on your monster?

Dane says we're all a work in progress. I don't mind working… when there's someone there next to me. Since the day I lost my parents, I felt alone.

I thought it was because I was in charge of Jude and there was no one to take care of me.

We should have taken care of each other.

Love is trust and respect.

Jude never respected me, and I damn sure couldn't trust him.

It makes me cringe when I remember all the times he mocked me to my face.

You only see the good in people...
You only see what you want to see...

I used to have that nightmare of Jude being sucked down under the sea. What I should have realized is that Jude was already gone. He drowned his soul the day he killed our parents.

I was clinging to what I wanted to believe I saw inside him. My greatest fear was losing the only person I had left.

My attachment to that false image of my brother is what kept me so alone. I loved a lie without ever understanding why it felt so hollow.

Jude had his fangs deep in my neck, and he drained me dry. He took without giving. He kept me just weak enough to always be afraid.

It was Dane who told me I was smart and strong.

Dane helped me not to fear the truth.

He's asked me to move in with him when I sell Blackleaf.

I said I would—as long as he gets rid of that damn perfume bottle.

I don't want to smell florals for as long as I live. But I walk with him to bury it in the woods.

We bury it far from the Midnight Manor, in a quiet spot beneath a hemlock tree.

Dane lifts the dusty bottle and inhales its scent one last time.

"I'm sorry, Lila..." he says as he sets it in the ground. "For every time I hurt you and all the ways I broke your trust."

He covers the bottle with clean, soft earth.

Right next to it, I bury the picture of Jude and me I kept on my nightstand.

It was a picture from a happier time, but when I look at it now, I don't see it quite the same. I can't forget what Jude's face actually looked like beneath his mask. And I see it now, leaking through. His teeth smile at me in the photo. But not his eyes.

I lied to myself about who my brother was.

I lied about our relationship.

And it caused so much pain.

I'm responsible for what happened to Tom and Gideon—responsible in a hundred different ways. I made so many mistakes.

And I'll make a million more. But different mistakes instead of the same ones. I'll never be perfect, but I can be better than I was.

"How do you feel?" I ask Dane when it's done.

He sighs. "I can't get her forgiveness. But at least I can know I've changed."

"How do you know?" I ask him because I'm wondering for myself. "How do we know when we've changed?"

"We'll know if we're honest with ourselves." Dane lifts my hand to his lips and kisses it. "In everything we do right and everything we do wrong—no excuses, reasons, or justifications. Because when is it okay to lie to you? When is it okay to hurt you?"

"Never," I whisper.

"That's right. And I won't."

He still hasn't. And neither have I. Which is pretty good for Doctor Death and the Black Widow.

When I visit the Midnight Manor, it all disappears. There, Dane and I can be exactly what we want to be—which is completely obsessed with each other.

We explore our darkest fantasies and strangest urges. I discover who I am beneath his fingers, and he trusts me to love who he is at his core, in all his beauty and imperfection.

On a stormy evening in November, when Dane's on call, I visit him at his private clinic.

I hoped he'd be alone because of the weather. Sure enough, there are no cars out front—only a single golden light flickering in his window.

I knock on his door, my hair whipped around in a tornado of dry dead leaves, the hem of my coat flapping.

Dane pulls the door open, his expression haughty and cool until he sees me. Then that wicked warm smile spreads across his face. "How can I help you this evening?"

"Doctor," I say, stepping inside and unbuttoning my coat. "I've got a horrible pain… I'm aching and throbbing…"

I open my coat and slip it off my shoulders, letting it fall to the floor. Underneath, I'm wearing only strappy black lingerie with open cups to show my bare breasts and the nipple rings that immediately draw my lover's eyes. Dane's golden eyes gleam, and his sharp teeth flash.

"I'm sorry to hear that. Let me take a look at you, and let's see how I can help…"

He's so handsome in his white lab coat, my heart hammers my chest. His clinic is warm enough to make me sweat, even in my skimpy clothes. The small space is all dark wood, with neat shelves of books, beakers, and instruments. Dane leads me to the examination table.

"Climb up here…" He takes my hand.

I sit on the edge of the table, my bare feet hanging down. I already slipped out of my heels.

The game is the heat all around us. It's the cool professionalism in Dane's tone against the temptation flickering in his eyes and the smile tugging his lips.

"Let's listen to your heart first…"

He sets his stethoscope in his ears and presses its disc against my breast. His warm hand cradles my back while he applies light pressure to my chest, always watching my face.

My heart throbs like it means to speak directly to him, like it will sing all my secrets, all my love…

He hears it pounding, and his eyes soften. He leans forward and kisses me on the mouth.

"I'm so glad you came to visit me..." he murmurs. "I've been missing you terribly..."

Then he straightens, and his amber eyes roam my body with wicked intent.

"Now, let's see what I can do for you..."

He bids me to lie back on the table, a pillow beneath my head. Then he pulls on a pair of latex gloves. The gloves cling to his shapely hands and give me a deep thrill with their shiny, antiseptic look. They make Dane's hands look more dangerous and almost inhuman.

"Lie still..." he murmurs in that deep hypnotic voice.

He sets my heels up on the table so my legs are butterflied and cuts off my thong with a pair of shears.

As he pulls away the material, his warm breath touches my exposed pussy. My knees tremble.

"You're a sensitive girl..." Dane places his gloved hands on my knees and presses them gently apart.

I've never let a man examine my pussy like this, with the lights on, a few inches from his face. I have to trust that Dane will touch me without hurting me, and most of all, I have to trust that he likes what he sees.

That's the hardest part—believing that I'm beautiful to him. That I don't have to be ashamed or afraid.

But when I take that leap of faith, and I see the deep-rooted lust in his eyes, the way his breathing deepens and his tongue wets his lips...then I've never felt sexier. Blood rushes through my body, and my pussy becomes so sensitive and aching that I'd give my soul for the brush of his fingers against my lower lips.

"You have the prettiest pussy..." Dane growls, his eyes trained between my thighs. "It's like the cleanest, softest little flower, with all the petals closed..."

He places his gloved fingers against my pussy lips. "And I can open them up so gently and find the very center..."

He spreads my lips open with light, soft pressure, a tiny bit at a time, so I can feel each millimeter of skin, each delicate nerve. He opens me up, bit by bit, layer by layer, until I'm throbbing and gasping and my clit is completely exposed.

"There it is…" His eyes burn. "My very favorite part…"

He takes his index finger and rests it lightly on the very head of my clit. And presses down.

It's like he's pushing a button that makes me sink to the center of the earth. The whole room collapses in on me and I fall and fall and fall…

He rubs his finger in small circles, pushing, pushing down. I visit Hades and return again, yanked back by the hook of Dane's gleaming golden eyes.

"That's a very good girl," he says when I've finished coming.

His latex-covered fingers are both clinical and erotic. They stick to my skin, part instrument, part human.

I'm remembering the first time he touched me, the first time he stood so close. The intensity of his eyes, the power of his hands…

I remember how recklessly I swung that hammer, and part of me wonders if deep down inside, I meant to put myself on the doctor's table.

Don't lie… You're getting exactly what you want…

"I wanted you to touch me like this from the moment I saw your hands."

Dane smiles, his dimple flashing into view.

"These hands?" He strips off the latex gloves.

Now, when he presses his fingers against my pussy, they're warm and velvety. I gasp and shiver as he spreads and touches and strokes. He licks my taste off his fingers and touches their wet tips against my clit, stroking up and down.

"Tell me what you like…" he instructs. "Tell me what feels best…"

"A little softer…" I beg. He lightens by half. "A little harder than that…now faster…now a little faster…"

Dane adjusts by degrees until the speed and pressure become momentum, a sensation that spirals and builds beneath his fingertips like pottery spun into shape until he creates my orgasm under his hands, and I'm lost inside it, spinning and spinning until I collapse.

He slides his fingers inside me. "Squeeze..."

I squeeze as hard as I can.

"Very impressive..." His eyes hold mine. "Now relax..."

I relax the muscles. Dane waits until I'm soft and loose. Then he begins to move his fingers, sliding them slowly and gently in and out of me while I try my best not to clench.

Trying to remain loose and relaxed makes me exquisitely sensitive. The friction of that soft, slow slide is like the swaying of a hammock—gentle, hypnotic, and irresistible. It builds and builds in an entirely different way, while I try to stay calm, but the climax requires convulsion.

"Now squeeze..." Dane orders, his eyes locked on my face.

I clench hard around his fingers and detonate. It's an explosion of gold that washes over me, warm fire in the color of his eyes.

Dane unbuttons his trousers, and his cock springs free, thick and hard and pale. Its head is slightly pink like his lips.

When he presses it against my opening, I groan.

"Beg for it," he growls, holding my eyes.

"Please..." I whimper. "Please..."

He slides it in partway.

"Oh god..."

"That's just the head." Dane smirks.

He slides in a little more.

His thickness and warmth make my pussy twitch and clench around him.

I make a noise I've never made before...a deep guttural groan.

"Almost there..." Dane slides all the way home.

I'm like a sock with a foot in it, stretched to his shape. My eyes roll back, and I don't know what noises I'm making.

Dane wets his thumb and presses it against my clit while his cock stretches me to the limit. He rubs slow circles while sliding his cock in and out of me an inch at a time.

Sometimes an inch is all you need. The head of his cock nudges against my deepest, tightest place. His thumb makes a whirlpool of pleasure.

I look into his face, and I see all the openness and intimacy and pure, raw lust of someone who has nothing to hide. He wants me. He loves me. And he's going to take care of me. But first…he's going to make me come.

I give in…all the way in. I let him take me wherever he wants to take me. I float in dark red bliss.

Because I trust him.

And I know he'll keep me safe.

Tom Turner gets off his crutches and immediately crashes his truck. I visit him in the hospital for the second time, where, thankfully, he's being treated for nothing worse than a scrape on his arm and a bump on his head.

"You've had more concussions than a quarterback," Emma informs him sternly.

She looks grumpy, but she's brought him an entire basket of her best muffins and croissants. Tom tears into them with both hands, his substandard hospital breakfast shoved to the side.

"It really wasn't my fault this time," he mumbles, his mouth stuffed with baked goods. "There was a woman standing in the middle of the road. I had to swerve…"

"What kind of woman?" Emma demands. "What was she doing? What was she wearing?"

Her eyes light up at the prospect of this new mystery while Tom recounts every detail of the apparition he saw on Route 88.

"I saw a ghost at the hotel once," Amy Archer says.

She seemed very keen to visit Tom with us and brought him a jug of her homemade kombucha.

"This is the second time I've seen one," Tom informs her proudly.

"Well, next time, don't swerve." Emma says. "Ghosts are already dead."

I murmur, "I don't believe in ghosts."

There was no phantom piano player in my house. The only vengeful spirit was my brother.

"I still do." Dane lays his hand lightly on mine.

Even Dane brought Tom a gift, a neat little shaving kit to take care of the orange stubble from his overnight stay.

Tom seemed surprised and grateful, but I don't know if he'll ever look comfortable around Dane. It doesn't help that Dane goes stiff as stone if Tom so much as brushes my hand. Or Emma either, for that matter.

My present is a set of keys.

"I left Jude's moped out front so you can at least get around until your truck is fixed."

"Don't give him that!" Emma shrieks. "He can't even drive his truck in a straight line."

"I can," Tom says. "As long as there aren't any ghosts."

Both the cousins are pleased when I tell them I'm planning to stay in Grimstone.

"It grows on you," Tom says, sinking back on his pillow with his arms cradled behind his head.

"Like fungus," Emma says dryly.

"I like it here." I look at Dane and smile. "It's…interesting."

"Better than being boring," Dane says, smiling back.

As Amy, Emma, and Dane file out of the room to let Tom take a nap, I run back to say one last thing to him.

"I'm really sorry. For leading you on, for going on that date…"

"Ah, it's okay." Tom gives me his grin just as sunny as Emma's, his carroty hair all in a mess. "Us miscreants will always help one another out."

When I drive back to Blackleaf alone, the house no longer looks like a broken-down beast. The shutters are trim and freshly painted. I've nailed on brand-new shingles and even made a signpost.

But it's empty inside.

No Jude. Nobody to take care of. No one but me.

I miss him.

I loved my brother, and it fucking sucks that he's gone.

That's the truth.

He didn't love me back. He'd hurt me to help himself.

That's also the truth.

Why do we admit the truth even though it fucking hurts? Because that's the way it won't kill us anymore.

It is painful to admit hard truths. But it's incredibly healing to be forgiven and loved in spite of them.

ACKNOWLEDGMENTS

I always have to thank Ry first because he is my business partner as well as the love of my life. He works so hard to keep the wheels on while I'm deep in the writing cave. Also, he's the one who taught me to meditate (though not as depicted here), which has been a huge boon to my mental health.

Thank you to Maya, who makes so many darkly beautiful things for me, and to Brittany, queen of all things organization, operation, and execution. We would be lost without you…at some book signing, without any of our stuff.

Thank you, Emily and Nicole, for outdoing yourself on the *Grimstone* covers—I want to turn them into wallpaper and cover my whole house.

Thank you, Kamrah and Kerry, for watching my little ones so I can work without worry, knowing they are loved and safe.

Much thanks to Katie for your incredible editing work—you've taught me more about grammar than all my English teachers put together.

And of course, thank you, Line, for the gorgeous, moody *Grimstone* art. I never feel my stories are complete until you've put your touch on them.

ABOUT THE AUTHOR

Sophie Lark writes intelligent and powerful characters who are allowed to be flawed. She lives in the mountain west with her husband and three children.

The Love Lark Letter: geni.us/lark-letter
The Love Lark Reader Group: geni.us/love-larks
Website: sophielark.com
Instagram: @Sophie_Lark_Author
TikTok: @sophielarkauthor
Exclusive Content: patreon.com/sophielark
Complete Works: geni.us/lark-amazon
Book Playlists: geni.us/lark-spotify